the rojocci papers

Hidden Within You
by
R. J. Graves, Jr.

This is a work of fiction. Names, characters, places and incidents are products of the author's imagination or are used fictitiously. Any resemblance to actual persons, living or dead, or to events and locales is entirely coincidental.

Cover design by: BETIBUP33 Designs

the rojocci papers
HIDDEN WITHIN YOU
Copyright© 2016 by R. J. Graves, Jr.
Published by R. J. Graves, Jr.
Pensacola, Florida 32503

Visit us at www.facebook.com/rojocci
www.therojoccipapers.com
ISBN-10: 0-9984073-2-1
ISBN-13: 978-0-9984073-2-6
Christian Fiction
$13.95 USD

Printed in the United States of America.
Second Edition

This book is dedicated to
the lovely Mrs. Graves, my sweet Susie.
The most wonderful and remarkable person I
know and the love of my life.

Acknowledgments

Several people have helped me with many aspects of this book, none more than my editor, Susan C. Graves, whose tireless efforts and extreme attention to detail have been a wonder to behold. Heartfelt thanks also to Kathy Coker, Sarah Whipps, and my mother, Betty Graves, for their most helpful input and encouragement during the many revisions.

Although I will no doubt, inadvertently leave many others out of these acknowledgements, I do want to thank my friend, Doug Gehman, who first suggested and encouraged me to consider writing.

"...the mystery which has been hidden
from the past ages and generations;
but has now been manifested to his saints,
to whom God willed to make known
what is the riches of the glory of this mystery
among the Gentiles, which is
Christ in you, the hope of glory."
Colossians 1: 26, 27

-prologue-

It was a few days after Hurricane Ivan in September 2004 when I first met the older gentleman with the kind eyes. Having moved the previous October, my family and I were recent transplants from the upper mid-west region to the beautiful white sand beaches of the Pensacola Bay Area. He was handing out bags of ice to so many of us who had been without electric power for more than a week. As I stood in line, awaiting my turn for the cold relief, I couldn't help but notice his warmth, toward even the most irate of inconvenienced citizens.

The somewhat frazzled mother in front of me was pushing one of those fancy double strollers, designed to accommodate two children. She had somehow fit her three little ones in the two seats and was balancing a case of bottled water on top of the handle. I offered my assistance, but she refused with an obvious suspicion that perhaps I had ulterior motives in my initiative. However, when she met the man with the kind eyes, she not only accepted his proposition to carry the two bags of ice, but she gladly welcomed his "unauthorized" extra case of bottled water for her noisy family, which he hauled to her minivan. It was an act of kindness matched only by the look in his eyes.

After receiving my allotment of one bag of ice and one case of water, according to the guidelines, I inquired as to his name and thanked him for his help in serving our fellow citizens.

He simply smiled and responded, "The Lord bless you today, my friend."

I never saw him again . . . until the next devastating hurricane hit our area.

In July of 2005, Hurricane Dennis blew ashore, again sending Pensacola and the surrounding area reeling. Five days later, my family and I had completely run out of ice. We were low on bottled water as well, so I headed to the distribution area to resupply these vital essentials. As I pulled into the parking lot, a familiar figure caught my attention. It was, in fact, the gentleman with the kind eyes. He was taking a break, eating a sandwich by the side of the massive ice truck. I approached him and asked if perhaps he remembered me. To my surprise he did, greeting me by name.

I asked if he would have time for a coffee someday along with a short cordial visit. He seemed appreciative, and after exchanging our contact information we set a time to meet a few days later at a local coffee shop. This initial meeting led to several more, including a few lunches. As his story began to unfold, I was almost mesmerized, not just by his personal saga, but also by the way he reflected what he expressed. He was demonstratively sincere, a somewhat rare quality in today's society. He also had a most grateful spirit, an essence that radiated from his person. His mannerisms and even the inflection in the tone of his voice had the very unique quality of graciousness, yet he seemed of a rugged character. Once I became aware of what he was going through personally, I marveled at the inner strength he possessed to be able to be out helping others.

After several weeks of reflecting upon our visits together, I felt compelled to write his story. The story you now hold in your hands. I am ashamed to admit, however, that amid the busyness of life it took me nearly eight years— until December of 2012— to start this work and well over three years to complete it.

I pray God's richest blessing on you as you read how the Lord worked in the life of one of us; a neighbor just like you and me.

R. J. Graves, Jr.
Pensacola, Florida
September 2016

~one~

I long to tell you a true story. However, the one who communicated it to me will not allow me to do so. "Only as fiction," he stated emphatically. Therefore, I am telling you a story where the names of characters and places have been fabricated, at least to some degree. It's a tale of a man, who today must be in his mid-sixties. Nonetheless, when these events happened he was decades younger and in possession of a dramatic personal problem. The type of which most everyone can identify within themselves. How he discovers the solution to this lifelong difficulty is why he will not allow me to reveal some of the names and places.

Consequently, I'll call him Alan. Alan Browne. For you see . . .

At some point in life, everyone longs for a quiet road. A stretch of life where the noise, hustle, and bustle have ceased, and a peaceful scene emerges, if only for a few miles. This was especially true for Alan. Never in his lifetime had he needed a tranquil setting more than today. From the cottage where he was staying, the road he walked down to arrive at his favorite spot was mostly quiet that sunny

October afternoon in 1995. Sitting down in the matted grass under the shade of his beloved oak tree, he gazed out across the serene waters of the Santa Rosa Sound. Somehow, the glassy smoothness had a very soothing effect on his storm tossed soul. As he considered the intense circumstances of the day, it seemed as though all of life was working against him. It appeared that he was always learning the same lessons over and over, yet never really quite grasping them.

A sailboat passed by a few hundred yards from where he sat under the enormous oak tree. Its branches, draped with Spanish moss, spread out over the water. The tips of the moss barely touched the water ever so softly, slowing the sway the gentle breeze had caused. It rather annoyed him that the boat had broken the calm of the water, just like the angst of the crisis in which he found himself disturbed the calm of his thoughts.

"Why?!" he grumbled out loud. "If only I could change the circumstances of life, so I didn't make the same mistakes all the time. If only I could somehow rework the last thirty years of my life, I wouldn't be tortured by these continual thoughts, these wretched thoughts. If only . . ." He stopped himself in mid-sentence.

Alan glanced back out over the beautiful turquoise water, the surface once again calm after the passing of the sailboat. He noticed how the turquoise turned to a rich sapphire hue where the water deepened. Then his eyes drifted upward to the brilliant blue skies completely devoid of any clouds or threat of storm. The deep cobalt color filtered through the dark green leaves and greyish brown limbs of the giant oak tree creating the illusion that the sky was an even deeper blue. The bright sunshine penetrated the canopy, falling upon his face as a gentle rain of warmth. He reached behind him and patted the trunk of the massive tree several times. "I would guess you've seen some storms in your day, my old friend. You mind me asking how you handled them?"

He paused a few seconds, as if expecting a reply from his ancient companion. Yet he heard nothing but silence with a faint whisper of the breeze through the dancing leaves. The stillness somehow subdued the turmoil of the storm within his soul.

"I absolutely love this place," he sighed to himself as if acknowledging it for the first time.

He lounged back upon his giant, untroubled confidant and closed his eyes. What a contrast this oak was to his life. Though angry winds may blow, it remained strong and steadfast without a hint of concern. He, on the other hand, continually battled feelings of insecurity and anxious thoughts, though "nary a breeze" of trouble existed. He was unusually suspicious of others even though they appeared friendly. He also had the self-destructive habit of looking for a double meaning behind what others said. Like the time years ago, when his friend remarked, with a smile, how he liked Alan's new running shoes.

Alan interpreted the friendly comment to mean, "About time you got some new shoes; the old ones looked like you pulled them from the garbage can."

Alan snapped back, "Well, your shoes look like you found them in the sewer." He would laugh as though he didn't mean it, yet the curt tone assured that it hit its mark.

Thinking back, he wished he had just responded, "Thank you."

Although he possessed a rather quick wit and good sense of humor, he had the unfortunate habit of blurting out the wrong thing at the wrong time. A number of years ago, he decided his clever way of stating the obvious, usually sarcastically, to an unsuspecting friend or relative was more of a curse than an asset. He could insult his closest ally without the slightest awareness he was offending.

"Why can't I just keep my mouth shut?" he questioned aloud.

Under the oak, his mind began to wander back over the years, pausing momentarily at those monuments in his memory; those temporary physical events which had occurred in the past but somehow had been transformed into permanent, vivid memories. These were forever etched upon his mind and would replay over and over again to the detriment of his chronic low self-esteem. The most damaging of these recordings were impossible to erase.

Laying there, an occasional grimace would cloud his face, giving the only outward evidence of the inward struggle. He grappled with the endless thoughts that moved through his mind as a ticker tape at the stock market.

"How can I make them stop? Please, where is the quiet place, that quiet road?"

A smile slowly broke across his face while he recalled the first time he heard the phrase "quiet road". Yes, indeed, it was a much simpler time. His mind, as a boat loosed from its roped mooring, began to drift with the tide into peaceful, still waters.

"Oh, just to be a carpenter again," he grinned as his mind floated upon the seas of his charted past. "Go to work, do your job, and come home. Yes, a mere worker-bee doesn't have any of these business problems that never seem to go away. That was definitely a much less complicated time."

It was back in September 1977 when Alan obtained his first full time job. He was fresh from his sophomore year at a small college in the Blue Ridge Mountains, just outside the Shenandoah Valley of Virginia. Physically, he was a strong young man of above average height and looks. He was very athletic, and that coupled with his good sense of humor caused no lack of attention from numerous young ladies. He had sandy brown hair, slate blue eyes, a huge smile, and an infectious laugh. Being lean and muscular, his mother often described him as wiry.

He loved almost all competition and especially enjoyed participating in many sports, but none more than running. For who doesn't like to engage in something they excel in? In high school, he was a member of the track and cross country teams winning many races, trophies, and medals, including the State Championship twice. However, more than competing, he preferred the long, solitary jaunts on the trails and roads of the Virginia countryside. He would start early in the morning and sometimes run for two to three hours or more. Alan found great solace and satisfaction in the exhausting efforts of the long run.

He wasn't particularly fond of academics, however, viewing them as more of an option than a necessity. In fact, that's why he needed a full time job. He had dropped out of college after the spring semester of his sophomore year. It was a difficult decision made easier by a lack of funds for tuition and textbooks. Try as he did, working summer jobs at the local grocery store and mowing lawns for his neighbors, he just didn't have enough money to enroll in his junior year. Now, his athleticism was put to more productive use as a carpenter's helper for his cousin, Dan Manford. Alan really wasn't interested in becoming skilled labor, but a job was a job and he needed the money.

"Besides," he thought, "working with my hands for Dan might be a refreshing change from the didactic labor of sitting in a classroom."

Cousin Dan, or "Dan the Man" as he was called by his employees, was a bigger-than-life kind of guy in both physical appearance and personality. His bushy, dark brown hair, eyebrows, and beard gave him more of a mountain man bearing than that of a savvy business owner. Even though he was only in his late thirties, he had developed a very successful construction company that built custom homes as well as a few small commercial projects throughout Northern Virginia. Dan the Man put Alan under the supervision of Jim Johnson, the job superintendent, on a palatial custom home in Great Falls.

Big Jim wasn't, but everyone called him that. As the story goes, although surely it has been embellished over the years, Big Jim stood his ground against an enraged mother bear as he was trying to rescue her cub entangled in barbed wire. The way Big Jim tells it, while on a hunting trip in the mountains west of Blacksburg, he came upon the cub, which appeared to be struggling to free itself. Trying to help, he began pulling on the hind legs of the furry little wiggler who couldn't remove its head from a bird's nest of barbed wire, left by a fencing company several years previous. Big Jim used calm, quiet tones as he attempted to ease the animal's fears as well as body from its trap.

The immature beast, who obviously didn't understand his rescuer's intent, was screeching a high pitch cry for help. Mama Bear evidently heard this plea and "came a runnin, with head down and nostrils flaring," as Big Jim would recount with a twinkle of delight in his eyes. When he realized his precarious predicament, Big Jim turned and faced the charging angry bear, threw his hands in the air, puffed out his chest to give himself the appearance of being "big", and sprinted toward the beast yelling like a Confederate soldier under Stonewall Jackson's command. The stunned creature halted in its tracks as if to say, "Maybe I should reassess this situation." Once Big Jim had determined it was safe to return to the rescue mission, he proceeded to free the little fur ball. The liberated cub then ran off to its behemoth begetter without even an acknowledgement of gratitude. Although, Big Jim swears he saw a wink of the eye from Mama Bear just as she turned away. If the story is true, Big Jim well deserved his "large" moniker.

When Alan arrived for his first day of work, he noticed the foundation of concrete and block was complete and the wood framing had just begun. There was a crew of five carpenters and Big Jim. Immediately after Alan hopped out of his faded red 1967 Toyota pickup truck, Big Jim barked in Alan's direction.

"Hey, new guy, move that stack of lumber over here! Now! We need it now boy!" Alan jumped to and grabbed a 2"x 12" board and started across the jobsite. "Not one, rookie!" came the admonishment from Big Jim, "Four!"

Alan's wiry build was well suited to the strenuous task, but the balancing act of lugging four long lengths of lumber across the muddy site was a bit tricky. He decided to carry two boards each trip. Then, he chose to run back and forth from the pile of lumber to the framing crew, thereby making up for the "lost time" of not carrying the required four pieces per load. Within a few minutes, he jettisoned his denim jacket and flannel shirt. By mid-morning, he had the task completed and realized a unique sense of satisfaction and accomplishment. Big Jim called him over. After handing him twenty dollars, he waved his hand in the general direction of the crew with the instruction to go get break materials.

"What in the world is a break material?" pondered Alan as he headed in the direction of the crew busily at work installing the 2"x 12" floor joists. He approached the first carpenter, who appeared to be about his own age. Alan thought he seemed to be the least intimidating.

"Break materials?" he asked.

"Yep, where you going?" came the reply.

"Uh, where do you want me to go?" It was much more a question of what constitutes a break material than where they are obtained.

"Hmmm . . . you better ask Stanley. He's the lead carpenter," he responded, pointing at the grey haired, muscular man kneeling on a newly installed section of plywood subfloor. It was more of a statement revealing the unspoken hierarchy within a construction crew than Alan recognized at the time.

Stanley Taft was dressed in blue jean coveralls and a tan chamois shirt with leather nail bags hanging from the widest red suspenders Alan had ever seen. He was looking at the blueprints when Alan inquired, "Break materials?"

"Where you going, son?"

"Well, I was kind of hoping you would tell me."

"I'm leaning toward Mickey Doogles. Okay with you fellas?" Stanley never looked up from the plans but all members of the crew answered as if he was speaking to them individually. Alan glanced around at the others as he stood there awaiting his yet unknown assignment.

"Maybe I should ask for directions to this supply warehouse," he cautioned himself. "How will I know a break material from any other material? Maybe it means it's broken or cracked. Yeah, that's probably it. They are less expensive because they're damaged but still useful. Then the carpenter can cut out the broken section and use the remaining piece that's undamaged," he reasoned with a sense of pride because he had figured out the mystery. "I hope Stanley gives me a list though."

"Got something to write on, son?" came the question from under the ragged Washington Senators baseball cap. Alan quickly looked around for a piece of paper or cardboard.

"Go get something to write on," The tone Stanley used this time expressed his patience had a limit.

"I think I have some notebook paper in my pickup truck. I could go get it. It would only take me a second," Alan's tone was apologetic.

"Here," quipped the elder carpenter holding up a block of 2"x 12" about half a foot long with a special pencil laid on top. The pencil wasn't round like the ones Alan was accustomed to using in school. Rather, it was rectangular with a very large lead protruding out one end to a point that appeared to have been sharpened with a knife.

Stanley continued, "I want a Sausage Egg McMuffin, hash browns, and a medium orange juice."

A huge smile broke across Alan's face as he realized he was in an entirely different world compared to his college classroom. It was most definitely a type of classroom. But one where they spoke an unfamiliar language as if from a completely foreign culture, words like: "joist", "sheathing", "stud", "rafter", "break materials", and of course . . ."Mickey Doogles".

"I think I'll enjoy this way of learning better than listening to lectures," he announced to himself while he drove to the break materials depot with the golden arches. Yes, it was hard work, but it was accompanied by a feeling of accomplishment that he hadn't experienced before.

"Besides," he declared out loud, "I'm learning a new language. I'm going to be bilingual." He laughed with an extra amount of twang to his Virginia drawl. "Yeah, I think I'm going to like this."

Every morning Alan arrived at the jobsite about an hour early, so he could unload the tools and electrical extension cords from the job trailer and ready them for the crew. Then, he would carry and stack the endless pieces of lumber the men would need for the next phase of framing. Floor joists were 2"x 12". Subfloor was ¾" tongue and groove plywood. All the plywood came in 4'x 8' sheets. The lumber needed for walls was 2"x 4" and 2"x 6" along with ½" plywood to cover as sheathing. Next, were the hundreds of long lengths of 2"x 10"rafters. And finally, he hauled more ½" plywood for the roof sheathing.

Carrying every single piece by hand across the often muddy terrain, Alan's boots, at times, were caked with as much as two inches of the thick Virginia red clay. He lifted each stick up to the crew on the first floor initially then, the second floor and third floors as the framing went higher. Finally, it reached the steep pitched roof. Day after day, five, sometimes six days a week, for several weeks, this was his responsibility. It was absolutely exhausting work.

"Keep the crew in lumber rookie!" Big Jim would remind him over and over. "Make sure they have subfloor adhesive. Don't forget the nails, hangers, and straps kid. Come on boy, get a move on!" he would bark.

Although Big Jim continually rode him and the work was strenuous, somehow it was very gratifying to Alan. He would lean back on the side of his pickup truck at the end of each day and marvel at the amount of "lumber in the air", as Stanley would call it. Alan was glad for the work and very grateful for the money, but he really wanted to learn more.

"How do contractors know how to employ the materials of wood, concrete, and brick in disarray on the ground and organize them into a building? I mean, how does old Stanley take the lines and words on several pages of paper and subsequently create a home the owner can enjoy?"

He marveled at the almost supernatural ability of the quietly confident lead carpenter. Whenever possible, Alan would ask him questions, trying to learn the source of this remarkable power that enabled him to build something out of nothing. Stanley would share with him, on a regular basis, the order of how things went together.

"You got to stay in sequence, son. If you get out of sequence, you're spinning your wheels, fixing a mess, and wasting time, son, you understand?"

Then he would show him what a symbol or line on the blueprint becomes in the structure as the principles are applied to the project. Alan loved the way Stanley took the time to answer his questions. His caring manner had quite an endearing effect on Alan. A couple of times each week, the two would linger after work at the jobsite going over everything from how to read blueprints to how to effectively use a hammer to drive a nail with a single blow.

"Efficiency is everything on a construction project," Stanley would repeat. "Always move in one direction to completion. Then, move back in the reverse direction. Never go back and forth. Wasted motion kills efficiency."

It appeared to Alan that Stanley enjoyed teaching him almost as much as he enjoyed being taught by Stanley.

"Remember, always be productive, son. Look for something that needs to be done before someone tells you it needs doing. You understand?"

Whenever Stanley asked if Alan understood, he would always put his hand on Alan's shoulder as if to say this was very important.

"Work hard, son, but remember to pace yourself. It's not a sprint. It's a marathon." With this admonition Stanley smiled and winked at his young protégé.

It all had a marvelous effect on Alan, creating within him a strong desire to discover more of this new mysterious world where he worked.

"Maybe I'll drop by that builder's bookstore on the way home and see if they have any carpentry books," declared Alan.

"Just make sure," remarked Stanley, "they aren't those 'Harry Homeowner' types but real professional carpentry books."

"Will do, Stanley, thanks and I'll see you tomorrow."

~two~

L iving with his parents and three siblings in a typical suburban Washington, DC, neighborhood, Alan was the oldest of four siblings. He had two brothers and one sister. His brothers were named Eddie and Bill. Growing up, the trio donned many nicknames because they were quite the characters when together. They had earned titles such as, "The Three Amigos", "The Three Stooges", and "The Three Knuckleheads", as well as a few others. However, they called themselves "The A.E.B.". It was an acronym that Alan had created in junior high school using the first letter from each of their names. It meant: All Evil Beasts. In reality though, they were much more mischievous than evil. In fact, if one hadn't thought of a way to get into mischief, the other ones would and vice versa. They were always daring each other to try the latest stupidity with little concern for the consequences. This, of course, fostered an extraordinarily competitive spirit within each of them.

What a contrast they were to their only sister Amy. Like one might suspect with three older brothers, she was somewhat of a tomboy, but she was still very much the "Feminita", as they used to tease her. (It meant they thought her to be a prissy girl.) However, they would protect her as their most valued treasure when she had a problem with one of her many male suitors. In the midst of a spat with Amy, it was an imposing sight to a young high school boy to spot the Three Amigos riding into town on their valiant steeds. Pulling up directly behind their Feminita, the stern looks on their faces clearly indicated to the young beau, "Now, you were saying?" Somehow this always solved every argument, at least temporarily.

Alan's parents were young when they married. His father had become a project architect in his mid-twenties with a commercial design firm located in Georgetown. Throughout the years, he had many offers from other companies, though he had never accepted any of them. He determined early on in his career that he was much more of a "company man" and didn't relish hopping around from one project to another in order to climb the invisible ladder to fame and fortune. He was a quietly analytical kind of guy who loved his job but hated the traffic congestion of his long commute.

Being the homemaker, Alan's mother was the rock of the family. With her duties at home and a part time job at the local elementary school, she was usually very busy. However, she always made time to listen to the latest crises from one of her "huddled herd" as she affectionately described them. She was a forceful woman, strong in mind and limb with high values and a strict sense of discipline. "Good Pilcher stock," she would remind her children, revealing the Scottish pride her father instilled in her. She possessed a very sincere type of kindness. Nevertheless, she wasn't hesitant to show the individual members of the A.E.B. the business end of her wooden spanking spoon, which they seemed to require on a regular basis while growing up.

Of late, Alan had acquired a great deal of respect for his parents. He had come to recognize how stressful it was raising a family of six in times when gas was sixty cents a gallon and the same amount of milk cost three times more. Out of necessity, his parents spent much time apart with his father working long hours and enduring the lengthy commute from Georgetown to their home in Oakton. Even so, Alan knew they had a deep love for one another and it meant the world to him.

"When you have an anchor at home," his father would proclaim referring to their marriage, "you can leverage a long way out."

He was using one of his frequent architectural metaphors relating how, without an anchored base, one cannot cantilever a beam, or a floor for that matter, very far past its pivot point. Alan always visualized the seesaw at the local park to help him understand his father's illustration. It was a wonderful analogy he had heard since childhood. However, it would take Alan years to fully comprehend it.

They lived in a four bedroom brick home. The fact that Alan was the oldest allowed him the luxury of his own bedroom. It wasn't always this way. As a youngster, he and his two brothers would share one room, his sister another, and the largest, usually with its own bathroom, was reserved for his parents.

His earliest remembrance was living in their small two bedroom home in Falls Church, just across the county line from Arlington. Then, they moved to Springfield during the summer between his fifth and sixth grade years. One year later, they relocated to Centreville, but his father decided the distance from work was too much to bear. Subsequently, before his freshman year in high school, the family, six Brownes in all, moved to Oakton where they found a place to call home.

That evening, after dinner, Alan immediately sequestered himself within his room. He was anxious to peruse the two carpentry books he had purchased on the way home from work. He'd discovered a building and engineering bookstore in Fairfax, and it supplied him with just what he was looking for. He selected the volume with the most photographs to read first. It was full of facts, definitions, and techniques. The illustrations were invaluable as they helped him visualize the process or skill explained in the text. He soaked it all up and was unable to put the manual down until he had devoured every last page, sometime after two a.m.

"I'm going to be exhausted tomorrow," he complained, chiding himself for not paying attention to how late it was getting. Then he smiled, "I'm going to need some more tools."

The alarm was extra loud and more obnoxious than normal as six a.m. came early for one who had closed his eyes at two a.m. But something was different. It was strangely quiet.

"Like a stillness had fallen over the house, the entire neighborhood," he mused half awake and half asleep. "It's almost like . . ." Alan leapt out of bed and rushed over to the window to pull back the shade and peer out into the predawn darkness. "Oh no," he cried, "not today!"

There on the window, the lawn, the driveway, his pickup truck, and everywhere else was the first snow of the season and lots of it. It was still falling heavily as he made his way out to his truck and through the four inches already lying on the ground. He started up the engine, adjusted the defroster on the windshield, and began the arduous task of scraping the windows. He glanced in the bed of his truck and noticed the few tools he possessed were covered in a blanket of the wet December snow.

"Great," he moaned. "It's ruined my tools too."

What had been an exciting evening of discovery the night before was quickly turning into a dawn of harsh, unpleasant reality. By the time he finally got into the driver's seat, he was cold, wet, tired, and a little more than impatient. He pulled out of their driveway sliding sideways, overcorrecting before he was able to straighten his truck as he headed down the street.

"Just what I need," he grumbled, "this white garbage all over everything, and I'm late to work."

He had personally established, two winters ago, that pickup trucks weren't made to drive in the snow. Although no one had gotten hurt, Alan and his cherished Toyota pickup truck had come to rest in a ditch on Dolley Madison Boulevard late one snowy night. It was after several three hundred-sixty degree spins and a series of maneuvers that more closely resembled bumper cars at the State Fair, than vehicles traveling upon a public road.

"Snow is no excuse!" Big Jim called out from the open door of the job trailer as Alan jumped out of his truck. "You're late! Let's get these cords hooked up. We got a nickel holding up a dollar." barked Big Jim with more than a hint of disgust in his voice.

"Greenhorn," he mumbled, referring to Alan's apparent lack of dependability, more than his actual lack of construction knowledge. It was a derogatory title no apprentice ever wanted to hear, especially not from the job superintendent.

"I'm sorry," groveled Alan, "but . . ."

Big Jim interrupted, "We'll have time for whining later. Right now, we need to get working."

Alan felt so discouraged and more than a little insecure. "As soon as I get these tools ready and move the lumber for the crew, he's going to let me go. I know he's going to fire me."

His troubled thoughts were almost loud enough to hear as if he were yelling them from across the jobsite. "Wasn't my fault I was sick one day last week. Man, now I'm late today because of this stinking snow. What will I tell Dad when he gets home? I know, I won't tell him. Ah, that won't work; Cousin Dan will call him to explain how I deserved to be fired."

"Lumber!" shouted Big Jim from the second floor of the nearly completed frame. "Come on boy, move it!"

Falling down more than he walked upright, Alan hauled the long lengths of 2"x 6" across the jobsite turned skating rink. He continually alternated between thoughts of frustration and excuses, to feelings of condemnation and vulnerability.

"What is wrong with me? Why do I always think this way about myself?" He had climbed up to the second floor using an extension ladder in the open stairwell. He moved over to the opening in the wall to pull up the pieces of lumber he had leaned against the outside of the building. It was excruciating work hoisting by hand the snow and ice covered sticks of lumber up two stories. His face was a picture of misery, more from the agony of his mind and emotions, than from the physical task at hand.

"You okay son?" It was the unmistakably low, steady tone with a hint of Southern Virginia drawl that could only be Stanley. "What did I tell you about pacing yourself?" Although there was a smile, it sounded to Alan like he was scolding him. "You look like you've run one of them marathons," Stanley was appealing to Alan's love of running. But when he noticed the look in Alan's eyes, he asked, "What's wrong son?"

Taking a deep breath of the cold, damp air, Alan sighed, "I think I'm going to get fired."

"What makes you think that son?" replied Stanley with concern in his voice.

"Well . . ." Alan must have gone on for more than five minutes complaining, agonizing, and defending the events of the last week or so. Stanley showed no emotion although Alan thought he looked concerned. Alan concluded his case by summarizing, "Besides, Big Jim hates me!"

Reaching up and placing his right hand upon Alan's shoulder, Stanley paused long enough to look directly into Alan's eyes. Then he delivered those prophetic words that would reverberate in Alan's mind throughout the rest of his life.

"Son," he said with a soft yet firm tone, "You need to find a quiet road. You need to find a **rojocci**, your own **rojocci**. You understand what I'm saying to you?"

"Oh yeah, sure," agreed Alan, showing more skepticism than any expression of affirmation. The comment carried with it a tone of sarcasm Alan had tried to avoid. "Thanks, Stanley," he resigned, trying to sound a bit more sincere.

Stanley patted him on the back and pulled out his framing hammer, ready to head back to work. He reassured, "Let me know if I can help you, Alan."

That was the first and last time Stanley ever used Alan's name. Before today it had always been "son" this or "son" that. It somewhat surprised Alan and had the effect of cementing in his mind the important words Stanley had so soberly spoken a minute before.

"Quiet road?" he repeated to himself on the way home that night. "And where are you going to find a quiet road in this busy city? What did he mean by a quiet road anyway? Why does Stanley think I need to find this so called quiet road? And what was that strange word, **roe-joc-kee** . . . or something?"

It was shortly after five a.m. when the phone rang the next morning. Alan could hear his father's voice from his parent's bedroom at the opposite end of the hallway. It became obvious from his tone Alan's father knew the caller on the other end. A few minutes passed and Alan started to drift back to sleep. He was startled by the knock on his door.

"Alan, you awake yet?" asked the voice from the other side of the door. "Alan, it's your cousin, Dan, on the phone."

Alan's feet hardly touched the carpeted floor of his bedroom as he jumped out of bed and jerked his door open. "Yes sir, I'm up," he verified, intentionally leaving out the "of course" as he headed for the extension in the kitchen. "Hello?"

The voice on the other end of the phone was loud, awake, and definitely that of his cousin Dan the Man. "Good afternoon Alan," came the sarcastic greeting. "You sleeping on your shirttails this morning?"

Before Alan could defend himself or even remind his cousin that it was barely five a.m., and he wasn't due at work for another two hours, Dan the Man bellowed, "I need you in Cherrydale today. You'll be working for Tiny. He's the job superintendent; he's, uh . . . well, you'll know him when you see him. The project's on Lee Highway about two blocks north of the fire station. Better get moving. They start at six o'clock down there."

Quicker than Alan could say thank you, ask why he was being transferred to another project, or even say good bye, the line was dead. He hung up the phone slowly as his thoughts started running at a trot.

"Big Jim hates me. I bet he wanted to fire me and now Dan is giving me one final chance. If I screw this up, I'm fired for sure."

He was putting way more pressure on himself than the situation actually merited. Try as he might, he couldn't avoid the well-worn ruts in his mind. As he glanced around the dimly lit kitchen, he decided his insecurities worked like the coffee grounds in his parent's fancy, new Mr. Coffee machine, which had just turned on automatically. No matter how pure the water that was poured into it each morning, it still came out coffee.

Developing a strong dislike for being late to work, Alan glanced at his watch as he pulled onto the jobsite. He was twenty minutes late. "Surely this superintendent will understand. I mean, Dan just called me this morning," he reasoned within himself although he was not one bit convinced.

He walked up to the makeshift plywood door of the old commercial brick building. Out of the corner of his eye, he caught sight of a man no more than four feet tall. The short fellow was pushing a wheelbarrow loaded with shiny pieces of scrap metal. His hands gripped the handles as they rested somewhat on his shoulders. It was a most unique sight, and one Alan found rather astounding. Continuing through the open door, within a couple of steps, he turned around and started back outside. He had decided that the barrow pusher must be the job superintendent named Tiny.

But before he fully turned, there was a call from inside the dust filled room, "Hey, kid!" He veered around but saw no one.

"Hey man, over here!"

This second beckoning gave Alan a chance to zero in on the direction from which the voice emanated. Lumbering toward him through the dust, was an enormous man, who was taller than Alan by several inches and who weighed at least three times more than his own weight.

As this huge man approached, Alan could begin to clarify his features. He appeared to be in his late thirties or maybe early forties. He had a long beard like those two ZZ Top guitarists and a long braided ponytail that swung back and forth as he somewhat waddled across the filthy floor. He wore typical construction work clothes under a black leather vest that appeared to be several sizes too small for him. He thrust forward his right hand, "You Alan?" he asked.

"Yes, sir. Sorry I'm late, but . . ."

"Ah, it's your first day; don't worry about it, man. But don't let it happen again," he frowned. Then he slapped Alan on the back as he broke into one of the biggest laughs Alan had ever heard.

"I'm just kidding you, man! Ha, I had you going though, didn't I, huh?"

Being unsure of what to make of this peculiar character, a cautious grin began to form on Alan's face. As they shook hands, Alan noticed his own hand disappeared in the huge meaty paw that engulfed his. He looked down at his hand. It was beginning to experience no small level of pain. He noticed the man had on black leather wristbands, each about two inches wide. They matched his small vest and the band on his left wrist had a watch attached by two enormous brass rivets. It all gave the appearance of a member of some ruffian motorcycle gang, even though there were no identifying emblems.

"Any trouble finding the place?" he quizzed Alan as he started back across the dust filled room to his original location. "Come on, man," he motioned with a flick of his head.

Alan thought the small, form-fitting Stars and Stripes cap looked quite odd with the black wide-framed glasses the man was wearing. This guy was definitely different from anyone Alan had ever met before.

Halfway across the floor he cocked his head toward Alan and beamed, "I'm Harry, by the way. But everyone calls me Tiny."

"Really?" queried Alan. "I mean, I thought . . ." He bit his tongue and quickly pulled back his thumb that had been pointing in the general direction of the guy pushing the wheelbarrow.

"What's that?" asked Tiny without turning around.

"Uh . . ." Alan paused for what seemed more than a few seconds. He desperately searched his quick wit for a better finish to his incomplete comment. It was the same quick wit that just moments ago almost got him into a very awkward situation.

"Uh . . . I thought this was a residential project. I don't have any experience on commercial work." Alan's face gave no hint to the relief he felt within.

"Don't worry about it, man. Dan the Man told me to teach you the ropes. He must have big plans for you. What, are you like his nephew or something?" he laughed. Then continued, "Come on, let's get situated."

The makeshift blueprint desk was in the corner of the main room of the building. It had a sloped top made of plywood with a set of plans spread across it. The plans had all sorts of notes written in red ink. At the top of the table, leaning against the wall, was what appeared to be a radio playing "Layla". As they approached, Tiny began to play an imaginary guitar with his hands while his rather oversized body moved with the beat of the song.

"Best stinking guitarist ever," he proclaimed with a smile.

"What?" demanded Alan. It was more a statement of disbelief than an actual question because everyone knew Jimi Hendrix was the greatest guitarist.

"Eric Clapton man," Tiny echoed pointing his bearded chin at the radio. "The man is un-be-stinking-lievable!" Tiny's corpulent mass was still rocking to the beat. "You got one of these, man?"

Alan looked at the radio again and for the first time recognized it was one of those new cassette players.

"Nah, I still have 8-Track," he complained.

Tiny just shook his head, although his imaginary guitar never missed a note. Alan noticed an open shoebox on the dust covered file cabinet next to the table. Inside, along with Derek and the Dominoes, were more cassette tapes. Names like, Led Zeppelin, Steve Miller Band, and Joe Cocker were right on top, giving evidence to those which received the most use. It was a far cry from "Sweet Home Alabama" which played a dozen times or more everyday on Big Jim's jobsite.

"Hey, man, you like Hendrix?" Tiny probed.

"Uh, sure, well I don't . . ." Alan replied with a bit of hesitation as if to say, "Aren't we supposed to be working?"

Tiny interrupted, "Yeah, second best stinking guitarist ever, right?"

Just then, a plumber walked by with a length of pipe as long as the man was tall. He swung it around and started playing as if he and Tiny were part of Eric Clapton's band. It was quite an unusual and, frankly, amusing sight.

Alan smiled as the thought crossed his mind, "This sure is a far cry from Big Jim's jobsite."

As if he knew what Alan was thinking, Tiny dropped his imaginary guitar and quipped, "Yeah, Big Jim runs a tight ship. He's a control freak. He's got that little man complexion thing going on."

Alan countered, "Don't you mean Napoleon Complex?" He was trying to use a tone that wouldn't sound as though he was correcting his new boss.

"What?" Tiny cracked as though he hadn't heard Alan. "Yeah, whatever. Let's get to work."

This last comment had given Alan an awful feeling inside again. It was the same feeling that had started to diminish as he was getting acquainted with his new superior. But now, it had found fresh fuel for its flickering flame and was returning to a full blaze.

"Why can't you just keep your mouth shut?" he silently reprimanded himself with disgust. "You idiot, you always have to say something that offends. Now look what you've done . . . and he's your boss." His internal rebukes were interrupted by Tiny motioning him closer to the blueprints.

"Here," he was pointing with his sausage-like finger assuming Alan knew what he was indicating on the drawings. "Move the bundle of metal studs outside by the forklift to right here." He was tapping with his finger for emphasis. Alan was quite lost as he had never read blueprints before, at least not for a commercial project.

"What's this going to be?" he asked, trying to distract Tiny from his inability to read blueprints.

"The fanciest stinking bicycle shop I've ever seen," declared Tiny.

Still attempting to make sense of the plans, Alan's eyes were darting all over the page, trying to take in as much information as quickly as possible before Tiny asked another question. He must have paused a little too long over the lines on the page because Tiny quizzed, "You got it, man?"

Alan stood upright and looked around the room. "Yeah, sure," and looked back at the drawings.

"Over there, man," Tiny relented, pointing to the opposite side of the first floor. "Stack them neatly over there, okay?"

"Yes sir," Alan mumbled as he started in the direction of his new task. Halfway across the room he heard, "Can't read plans, man?"

"No, sir," he replied without turning around as he continued across the floor.

"Don't worry about it, man. It's easy, I'll teach you. You just got to learn the language, that's all."

A grin broke across Alan's face as he turned toward Tiny. "Thanks, Tiny, I really appreciate it."

"You're gonna love it here, man," he cajoled with a smile. "Now get to work!" he shouted as his smile became a huge laugh again

-three-

I t wasn't until late April 1978 that the bicycle shop project was finally nearing completion. Tiny was right, Alan absolutely loved working there and working for Tiny. He had a casual leadership style that never seemed to get flustered no matter what the problem. It appeared to Alan as though Tiny didn't care, and yet he had an exacting eye for detail. He was quite the unusual character. However, Alan had developed a great deal of respect for him and considered Tiny a friend. He also had thoroughly enjoyed becoming friends with the bike shop owners. Dropping by two or three times a week to check on the progress, they often took the time to visit with Alan.

The owners, Frank and Carol, were a married couple in their late forties. They had a younger partner, Bruce, who had been a professional bicycle road racer in Europe. Although Bruce had never raced in the big events, like the Tour de France, he was incredibly strong by American standards. The three partners talked of cycling with Alan, trying to sell him on the sport more than attempting to sell him a bike. Perhaps their tactics would change after their shop was open. Alan always defended his love of running and retorted that cycling was just way too expensive for him. This usually had the effect of putting the trio on the defensive, which was precisely why Alan did it. He liked them though, and they seemed to enjoy him as well. These were friendships that would last for years.

One Friday afternoon, as Alan was finishing some final touches on the restroom hardware, he heard the jobsite telephone ring. A few minutes later Tiny asked Alan to remind him to tell him something at the end of the day. Tiny was always doing that. Alan thought it was more of a psychological ploy Tiny used to make Alan feel important, than the fact that Tiny actually couldn't remember something. Regardless, Alan usually went along with the game. Therefore, after putting away all the tools in the job box, he asked Tiny what he was supposed to remind him of.

"Huh? Oh yeah. Your daddy, Dan the Man, called," he teased. "He wants you to report back to Great Falls on Monday. You're heading back out to Big Jim's job, alright, man!"

There was more than a hint of sarcasm in his voice. Tiny knew, from their numerous talks together, that Alan really didn't like the way Big Jim managed a jobsite or how he always talked down to him as if Alan was completely lacking any common sense.

"Good luck, man," he mumbled as if resigning himself and Alan to the fact that Alan was going to be miserable.

"Nice knowing you," Alan sighed, matching Tiny's level of sarcasm as he turned to open the newly finished door to the bike shop. "Have a great weekend. Tell Frank, Carol, and Bruce I'll still drop by for the Grand Opening." Alan was almost to his truck before he realized he never heard the door close behind him.

"Hey, Alan, man!"

He swung around hoping Tiny was going to tell him it was all a big joke.

"It's been really great working with you. You got a lot of potential. Don't let that little man get to you, okay? He's just got that Napoleon Complexion thing going on, man." He leaned back letting out one of his huge laughs, which almost matched the size of his body.

Alan smiled back, acknowledging more the sincerity of what was expressed than the words used. "Thanks, Tiny," he waved as he hopped in his truck and started for home.

It was one of the shortest weekends on record. At least it was from Alan's perspective. It still had the same number of hours, but the hours undeniably had fewer minutes. The heaviness he felt Friday afternoon since the "Oh, by-the-way announcement" he received from Tiny gradually became as heavy as an elephant sitting on his chest. By Sunday evening, Alan had worked himself into such an unbearable mega-city-of-anxiety that he was completely distraught as to which street to turn onto for relief. Every door on all of the buildings had the same dreadful look, and the entryways led to rooms decorated with the same insecurities, his insecurities. He desperately needed another city, another neighborhood where his mind could dwell. "Something with tree lined streets and green lawns," he imagined as he lay on the floor in his bedroom gazing at the ceiling.

"Ah, yes, a quiet neighborhood . . ." He paused and closed his eyes, letting himself drift to that idyllic setting in his mind. "With quiet streets . . ." He allowed himself to float into the peaceful picture, which was beginning to have the calming effect he so longed for. "Big shady trees with beautiful emerald green lawns accented by the rich colors of spring."

He envisioned the bright red tulips, pastel yellow daffodils, and his favorite, the wonderful mix of white, pink, and red azaleas. The more he mused upon the imaginary scene in his mind, the less he actually felt the heaviness in his chest. He felt lighter. He groped for the words to describe the sensation. A smile slowly began to form upon his face as he mustered the courage to allow it. "Mmmm . . ." he released the sigh as if it had been trapped in a deep place a great distance away. "It was a serene street, a quiet road with big oak trees arching across the top creating more of a leafy tunnel than a shade filled channel."

As he lay on the floor, suddenly something surprised him in such a way that his eyes opened wide in a sense of awe and amazement, which sent him reaching for his desk chair to pull himself up. "What?" he contemplated aloud. "What was the thing Stanley said to me months ago on my last day at Big Jim's job?"

Recalling the snowy day, Alan remembered how he had arrived late to the jobsite because of it. He had jumped out of his truck only to be met by the harsh comments from Big Jim. His mind rehearsed the conversation on the second floor between Stanley and himself. He repeated the words over and over trying to recreate the exact quote from Stanley. He leaned forward on his desk chair as if leaning into the answer, his head down, held in one hand as the other grasped the back of the chair. Several minutes passed before his mind, searching the mental file cabinet, opened to the correct folder.

"It was, 'you need to find a quiet road. You need to find the . . .'" He stretched the cranial folder a bit wider as if to see the next page in it.

"What exactly did he say?" he questioned, imploring his mind to turn to the page which would reveal the word. "Wasn't it jockey something? Or was it something jockey? Yeah, I think it was something jockey."

Scurrying through as many combinations of the word as he could, Alan started with the letter "A". "Was it 'able jockey, alphabet jockey, apple jockey?' No." Then he went on to the words beginning with "B". "Maybe boy jockey, boat jockey, bull jockey? Wait a minute," he interrupted his theoretical interrogation. "Boat jockey sounds right . . . well, kinda. Coat jockey? Float? Goat? Goad?"

Alan escalated the volume as if he would hear it better. "Toad?" His mind, now running a thousand miles an hour down his cerebral pathways, sought the right combination of sounds, which would match what his memory had stored.

He backtracked. "Toad jockey?" he laughed out loud. "Really, toad jockey? Yeah right." Then he mocked himself using a Scottish brogue, "He rode into town on a green frog. The villagers cheered, 'Here cometh the toad jockey!'" As his laughter tapered off, he began to recognize something familiar in the reverberations in his ear.

"Wait a cotton picking minute," his tone having completed a total transformation from humor to an astonished sense of discovery.

"It's road jockey!" he shouted. "That's it. Road jockey. I can't believe I didn't remember road jockey." He repeated the words several times to assure himself he wouldn't forget what he had just recalled. "I can't wait to see Stanley tomorrow. I am definitely going to sit down with him at lunch and ask him why he said I needed to find a quiet road. And what in the world is a road jockey?" At that precise moment, Alan realized something within him had changed dramatically in the last few minutes. "Strange," he marveled, "now I'm really looking forward to tomorrow."

Flopping down on his bed he smiled while staring at the ceiling as though he could see right through it to the sky above. "I can't believe this," he mumbled in amazement. "I'm really looking forward to going to work tomorrow even in spite of having to work for Big Jim. What on earth just happened? I was totally discouraged, and now I'm almost excited."

Still smiling, he closed his eyes for a few seconds and then opened them wide. "How'd that happen is the important question. How? Nothing changed on the outside of me. I'm still going to work tomorrow. I'm still going to have to do what Big Jim tells me. I still have to deal with his rotten attitude toward me. Everything is still the same, but inside I feel totally different. I feel really happy. How did that happen? Nothing changed except something within me. But how did it happen?"

Allowing his eyelids to slowly close, Alan set his mind to figuring out this new mystery. This was an absolute wonder he was experiencing. Something he wasn't sure he had ever considered before. If he had, he hadn't realized it at the time, and it certainly wasn't something he remembered. Regardless, it was a remarkably peaceful place to be.

Awakening well before his alarm went off, he got up, showered, and gobbled down breakfast, enabling him to be on the road a full thirty minutes early. It was more an excitement of seeing Stanley, than a concern of being late which motivated him. He had planned that he would try to sit next to Stanley at lunch. This would give Alan the opportunity to ask him questions about the curious comments he had made months before.

"It sure will be good to see him," he echoed several times on his way to the project in Great Falls that morning.

No sooner had Alan arrived, than he could see the jobsite was a beehive of activity. Apparently, the project was several days behind schedule and Big Jim was riding everyone more than usual. He was talking with Stanley and two other men Alan didn't recognize. So he moved right for the job trailer and started hooking up the electrical extension cords for the carpenters.

"One in the garage and one in the kitchen, kid," came the call from Big Jim.

"Yes sir," was Alan's reply. He moved as quickly as he could so he wouldn't give Big Jim any cause to hound him. Glancing in their direction several times, he made everything ready for the carpenters. Just then, a large truck from the lumber yard arrived. Alan ran over to see what was being delivered.

"What you got?" asked Alan.

"Thirty-three, eight foot tall, solid core black walnut doors and matching trim. There are more pieces of molding than you can shake a stick at, buddy."

It took Alan and the driver most of the early morning to unload all the doors. They placed them by each opening where they would be installed throughout the mansion. Then, it took another forty-five minutes to move all the trim lumber into the garage. It was mid-morning when the truck finally drove off the jobsite. Alan opened the door to the job trailer and placed the receipts on Big Jim's desk. His boss didn't even acknowledge Alan.

"Break materials, kid, go get break materials. I want orange cupcakes and chocolate milk." Without looking up from what he was doing Big Jim slapped down three dollars on his desk. "Hurry back."

Being a bit dismayed and confused, Alan jogged to the house to look for the carpenters. "I know he hates me. Why only three dollars? He better not think I'm buying. I don't have enough money for all these guys."

He moved through the first floor, which was fully drywalled and painted. He could hear voices coming from the kitchen. As he turned the corner, he found Stanley and another carpenter installing the cabinets.

"Break materials?"

"Yeah, hang on just a second, son." Stanley's voice was strained from the effort of holding up a wall cabinet and trying to set a screw at the same time. Alan strode over to help alleviate the load and free Stanley to focus on setting the screw before the cabinet moved.

"There. Thanks, son. Where you going?"

"Big Jim wants orange cupcakes and chocolate milk, so I guess I'm going to 7-Eleven."

"Okay. Get me a honeybun and a small coffee." Then, he turned to continue installing the wall cabinets.

"Uh . . . Stanley," Alan stumbled, "He didn't give me enough money, uh, you know, for . . ."

Stanley interrupted, "Oh, I'm sorry. Here you go, son. Get something for the other fellas too, okay? And if there's anything left, put it in your gas tank."

"Thanks Stanley," his voice rang out much louder and stronger. He turned to the other carpenter, but before getting his order he looked at Stanley. "Would you have a few minutes today when I could ask you a couple of questions?"

"Sure, son, anytime," was the reply from the elder craftsman.

"Great," smiled Alan.

However, the rest of the day, as well as the entire week, was so busy that Alan was unable to get a few minutes to sit down and visit with Stanley. It seemed that Stanley was really pushing as he went from finishing the cabinets in the kitchen, to those in the six bathrooms and then, started to install the doors, before working on the trim. Alan had to drive to the lumber yard in Fairfax and the hardware store in Falls Church at least once every other day. Along with getting snacks and lunch for the carpenters, he spent almost all of his time behind the windshield. It was early Saturday evening when he finally saw Stanley alone by his truck.

"Hey, Stanley, got a minute?"

"Son, can it wait? I am so beat I can barely stand up. If it's okay with you, I really need to get home and fall into bed." He appeared out of breath while he pleaded with his young friend.

"Oh, it's okay. I wanted to ask you about the "quiet road" you mentioned last year and, uh . . . that road jockey thing."

Giving a weary grin, Stanley placed his hand on Alan's shoulder. "I would love that, son. I'm just too tired to share it with you right now. It takes some time to discuss it. You understand, don't you?"

Alan felt guilty for pressing the exhausted older man. Stanley did look extremely tired, and he was sure it could wait until Monday. "Sure, sure, Stanley, I'm sorry for asking." He was trying to muster every ounce of sincerity within him, so Stanley wouldn't notice his disappointment.

"It's this project," Stanley started. "It has to be completed by . . ." He stopped mid-sentence as if he was just recognizing Alan was fine with waiting until Monday for their visit.

"Thanks, son. Have a good weekend, or should I say, have a good Sunday?"

"Yeah, that's right only tomorrow to rest up. You too, Stanley."

Sunday afternoon was the annual Browne family picnic. Usually the entire Browne family, including Alan's aunts, uncles, and cousins travelled to a local park or to one of his relative's homes, but this year it was in Alan's backyard. Sunday morning, his mother and father scurried about making sure there was enough of everything and moving tables and chairs around to accommodate all the extra people who invariably telephoned at the last minute, stating they would actually be in attendance. After one such call, Alan's mother was in a near panic.

"Alan," she called across the house from the kitchen, "Alan, come here now!" As Alan entered the kitchen she handed him a small piece of paper with three, ten dollar bills on top with the instructions to hurry. "Just go to Safeway," she explained with the repeated admonition, "Hurry."

Wandering up and down the aisles at the local grocery store was not Alan's idea of how he wanted to spend a Sunday afternoon. With about half of the seventeen items on his mother's list secured in his cart, Alan paused in front of the beer case to ponder how his mother would react if he used some of her money for a six pack of Schlitz. He smiled, as he thought about her voice screeching out, "Oh, Alan, honestly!" then he heard a voice behind him.

"Can't decide on how many or is it the brand?"

He swung around to find the Youth Pastor from the church he hadn't attended in more than a year smiling back at him. In fact, the last time he had visited was during Spring Break the year he dropped out of college.

"It's good to see you, Alan. How have you been?" Although the pastor wasn't leaning forward, it felt to Alan as though he were.

Alan leaned back a bit, "I'm fine, how are you, Fred?"

Fred Howard was a very nice man. However, the setting in which the two were standing, and the fact that Alan was gawking at the stacks of adult beverages made the get-reacquainted-session more than a little awkward.

"I'm doing fine Alan. I've missed seeing you around church. Are you attending somewhere else these days?"

"Well, no, not really. I had to drop out of school and started working full time, so I'm pretty tired on the weekends. I still read my Bible and pray and stuff though." Alan almost sounded apologetic.

"Hey, I'm not asking for an explanation Alan. I just want you to stay plugged in somewhere. It doesn't have to be our church. But stay involved okay? You have some really great gifts, and others are drawn to you." Fred had that kind of half-smile-half-frown face on. It was the same face he used when he wanted the youth group to know the point he just made was important.

"I appreciate that, Fred. It means a lot. I'll get back soon, but I can't this evening because we're having our annual Browne family picnic at our house. In fact, I really need to finish shopping and get back home." Now Alan had a contrite tone.

"It's really nice to see you again, Alan. Don't be a stranger." Fred expressed as he walked away.

"Nice to see you, too!" Alan called back. Alan felt awful as he watched Fred turn the corner and head out of sight.

"Well, that was awkward." he whispered as he once again looked toward the beer racks. He shook his head and glanced down at his mother's list then started for the potato chips. While still gazing at the list, he turned the corner and found himself face-to-face with Fred.

"Oops," Alan chuckled as he quickly backed up.

Fred laughed, "Alan, I came back to tell you something. Memorial Day weekend is coming up, and we are having a college age retreat for all students returning from school. All the high school graduating seniors are invited too. Alan, it would be really great if you could come." The tone was friendly, but he was definitely pressing. "Come on, what do you say? There will be many from the old gang there. I'm sure you'll know almost everyone. It'll be fun."

"Oh, I don't think I can make that weekend. I have a lot going on right now."

Alan's quick wit was failing him. He was sure Fred would know it was just an excuse, a front to hide the fact that he didn't really want to see any of the old gang. Most were still in school. Some had graduated and received their degrees. And as far as he knew, he would be the only dropout among them. This was not something his fragile self-esteem needed. Not now anyway.

"Thanks, Fred, but I really can't make it. Say 'hi' to the gang for me though, okay?"

"Will do. Really nice to see you again, Alan. Stay in touch, and if you change your mind just give me a call, okay?" They waved at each other as they continued on their separate ways.

"It would be nice to see some of those guys," he acknowledged on the way back home. "But not on a retreat. That would be incredibly difficult to sit there for hours on end wondering what to say. Then, I'd make some smart-alecky comment that I would end up regretting for years. It's like the high school class reunion. There are so many people I would really like to see, but I would much rather just run into them individually on the street somewhere. In a big gathering, everyone knows they'll be seen by others they haven't seen in years, so they dolly themselves up. No, I don't want to go to something like that. Not now, not ever!"

-four-

By the time the family picnic, which had turned into a game night, was over it was well past eleven o'clock. Alan, his brothers, sister, and parents cleaned up most of the mess before going to bed sometime just before midnight. As he set his alarm clock, allowing himself an extra thirty minutes of sleep, Alan reminded himself not to be late for work.

Monday he dragged himself around the jobsite but tried to appear energetic in front of Big Jim. He knew if Big Jim suspected he was exhausted, he would ride him relentlessly. "Go here, do this, go there, do that," he could almost hear the words as he endeavored to give the impression of being busy.

Sometime after nine o'clock, Big Jim called the entire crew over to the job trailer. They gathered at the foot of the metal stairs with Big Jim standing at the top like a preacher in his pulpit. Alan was sure Big Jim relished his perch where he could announce his latest decree to his peasant subjects below. Although he faced Jim, Alan's eyes darted around looking for Stanley. "He must still be working on the trim inside the house," he thought. Then he noticed Stanley's truck wasn't in its usual spot.

"Guys, bad news," Big Jim paused, allowing the men a chance to prepare themselves for the next words, "Stanley had a stroke."

The words traveled through the air carrying with them a rush of emotion. Stanley was well-liked and admired by everyone. Alan turned in disbelief, he began walking slowly back toward the house and his duties because he didn't know what else to do. He heard one of the carpenters behind him ask if Stanley was at home or in a hospital.

"He's in Arlington Hospital. You know, he and Betsy have lived down there since the early 1950s. It's not good. They're not sure he's going to make it."

Whirling around, Alan marched back to the trailer, and called out, "Do you know if he can have visitors?"

"Not sure, kid, you'd have to call the hospital. I think he's in intensive care though," Big Jim sounded like he was sympathizing with Alan. Several more questions were asked as the entire crew groped for more information regarding the condition of their admired leader. The urgent requests far surpassed the level of information actually possessed by Big Jim.

"Look," he conceded, "I don't have any more details. I just heard the news myself a minute ago from Dan the Man. Come on, you guys, let's get back to work. There's still a lot to be done to finish this house . . . and now we have to do it without Stanley."

On the way home, Alan finally let the tears out that he had held back all day. At one point, he pulled his truck off the side of the road since he was having difficulty seeing through his blurry eyes. He then remembered a park close by where he used to go for long runs. Pulling his truck into the gravel parking area, he stopped under the shade of a beautiful dogwood tree in full bloom. He half-prayed and half-talked while he thought about poor old Stanley. He had really grown fond of him. He reminded Alan of his great-grandfather Browne, who had been very kind to him when he was a child. Alan called him Great Papa. In fact, up to this point in his life, Great Papa's funeral was the only funeral Alan had ever attended. He was eleven years old at the time and could remember it like it had happened last week. The memory of Great Papa caused Alan's eyes to continue to fill with tears.

"Great Papa is gone. Stanley's gone. I wonder who's next?" he sniveled, pitying himself more than he should.

Just then an attractive girl, who appeared to be about Alan's age, jogged by in her running outfit. Alan quickly sat up in his seat. Managing a wry grin and hoping to catch her attention, he pointed one finger from the hand that was resting on the top of the steering wheel. He watched her head down the same trail he used to run on for his longest loop in the park.

"You're next," he chided himself. "Great, the first cute girl you've seen in months, and you're sitting here feeling sorry for yourself." His eyes still followed her as she jogged down the trail and out of sight. "And she's a runner," he complained out loud. Alan was especially interested in girls who enjoyed running.

All week he thought about Stanley and wondered how he was doing. Occasionally, he asked Big Jim if there had been any word. The reply was always a blunt, "Negative!"

By Friday afternoon, Alan had made up his mind to visit Stanley over the weekend at Arlington Hospital. Driving down Saturday afternoon, he tried to prepare himself for what he might see. He'd never been to visit someone who had suffered a stroke before. "I think my grandfather Pilcher's sister had a stroke a few years back when I was a senior at Oakton High. She's still alive and doing pretty well." Alan was trying to reassure himself that maybe Stanley wasn't as bad off as he was anticipating.

Walking the halls of the hospital with a general feeling of uneasiness, Alan quickly concluded he wasn't fond of these medical institutions. He didn't like the way people eyed him either. "Granted, I must look somewhat lost, but I'm not sick or anything." He eventually found his way to the intensive care unit and approached the desk where several nurses and a doctor stood. After a couple of minutes had passed, he summoned the courage and stammered, "Uh . . . pardon me?"

A courteous, attractive nurse with grey hair turned to Alan, "How may I help you, baby?"

Alan smiled, "I'm looking for Stanley Taft. He's a patient here."

"Oh sweetie, they sent him down to regular care last Wednesday."

"Where's that?"

"Let me see which room they moved him to."

She opened a big binder filled with dozens of sheets of paper. "Hmmm," she rubbed her chin with her free hand. "He's not in here. Y'all know where they sent Mr. Taft?" she asked without even looking up from the binder.

"Home," came the reply from someone in the group of nurses gathered around the doctor.

"He was released this morning," added another nurse.

Alan smiled and thanked the nurse for her kindness. Just before leaving he asked, "Do you have his home address?"

"Oh, sugar, we aren't allowed to give out personal information." Then noticing the disappointment on Alan's face, she held up one finger as if to say, "But wait just a second." Reaching behind the countertop, she pulled out a phone book and proposed, "Maybe you could look him up." As he flipped to the "T" section in the massive book he thanked her again.

The Taft's house was not at all what Alan had envisioned. It was a small, brick single story home, painted white, with a deep crimson front door and shutters. The short driveway on the right led to a single car detached garage with white clapboard siding. A generous screened porch was on the left side, opposite the drive. Heavily laden with white blossoms, a large dogwood stood near the porch while the yard had more brilliant azaleas than lawn. It was entirely surrounded by a short white picket fence. Alan thought it was like something one would see in a Better Homes and Gardens magazine. He parked on the street in front of the gate that had a small sign on it which read, "Friends always welcome," with an insignificant arrow pointing toward the driveway.

With each step he took, his running shoes made a scrunching sound as they landed on the minuscule stones that formed the two tire tracks of the driveway. Alan chose to walk on the middle strip of green grass instead. "This place is immaculate," he whispered to himself as he knocked on the wooden screened door at the side of the house. It rattled with each blow from his knuckles. Alan could see through the screen that the inside door was open.

"Come on in," sang a female voice. Alan wasn't sure what to do, so he waited. "Bernie, I said . . . oh!" the female voice appeared from around the corner of the open door.

"Hi, my name is Alan Browne, I work with Stanley."

"Oh, my goodness, yes. Well, come right on in, Alan. I'm Stanley's wife, Betsy. Come on in, honey." She immediately gave Alan the impression that she must be one of the nicest grandmothers ever.

"Please have a seat, dear," she motioned toward the direction of the small table in the corner of the tiny kitchen. "Stanley has told me so much about you," she smiled. She jumped back to her feet, "Would you care for something to drink? How about some iced tea?"

"Uh, sure, thank you very much." Alan's mother had always told him to accept something offered when visiting someone. "It's the polite thing to do, even if you don't want what's offered," she had instructed.

Watching Betsy, Alan observed how she opened the old refrigerator and then the cabinet to get a glass while she continued talking. "I bet she's done that thousands of times. She doesn't even have to think as she goes from one place to another in the kitchen. It's like she does it by instinct."

Betsy was a short, stocky woman who possessed one of the friendliest personalities Alan had ever seen. She made him feel right at home, like they had known each other for years. She wore a flower-print house dress and black shoes with a small heel. Alan smiled while she went on about this thing or that. At one point, she paused for a second or two, as if to say, "Okay, your turn to talk." After fumbling for a topic, Alan queried, "Uh, who's Bernie?"

"Oh, good heavens, I almost forgot," Betsy glanced at her watch. "Bernie's my brother. He lives in Sleepy Hollow and should be here any minute. We're going to talk about how to care for Stanley here at home."

"Can he have visitors?" Alan was anxious to see him.

"Well, he's sleeping right now. But maybe we could poke our heads in and take a peek," smiled Betsy patting Alan's hand. With that she started out of the kitchen. "Follow me," she whispered.

Alan couldn't help but notice how sunny Betsy's disposition was under what must be the cloudiest of circumstances. He followed her through a little living room filled with what Alan thought were antiques. They went down a short hall to a door cocked open just a bit. She turned to Alan and put one finger on her lips. "Please be quiet, Alan, okay?" He nodded his compliance.

Opening the door slowly, she revealed a room with very little light coming from a shaded window behind the bed where Stanley lay sleeping. Alan could hear the labored breathing even before his eyes were able to recognize where it was coming from. As his eyes slowly adjusted to the darker atmosphere, Stanley came into view. Just then he heard a rattled knock on the wooden screened door in the kitchen.

"Oh, that must be Bernie," Betsy whispered, tapping Alan on the arm before she left Stanley's room.

Alan had a difficult time taking it all in. Stanley was a man he had come to know, respect, and appreciate. He admired how strong and knowledgeable Stanley was. Just last week he was out working alongside him, and now he lay listless upon this bed. He peered through the dim light trying to gain a clearer glimpse of his informal mentor.

"You okay, Stanley?" he barely allowed his words to be audible. There was no sound in reply other than the labored breathing. Stanley's face appeared contorted. His head was cocked over to one side, almost laying on his shoulder, which seemed to be in a permanent shrug. Alan felt tears welling up in his eyes. "I'm so sorry, my dear friend."

"Alan?" Betsy was quietly trying to get his attention from the hallway. Wiping the moisture from his eyes he turned around and walked out of Stanley's room.

"I would like you to meet my brother, Bernie Himmel," Betsy motioned with her hand in the direction of the man standing across the living room.

"Nice to meet you, young man," smiled Bernie.

"The language was English but had a rather thick accent of some sort," thought Alan. "Very nice to meet you sir." Alan stuck out his hand in greeting although he looked toward Betsy.

"Our parents migrated from Germany when we were just little ones," she explained. "Bernie is the oldest, so he has retained the strongest German accent. I don't really have much of one because I was so young when we came to America."

"Oh," Alan nodded. "Well, I really should be going. Thank you so much for the iced tea. That was very kind."

Alan knew that Betsy and her brother needed to be alone for the very serious conversation that was to come.

"Okay then, honey, if you have to." Betsy walked Alan to the door. As he stepped out onto the gravel drive, she said, "Please visit again soon. Anytime, Alan, I really enjoyed meeting you."

"Yes ma'am, I will," Alan smiled back.

"Now, Alan," she teased, "You call me Betsy. No more of this ma'am nonsense, okay?"

Alan laughed. "Yes, Betsy. And please, when Stanley wakes up, tell him I dropped by, okay?" he pleaded as he started down the driveway.

"I will," came her reply.

Looking back, something came over Alan like a warm flood of liquid emotion invisibly being poured upon him. He turned around, walked up to Betsy, and put his arms around his new found friend. "Thank you, Betsy. God be with you," he whispered in her ear.

"Ah, thank you, Alan. You've made an old woman's day."

He gave her a kiss on the head through her curly grey hair. Leaving he waved and announced, "I'll be by after work one day later this week."

On the way home Alan decided Wednesday would be a good day to visit Stanley and Betsy. Then he could visit once during the week and once on the weekend, until Stanley got better. Selfishly, he was guessing Betsy would have dinner for him if he dropped by after work. He was assuming that Stanley would be well enough to talk, at least a little, by the middle of the week. He was secretly hoping to ask him about the "quiet road" and the "road jockey" thing. It had really piqued his interest.

That week seemed to fly by as everyone was carrying a heavier load than usual without their skilled leader. The carpenters took on the trim, the apprentices did more of the door and window hardware, and Alan was swamped doing everything from carrying trim, to running to the hardware store, to touch up painting. Before he knew it, it was Wednesday. He had determined to ask Big Jim at lunch if he could leave an hour early to go down to Arlington to see Stanley. However, at about eleven o'clock Dan the Man showed up to walk the project. Then, he and Big Jim left for lunch and didn't return to the jobsite until just before time to go home.

Calling the crew over, Big Jim climbed the four steps to his pulpit. Everyone was there, except Stanley, of course. "Men, last night our dear friend departed for greener pastures."

Big Jim's voice almost broke; he was obviously upset. Two of the carpenters asked when and where. Alan was a bit confused as to what exactly Big Jim was referring to. He leaned over to the carpenter standing next to him and asked, "What's he talking about?" The carpenter just shrugged his shoulders. Big Jim could tell that Alan wasn't the only one who was in denial.

"Boys . . . Stanley died last night in his sleep at home. The funeral will be this Friday, two p.m. at Arlington Christian Church on Wilson Blvd. Dan the Man says that whoever wants to go can have the afternoon off with pay."

Alan was in shock. He turned away and walked slowly to his truck. Getting in, he quickly drove away. He arrived at the same park he had gone to the first time he received the terrible news about Stanley's stroke. But this time he got out and started walking down the trail. Once he was out of sight of the parking lot, he started running. He ran as hard and as fast as his work clothes and boots would allow. He made it all the way to the creek. Then he dropped to his knees on the stony bank and started yelling out loud.

"Why? Why take this good man? Why?!" he shouted. He was more angry than sad.

Picking up a rock, he threw it with all his might into the water, then another, and another. Yes, he was angry Stanley had died. But he was also angry he had passed away before he could get back to see him. And deep down inside, he was angry that he would never find out the secret he felt he desperately needed to know. What had Stanley meant when he told him to find a quiet road and to be a road jockey?

"Or something like . . . I don't even know what it was anymore," he shouted.

"I wish I knew," he said softly as he began to weep. "Stanley's really gone this time. He's really gone forever." He put his head in his hands and sobbed, "He's gone forever."

~five~

All spring days should be like May in Virginia. "If you have to have a funeral, you want it to be on a day like this," Alan thought as he drove to the church. He learned from the Pastor's eulogy that Stanley and Betsy had been married over forty years. They never had children of their own, but took care of a nephew off and on throughout the years as well as a few foster children on occasion. He painted a picture of a generous, kind, and caring person who tried to quietly live by his beliefs. He said Stanley was always ready to help anyone in need and shared a couple of poignant stories to illustrate.

"Funerals are never easy, but if you have to go to one," Alan thought on his way to the wake at Betsy's house, "at least this was a pleasant one."

The gathering was in the Taft's back yard. Immaculately maintained, like the front yard, it had two huge oak trees to shade the beautifully manicured lawn. There was a modest vegetable garden in the far corner up against the rear picket fence. Alan proclaimed, more than once, to whoever would listen, how beautiful the setting was with all the assorted colors and varieties of flowers. Making his way over to the three picnic tables covered with white cloths, he poured himself some bright red punch and stood off to the side.

Even though he tried to avoid being noticed, Alan met all of Stanley and Betsy's family and several of their friends. Each one took their turn consoling Betsy, who actually seemed to be doing most of the comforting.

She was a remarkable woman to watch. She would immediately turn a gesture of consolation by a friend into a word of care and love for another. "I would like to be like that," he marveled. "I really want to care for others more than I care for myself." He was considering it more wishful thinking than something he could actually achieve. "How does she do it? She's got to be hurting, yet she loves on others who are hurting too." I wonder how you go from being as self-absorbed and self-conscious as I am, to being so caring, so others-focused like Betsy?"

He reasoned while watching her, "She must have been born that way. She must have had warm and loving parents. Yeah, everyone is a product of their environment." At least that's what his Psychology professor had declared. "She must have had it easy growing up. No wonder she's so nice," he reassured himself, while also justifying his own self-absorption. "Although, come to think of it, I didn't have a rough childhood, so what's my excuse?"

After an hour or so, he made his way over to say goodbye to Betsy. They exchanged a few polite words, but it was obvious to Alan she was more concerned about her other guest's well-being than having a conversation with someone she hardly knew. As he walked down the gravel drive toward his truck, he felt an emptiness, an aloneness, a heavy sadness that bordered on depression.

"Maybe I shouldn't have come," he confessed. "I think I'll go by . . ."

"Oh Alan!"

He turned to see Betsy half jogging down the driveway.

"Alan, you promised to drop by."

"I know I am so very sorry. I feel absolutely terrible."

"What? No, no, dearie, you misunderstand me." Betsy was using her grandmotherly-kindness tone. "Please drop by any time, okay? I have something I would really like to talk to you about. You have any time this weekend?"

Alan smiled a smile that came from way down inside of him somewhere, "I'll drop by tomorrow, if it's okay? Or would Sunday be better?"

"Let's make it Sunday afternoon. Three o'clock?"

"Three o'clock it is," beamed Alan. "I'll see you then Betsy. I'm really looking forward to it!"

"Me too. Be careful driving home now, dear."

On the way home, he decided to stop by the church where he used to attend before heading off to college. He was looking for Pastor Fred and found him in the Youth Center, which was more of a basketball court than a meeting hall. Pastor Fred was an athletic man with a kind heart. He enjoyed beating someone on court almost as much as comforting him afterwards.

When he saw Alan approaching from across the room, he jumped up, shouted, "Hey, Alan!" and threw a basketball his way. "How you doing? Long time no see," he teased, crouching down in a defensive posture.

Alan took a long shot from on top of the key. It bounced off the rim and Pastor Fred tipped it back in with a jab.

"Two points," he bantered.

"Fred, do you have a minute?" Alan was hoping to be a bit more serious than playing a one on one basketball game would allow.

"Sure, Alan, what's up?" Then, moving toward the chairs along the side line, he said, "Have a seat."

Without a whole lot of detail as to why he was not attending church or an explanation for their last conversation in the grocery store, Alan came right to the point of his impromptu visit. "Is there still room on the college retreat for one more?"

"Why sure! In fact, I'm in need of someone over twenty-one to drive the church van. Would you be willing?"

Alan thought Fred was pressing his luck and was about to reply, "No thank you," when Fred blurted out,

"The driver gets half off the cost of the retreat."

That last little piece of information caught Alan's attention. He thought for a few moments then conceded, "Oh, alright. I guess it will be fine."

"That's great, Alan. I can't wait to tell everyone the great Alan Browne is going on our retreat! They'll all be thrilled."

"Now, wait just a minute there, Fred," Alan rebuffed. "I'm not going to be a side show or anything. If that's the case, I'm staying home!"

"Ah, Alan, I'm just kidding. Although, I know everyone will be very happy to see you. You've made quite the impression on many of our young people. You are somewhat of a legend to them, you know."

Alan smiled, "Like they say in that new movie, *Star Wars*, That was . . . 'a long time ago in a galaxy far, far away.'"

"Maybe we'll have another touch football game at this retreat?" Fred was testing the water more for Alan's receptivity than actually planning a football game.

"It's baseball season," proclaimed Alan. "You can't play football during baseball season." They both laughed and agreed if a game was to be played on the retreat, it would be baseball.

As they walked across the floor together, Fred gave Alan the details of the retreat. They would leave next Friday at five p.m. from the church. The retreat center was in the mountains of Western Maryland. They were hoping to arrive there between ten and eleven that night. Because it would be Memorial Day, they would return to Northern Virginia on Monday afternoon. Fred insisted, since Alan would be driving the van, he would need to be at the church early on Friday. Alan acquiesced as they shook hands and said goodbye.

"Well, that wasn't so bad," He declared to himself on the way home from the church. "Maybe it's the first step to a different me." Little did Alan know how true those words would come to be.

He left early for Betsy's on Sunday afternoon because he wanted to drop by the grand opening of the bicycle shop he helped Tiny build. Since both were in Arlington, he thought he could knock out two birds with one stone. The parking lot at the new Cycle Sports Pro Shop was packed with cars and people riding bikes.

"Wow, this place is really popular." he chuckled with delighted surprise. He was greeted at the door by Bruce, who soon had Alan looking over the latest aluminum bikes from a company called Cannondale.

"This is not your father's bike, Alan. Give it a try in the parking lot. You're going to love it, dude." Bruce was trying his most recently learned sales tactic on his latest victim.

Alan was absolutely amazed at how the bike handled. It responded to his every move, whether he was steering, or pressing on the pedals. "That's un-be-stinking-lievable man!" he shouted as he rode past Bruce, who was still standing at the front door. Alan frequently used the wonderfully descriptive word he had learned from Tiny.

"I knew you'd love it!" Bruce laughed back.

"You're right. This is nothing like I have ever ridden before." Alan stopped in front of Bruce. "How much?"

Bruce looked down at the bright green frame, then looking back at Alan, "Six hundred dollars, uh . . . plus tax." After looking away, he glanced back at Alan, who had an expression of shock on his face, his mouth hanging wide open.

"Not my father's price tag either, eh Bruce."

"Well, I'm sure, for you, we could come down a bit."

"How much?" Alan amazed himself he was even considering buying such an expensive bicycle. Especially since he only paid three hundred-fifty dollars for his pickup truck.

"I'm sure we could make you a really great deal. Let me ask Frank what we can do, okay?"

Bruce walked across the wood showroom floor to the sales counter where Frank and Carol stood. Alan, holding the shiny Cannondale near the front door, watched the owners haggle over how much of a discount they were going to give him. It must have been Bruce mentioning Alan's name which triggered the three to look in his direction and immediately head toward him.

"Hey, Alan," they exclaimed in unison.

Then Frank, smiling at his wife, asked Alan, "How have you been?"

Alan gave them the Reader's Digest version of the events that had affected his life of late: how Stanley had died and how his job was going. "All in all, *comme si comme ca.*" Alan nodded in Bruce's direction knowing he would appreciate his use of French to describe his overall well-being. "I'm sure that's more than you wanted to know, but suffice it to say, it's been good and bad lately." Alan tried to avoid sounding like he was complaining.

Frank continued, "Actually, we were wondering about you, Alan. When we came back that Friday, Tiny explained you had been transferred to a project in Great Falls. He said you weren't happy."

"Yeah, well . . . it's not the same as working for Tiny."

Frank smiled and patted Alan's shoulder, "How would you feel about coming to work for us Alan?"

"What?" The offer pleasantly surprised Alan. He tried to hold back the smile that was forcing its way onto his face. "Well . . . I, uh . . . I'm not quite sure what to say."

"How much do they pay you at your current job as a carpenter's helper?" queried Frank.

"I make four twenty-five an hour," replied Alan. "I just got a raise a few weeks ago," he furthered with some pride in his voice.

"We can pay you the same per hour. Plus we'll pay you five dollars extra for every bike you sell." Frank was really pouring on the pressure. "And," he continued, "if the sales price is over five hundred dollars, we'll make the commission ten dollars. What do you say, Alan? You interested?"

"Wow, that's very kind of you. I'm not sure what to say. Could I have a couple of days to think it over? Maybe I should talk to my parents about this. Is that okay?"

"Sure. Just give me a call and let me know as soon as you can, okay?" Frank had backed off of his high pressure tactics, but had one last thought for Alan. "We're really busy and need to hire someone quickly. So let me know by Tuesday, okay?" Then, putting his hand on the handlebars of the bike Alan had been holding, "Employees get bikes at cost."

"Thanks, Frank, I'll get back to you as soon as possible." He rolled the bike toward Bruce stating, "I think I'll hold off on this purchase just yet."

Alan's mind was a whirlwind of activity during the drive to Betsy's house. Pondering the job offer from Frank brought a smile to his face. "I wonder if I could make it work? It would be nice not to have to put up with Big Jim's attitude every day. Hmmm . . . the commute is longer though. I can't wait to hear what Mom and Dad have to say about this."

It was really nice to see Betsy again. She seemed quieter than the day of Stanley's funeral. She explained to Alan that it had been a really difficult couple of weeks, and she was a bit tired.

"I can come another day if that is better for you Betsy."

"No, no, dearie today is fine. Would you care for some iced tea?" She always smiled when she asked Alan a question. "Please sit down Alan."

"Sure, thank you, Betsy. You doing okay today?" he questioned once he sat down at the kitchen table.

"Well, I'm feeling drained, Alan," she explained, placing the glass of cold tea down in front of him. "It has been a very emotional few weeks, dear. I just need a good night's rest, for tomorrow will be a brighter day. Now, the reason I asked you over today," she continued with a more concerned tone, "is because I wanted to discuss something very important with you."

Alan moved forward in his seat and encouraged, "Yes, ma'am?"

Betsy gave him a look as if to say, "What did I tell you about calling me ma'am!" However, she said nothing.

"I've decided, since Stanley and I never had any children, and since I sure don't know how to use them . . . well, I want you to have his carpenter's tools. I know Stanley would want you to have them too." Betsy was smiling but there were tears in her eyes.

"Wow . . . uh, I don't know what to say, Betsy. Are you sure? I mean, don't they hold some sentimental value or something?" Alan was trying to talk her out of the generous offer although, deep down inside he was jumping up and down with excitement.

"Oh, no, honey, there's no sentimental value for me. I don't even know what he's got out there," she was motioning in the direction of the little detached garage in the backyard. Rising to her feet, she patted Alan on his hand and exclaimed, "Let's go see!"

Pulling outward, the two explorers opened the heavy, wooden doors to the garage. They peered into a floor to ceiling mess of scrap material, tools, spare parts, and the like.

"Stanley didn't have German parents," Betsy stated frankly, as if that explained the reason for the messy sight before them, and why the rest of their property was so immaculate. Then she smiled, "I was never allowed in his workshop."

Alan looked at Betsy just long enough to see her wink back at him. She laughed, "God love him. He was a wonderful husband and my dearest friend, but boy was he a mess." Alan laughed too. He put one arm around her and held her tight. The two mourners had quickly become good friends.

"Now, just the carpenter's tools, okay, Alan? Bernie told me he may want some of the other junk in here."

"Of course," he nodded in agreement with his eyes widened, like those of a sweet toothed kid in a candy store. "Okay to back my truck up the driveway?"

"Sure, dearie," she sighed and smiled all at the same time. "I think I'll lie down for a few minutes. Have fun, Alan." She patted him on the back. Afterwards, she turned to walk toward the house.

"I won't take anything unless you approve it first, Betsy," he called after her. Opening the wooden screened door, she waved back as if to say that was fine with her.

Alan spent the rest of the afternoon in Stanley's garage, which had really been used more for a shed. Amid the mounds and stacks of junk, he occasionally discovered a beautiful wood chisel or an old handsaw at the bottom. It was filthy work, but he loved every minute of it. Hours later, Betsy brought out a plate of meatloaf, mashed potatoes, and sweet peas. After he washed at the outdoor spigot, they both ate dinner at the picnic table under the awning attached to the side of the garage. He had never met anyone as kind as Betsy in his entire life.

"Here she is in mourning, and she is serving me." He was continually amazed at her selfless and caring ways, causing him to wonder at the source of her seemingly endless inner strength.

After dinner, he concentrated for an hour or so on the tool bench area. "There," he allowed himself some satisfaction. "Spare parts in that pile, scrap wood over there, pipes and, uh . . . pipe stuff right there, carpenter tools by the door, and oh, yeah, all the other tools on the work bench." Just then, Betsy came out with a plate of chocolate chip cookies and a tall glass of cold milk.

"Lookee there!" she exclaimed in amazement, "There's a concrete floor in that garage. I was positive it was dirt." They both laughed out loud.

It was already dark, but Betsy assured Alan she could see the tools he had laid out for himself. She looked them over carefully, more at Alan's request, than for her own benefit. "I think that's fine, Alan. I'm glad someone will be putting them to good use. I mean, you'll use them won't you?"

"Oh, absolutely, I'll use them every day at work and on projects at home," he blurted out without stopping to think. This posed a bit of a problem for Alan because he was seriously considering the job offer from Frank at the bike shop.

"When you're done, Alan, please lock up the garage for me. I really need to get to bed now. I'm so glad you came over, dear. Please be careful on your drive home."

"I will, Betsy. And thank you, thank you, thank you so much." Alan gave her a big hug to show how much it all meant to him. "I'll make Stanley proud."

He watched her as she slowly walked back toward the house with the empty plate of cookies and glass of milk, both of which Alan had devoured in short order. "What a precious lady," he mused aloud.

"Lord, bless dear Betsy and please comfort her in these days. I'm sure she is hurting more than she says." He was doing his half-praying, half-talking thing he used to do all the time. He had drifted away from that for some reason. He wasn't sure when, but at least he did it today.

"Wow, what a day this has been," he bellowed, turning to the pile of tools on the floor. "Well, let's get you guys loaded up."

It was after nine o'clock before he had all the tools loaded in his pickup truck and started for home. No more than a couple of miles from Betsy's, it suddenly began to rain and continued to pour all the way home. Pleased to find that his father had not parked the family station wagon in their garage, he quickly backed his truck into the driveway. Alan moved all of Stanley's soaking wet tools into the garage and closed the door. "Oh no!" he cried, starting to pull the waterlogged items out of the truck bed. "If I don't dry these off tonight, by morning they'll be rusted and will certainly be ruined."

Turning on the fluorescent overhead lights, he immediately started cleaning and drying the saturated instruments and equipment. With the job almost complete, and the hour approaching midnight, Alan came across a small flat leather pouch, no bigger than the palm of his hand. At one end it had an opening cinched closed with a leather draw tie. It lay at the bottom of a hand built wooden toolbox in a puddle of rainwater. Alan recognized the toolbox as Stanley's favorite because it was the one he had kept by his side at work every day.

"What's this?" he inquired out loud. He got a clean cloth from his father's box of old rags and began to dry off the little soggy satchel.

"Whaaat?!" He couldn't believe his eyes. There, embossed diagonally upon one side of the leather pouch, was a single word, all in lower case letters. Alan's eyes widened in excitement, yet he wiped the piece several more times to reassure himself of the word he thought he saw. He pulled the cloth slowly over the word one more time as if to give it a chance to change itself. There, staring back at him, was the word: **rojocci.**

six

Under the light by the box of rags in his garage, Alan stood for what seemed to be several minutes. He was in a state of quiet shock, almost frozen, as he stared down at the soaked leather pouch. "So that's how you spell 'road jockey'? I guess it wasn't 'road' after all. I was sure that Stanley said 'road jockey' though. If not, then what did he mean by me needing to find a quiet road? This doesn't make much sense."

Moving over to the open tailgate of his pickup truck, he dried off the wet surface and spread out the damp cloth he was using like a place mat upon the metal gate. Next, he laid the still moist leather satchel gently on the makeshift examination table. After retrieving another dry cloth, he cautiously loosened the calfskin drawstring. When he picked up the pouch, water trickled out from its interior cavity. He carefully took the dry cloth, as an expert forensics specialist might, and dabbed the inside of the pouch. Gingerly drying the opening, he discovered what appeared to be a folded piece of paper inside.

"What's this?" he questioned out loud as he quickly reached inside with his thumb and index finger to pull it out. To Alan's amazed disappointment, the paper was so saturated by the rain water that only a torn portion was removed from its soaked leather tomb.

"Ah, man," he complained out loud. "How am I ever going to get the rest of it out of there?"

He looked around the garage for any ideas that might work. Glancing down at Stanley's tools he had recently finished drying, he saw a pair of small needle nose pliers. "Yes," Alan exclaimed, "Those will work."

Again he laid the pouch flat upon the examination table which was the tailgate of his pickup truck. Gently squeezing the seamed sides of the leather satchel, he caused the opening to gape wide. While holding it steady in his left hand, he ever so slowly moved the needle nose pliers into the miniscule womb. Grasping the fragile, waterlogged remnant, he gently pulled it toward freedom. Just as the remains of the torn piece were being loosed from its bonds, the tips of the pliers ripped it in half.

"Oh, no," barked Alan. Reaching one more time with the pliers for the soaked paper, now protruding from the opening, he tenderly slid it to freedom. At this precise moment, he heard the living room clock strike midnight.

 "Whoa, that's spooky," he chuckled sarcastically. He tried to laugh off the precise timing of the esoteric event, yet it had a peculiar, unsettling effect on him.

"Now, let's see what we have here."
Alan moved the embossed leather pouch to the side and began to very carefully unfold the torn pieces of paper. After several minutes of an extremely genteel technique, he laid before him the tattered results of his exploration.

"Hmmm . . ." he breathed.

He could barely recognize letters handwritten in pencil on the three pieces. He moved the fragments to align the original edges of the paper. After more than one attempt, finally the completed puzzle and the full picture of the letters came into view. Everything was so wet that all the characters were terribly smudged and most were absolutely unreadable.

"Ah, come on, man," Alan complained as if the cause of his complaint was standing in the garage with him.

Inspecting his curious treasure gave him a rare mixture of apprehension and delight. He picked up the leather satchel again to reassure himself that the word embossed upon it was actually the word he thought he heard Stanley utter last December.

"That's got to be it. I'm ninety-nine percent sure that's the word. But what does it mean, and why did Stanley think I needed to find it?"

Turning his gaze back to the three wet pieces of torn paper, he scratched his head. Still peering at the fragments, he spelled the word out loud very slowly as if to let it sink deep within him.

"r-o-j-o-c-c-i"

Like a seasoned sleuth, he lingered over his investigation expecting the clues to speak to him from their silence. He leaned forward. "It's all too wet. Hey, wait a minute."

To avoid waking his family, he stealthfully ran into the house and up the stairs. In the hall bathroom he found Amy's hand held hair dryer hanging on the towel rack where she always left it. This usually annoyed Alan when he was trying to dry his hands, but this time he was happy it was so easy to find.

Back in the garage, he rolled out one of his father's electrical extension cords and plugged in the blow dryer. He held down each torn piece individually as he took low powered, sweeping flows of warm air across them. After a few minutes, he repeated the process on the reverse side. Flipping each one over very softly, he meticulously realigned the edges bringing the three together as a whole once again.

"There," he congratulated himself. "Now, let's see what we have here."

After many minutes of close inspection, Alan decided he needed more magnification. Running tiptoed once again through the darkened house, he found his mother's purse on a chair under the dining room table.

"I knew it!" he grinned. Digging through the vast cavern full of motherly paraphernalia, he grasped the object of his short search. "Yes," he whispered as he jogged back to the garage.

Once again, he leaned over the paper artifacts, this time with the item borrowed from his mother's purse. Catching a glimpse of his face in the rear window of his truck caused him to chuckle. His masculine features contrasted with the winged tipped, cat-eyed black framed reading glasses, mounted upon his beak, made quite the sight.

"Ah, the little fake diamonds give it just the right touch," he pronounced with a smirk. Then, looking down at the objects at hand, his expression turned more somber.

"Oooo . . . that's better. Yes, I think I see a . . ."

Suddenly, he jumped toward the passenger side of his truck and threw open the door. Scrounging around the items on the bench seat, he found a notepad and a carpenter's pencil. He laid them next to his makeshift laboratory on the tailgate. He squinted through the feminine spectacles trying to decipher what appeared to be letters. Leaning further forward, his nose just a few inches from the surface of the paper which had turned parchment, he began scribbling his findings upon the notepad.

Finally, after several close inspections, Alan was convinced he had gleaned all the artifact would release. He slowly turned to the little pad to review his findings. As he removed his mother's glasses, his curious amazement transitioned into somewhat of a guarded disappointment. Tearing out another sheet from his notepad, he wrote down a more legible rendering of his new discoveries.

The word **rojocci** was printed in lower case and in a diagonal fashion. However, only the "o-j-o-c-c" letters were actually discernible. There appeared to be smaller words emanating from each of the individual letters, as if the larger letters were the first letter in the represented word. None of these were even remotely recognizable with the exception of those aligned with the second "o" and the first "c" in the diagonal.

"This is the most curious thing I have ever seen," he declared out loud.

To confirm his findings of the two smaller words, he once again mounted the stylish lenses upon their youthful perch. "Yep, I think that says something like, '**overlook**' and the other one is definitely the word '**cherished**'. What in the world is that? I mean, I know what an overlook is, but why would an overlook be cherished?"

He headed back toward the door leading inside the house. He made his way carefully through the dark maze of the family room over to the bookshelves adjacent to the fireplace. Feeling on the lowest shelf with his hand, he came upon the largest book which could only be the dictionary. He carried it back out to the garage, stopping in the kitchen for a glass of cold milk.

Alan opened the big book on his tailgate and turned to the "C" section, there he came across the word "**cherish**". He repeated what he read several times to let it sink deep within. "To hold or treat as dear; to feel love for; to cling to fondly." He combined this definition with "**overlook**", which he found to mean, "To fail to notice; to disregard or ignore; to afford a view over."

He ran the combinations over and over in his mind working it several times until he proclaimed, "I'm not sure what it means; "**overlook** and **cherished**?" He read the definitions again combining them into a sentence. "To treat as dear something that is disregarded or maybe has a view over something." He was completely confused and yet absolutely determined to discover the answer to this mystery.

"And this **rojocci** thing," he pondered aloud as he sat down on the tailgate. "Maybe it's an acronym and not a word at all? I wish Stanley was still around so I could just ask him. I'm sure he would be happy to fill me in."

His mind wandered over the past several days as he reviewed all that he had discovered in the last few hours.

"Wow, what a day this has been: first, Frank's job offer down at the bike shop, then, dear Betsy giving me Stanley's tools, and now, this . . . road jockey, uh, I mean **rojocci** thing. Man, what a day. I wonder what this has to do with finding a quiet road. Hey, maybe **rojocci** is the quiet road? Or . . ."

He paused for a second or two.

"Or is the quiet road the **rojocci**? Boy, I sure wish Stanley was still alive. If only I had asked him sooner. If only I . . . wait a stinking minute!" He was using that descriptive word again. It was the same word Tiny used in almost every sentence when he needed to describe how he felt about something or someone. Alan was sure it was Tiny's second most used word other than "man". And now, Alan was using it in a moment of amazement, because he realized Betsy might know all about this.

"Surely Betsy would know the meanings of all the words and letters. She must at least have an idea of how the things Stanley said to me are related. I would guess she can make some sense of all of this. I have to get to her house tomorrow after work . . . tomorrow?!"

He peered down at his watch in disbelief. "I mean today. Oh man, I can't believe it's after one o'clock."

Monday flew by as well as Tuesday. For Alan was extremely busy helping the carpenters finalize all the details on the Great Falls house. On Wednesday, he left at a more reasonable hour and drove immediately to Betsy's. He knocked on the unlocked wooden screened door of her house several times, but no one answered. Her car was in the driveway, but there was no sign of her anywhere.

"Hmmm . . . maybe I'll leave her a note with my phone number."

Finding a roll of duct tape in the pile of junk on the floor of his truck, he attached the paper to the screened door with a small strip. Upon arriving home, he found his family already seated at the kitchen table eating dinner.

"Get cleaned up, honey, and I'll set you a plate," his mother said with an understanding tone. "Work late again?"

"No, ma'am, finished on time today but headed down to Betsy's in Arlington for a few minutes."

"Arlington?" questioned his father, "Where does she live down there?"

"Kind of off Quincy Street and Old Dominion Drive in Cherrydale," Alan shouted from inside the hall bathroom just off the kitchen.

His father glanced around at his other children seated at the table as if to say, "You know anything about this Betsy?"

Just then, everyone at the table heard a loud "Bam!" from inside the hall bath. It was quickly followed by a loud "Oh, man!" from Alan. It sounded like the toilet seat had slammed shut again.

Alan's brothers exclaimed in unison, "Guillotine!"

"Honey," his wife pleaded, "Would you please fix that toilet lid before one of our sons becomes a eunuch?"

The entire family, with the exception of Alan, burst into an uproar of laughter. Just then, Alan emerged from the bathroom and walked into the kitchen.

"What's so funny?" he begged as he sat down at the table.

"Well," chuckled Eddie, "Mom was just telling Dad to fix the toilet before one of us boys ends up a bit short one day." The family, this time including Alan, erupted into another round of laughter.

"Yeah Dad, the guillotine almost got me!" chuckled Alan.

"Who is Betsy, son?" Alan's father was quick to change the subject from another "to do" item that would now undoubtedly be on Mrs. Browne's list for the upcoming weekend.

"She's Stanley Taft's widow," Alan explained. "Remember the funeral I went to last week? It was for the guy at work I told you had been teaching me so much about carpentry and building. His widow gave me some of his carpenter's tools."

"Yeah, I noticed the mess you left in the garage. After dinner, get in there and clean it up, son." Alan's father was really trying to keep the focus on issues other than his wife's "to do" list.

"Yes, sir," smiled Alan. "Sorry about that, Dad."

"Oh, Alan," his mother interrupted, "Betsy called for you while I was fixing dinner."

"She did? What did she say?" he quizzed looking up from his plate of spaghetti.

"She expressed she was sorry she missed you but was having dinner with her brother and his wife. I think that's what she said anyway." His mother had leaned over on one elbow with her fork in the air. "Anyway, she left her phone number. It's by the phone on the countertop."

"Thanks, Mom." Alan turned around to see where she had laid the note.

"So who is this Betsy?" his father asked wanting to assure the subject had no chance of returning to weekend tasks for him to complete.

"Well," Alan consented laying his spaghetti laden fork on his plate. "She is an incredibly nice lady who just lost her husband. She's probably in her late fifties, or I don't know maybe she's sixty-something. I really liked her husband Stanley. He was a great guy who was really kind to me on the Great Falls project. Then last Sunday, she gave me some of his tools. So I feel like I should help her if she needs anything. You know what I mean, Dad?"

"Good for you, son," his father smiled. "It's always important to help widows whenever you can."

"Hey, Dad?" Alan paused, so he could shovel the waiting fork full of spaghetti into his mouth. "You ever heard of something called **roe-jock-ee**?" He was a bit hard to understand with a mouth full of vermicelli and marinara sauce.

"Road jockey?" posed Amy with one of her inquisitive looks.

"No, it's **roe-jock-ee**." Alan emphasized the "**roe**" portion of the word.

"How do you spell it Alan?" asked his mother.

"**r-o-j-o-c-c-i**" He glanced around at the faces staring back at him. They appeared as if they were waiting for Alan to explain the meaning to them. Alan's eyes stopped at his father's face, "Dad, you ever heard of it?"

"Doesn't sound familiar, son. Have you checked the dictionary and encyclopedia?"

"Yes sir, but I didn't find anything."

"Where did you see it?" his father queried although he didn't look up from his plate, so Alan wasn't sure if his father was interested in continuing the discussion.

"Ah, it was just something Stanley had mentioned to me some time ago. It's no biggie." Alan offered an apathetic tone, more to see if his father was still interested in the topic, than because he wanted to drop the discussion altogether.

Just then Amy, who was at the completion of her sophomore year, spoke up about her high school's Junior Prom and the dress she would be wearing. Alan thought she had probably been waiting for a break in the conversation. It was just as well, nobody seemed to know anything about his topic anyway.

When Amy finally finished her colorful description, ending with her shoes, Alan told his parents about the job offer he had received from the bike shop. After many questions and more advice than he was expecting, Alan determined that both his parents thought it would be wiser to stay in Cousin Dan's employ, than to work at Cycle Sports Pro Shop. It went back and forth for quite some time, and long after the plates were cleared from the table his parents agreed that perhaps a part time arrangement would work. It was an idea his mother brought up, and it actually made a lot of sense to Alan.

"See if they'll let you work one or two evenings a week and maybe on Saturday," she proposed. "Then, you can still learn construction but have another option if it doesn't work out later on."

The three of them agreed it was a good solution if the proprietors of the bike shop would allow Alan the opportunity. Alan told his parents he would talk it over with the owner sometime that week and let them know how it went.

Once their conversation had ended, Alan telephoned Betsy. After the initial pleasantries, which usually took several minutes whenever he spoke with her, he asked if she had any time available before the weekend when he could drop by.

"How about Friday after you finish at work, dearie?" offered Betsy.

"No, I'm going on a retreat for college kids this weekend, and I have to be at the church no later than four o'clock. Would tomorrow work?"

"Yes, that sounds real nice, Alan. And now you have my phone number, so you can call me if you won't be able to make it, okay?"

"Oh, don't worry, Betsy, I'll be there. Hopefully no later than six o'clock," he assured her.

"That sounds fine, dear." Betsy went on to ask him how he liked Stanley's tools and if he was putting them to good use. After he spent several minutes explaining how he wasn't exactly a full-fledged carpenter yet, but he did use them whenever he could, she replied, "Oh, I see." She seemed a bit more resigned and finished the conversation with her kind hearted way of expressing concern for Alan's well-being.

"Bye bye now, Alan, you be careful driving here tomorrow."

"Yes, ma'am, I will. I'm really looking forward to our visit." Alan was trying to end their conversation on a more upbeat note than the low one he thought he was sensing from her. The last thing he wanted to do was offend Betsy.

"Me, too, Alan. Bye bye."

"Bye, Betsy, see you tomorrow." Alan listened until the phone clicked on the other end. He now had a heaviness in his chest. It was the same feeling he got whenever he thought he may have offended someone, especially someone he cared for. And he really cared for Betsy.

~seven~

Thinking his day would never end, Alan finally got behind the wheel of his little pickup truck at four forty-five. Because he was trying to avoid the rush hour traffic, he made his way to the bike shop using all the backroads he knew. He looked down at his watch as he parked his truck in the parking lot. It was ten minutes after five o'clock. Even though he was anxious to get to Betsy's house, he wanted to be sure that Frank understood he appreciated the job offer. It took several minutes for Alan to explain his situation with his current job, how the owner was his relative, and what his parents had advised him to do. Although Frank seemed disappointed, it appeared to Alan that Frank understood.

Then, Alan suggested a part time solution. "I could work one or two evenings each week and Saturdays if that would help you, Frank."

Frank reclined back on the sales counter where they had been talking and nodded his head, "Yes, that might be just the solution, Alan. We are open until nine o'clock on Thursdays. Saturdays are from ten o'clock until six o'clock. If you could work a full day on Saturdays and come in right after you get off from your construction job on Thursdays, I think that would work for me. Are you sure it would work for you?"

Alan smiled, "Well sure, I have plenty of free time when I'd rather be working and making some money. I mean, it's not like I have a girlfriend or anything."

The two shook hands and agreed Alan would start at five o'clock, one week from today. "Thanks, Frank, I really appreciate the opportunity. See you next Thursday."

Alan was in a hurry to get to Betsy's. "Man, it's almost six o'clock." he whispered as he ran out the door to his truck.

It was just after six by the time he arrived at Betsy's house. He ran up her driveway and knocked on the wooden screened door. He looked himself over and determined he was too dirty to enter her always immaculate home. She greeted him at the door and invited him in.

"I better not, Betsy, I'm filthy from working all day. Would it be okay if we sat at the picnic table under the garage awning?"

"Sure, sweetie, let me get my sweater." When she returned she posed, "You hungry, Alan? I have some chicken-n-dumplings with biscuits?"

"Yes, ma'am, that sounds wonderful."

"Here." She handed him several placemats, two plates, and some utensils rolled up in napkins, through the partially opened screened door, "Iced tea okay?" she asked as the door bounced shut.

"Perfect," Alan called from halfway to the garage.

It was a very pleasant evening as the two of them enjoyed one another's company over a scrumptious dinner.

They set the plates aside as if they both knew that Alan had something really important he wanted to discuss. He poured them both some more iced tea. Then leaning forward, he took a deep breath. His antics piqued Betsy's curiosity and she broke the silence.

"Yes, Alan?"

"Uh, Betsy . . . uh . . . Stanley mentioned something to me one day at work last December. It was an unusual comment. However, before I had a chance to ask him what he meant by it, I got transferred to another job site. And, uh, although I visited him several times after work, the topic never really came up again until . . ." Alan paused as he looked across at Betsy with an expression that he hoped appeared sympathetic.

"Until?" coaxed Betsy.

"Well," Alan continued, "until I was transferred back to working with Stanley. But we never had a chance to talk about it and now he's . . ." This time his pause was more from choking back his emotions than from not knowing what he wanted to say.

After several seconds, Betsy patted his hand that was resting on the table. Then, she gently squeezed it and implored, "What is it Alan? It's okay, what's bothering you, dear?"

"Ummm, maybe it's more of how he expressed it, than what he expressed." He wiped the tears from his eyes. Looking up from the table top, he gazed across at Betsy, who sat quietly nodding her head.

"Yes?" she whispered, "What did Stanley say to you, honey?"

"Well, uh . . . Betsy, has Stanley ever mentioned to you anything about a quiet road? Or maybe something he called **rojocci**?" With this last word he looked directly into her eyes to determine if they would give away any indication she recognized the word.

"Oh sure, Alan," she smiled softly. "Is that what's troubling you?"

"Yes ma'am. I have no idea what Stanley was trying to say to me and now . . . it's too late. Can you help me with this? Do you know what he was trying to tell me?" Alan was leaning far forward now, so far forward his chest was pressed up tight against the edge of the picnic table.

"Tell me what you know about **rojocci,** Alan?" she negotiated with a gentle smile.

"Nothing really. However, I found this little leather pouch in the bottom of Stanley's wooden toolbox. It had a sheet of paper in it."

At this point in Alan's explanation, Betsy's eyes widened as if to say, Alan may have discovered something that he shouldn't have. Alan continued without giving a hint he had noticed the change in Betsy's expression.

"The paper was soaking wet because it rained all the way home that night. Everything was in the back of my pickup truck. I didn't have anything to cover Stanley's tools to keep them from getting drenched," he offered in an apologetic tone.

Betsy's eyes focused on Alan's eyes, and she responded in a most serious tone, "What exactly was written on the paper, dear?"

"It appeared to be the word **rojocci** handwritten in a diagonal fashion with several other words proceeding from each letter. Although, I'm not really sure, I think the word might be an acronym. Do you know anything about it, Betsy? Or for that matter, do you have any idea what Stanley meant by it, or by me needing a quiet road?" He gave her a winsome smile hoping it would help coax an answer from somewhere within her.

Betsy paused and then after smoothing out her housedress, scooched forward, quietly acknowledging in the same sober tone, "I think I can help you in your quest, Alan. But first, tell me what words you read proceeding forth from **rojocci** that were written on the paper you found."

"Well, it was so messed up! I'm so sorry, but the paper tore in three pieces as I was trying to remove it. Everything was sopping wet, and most of it was so smudged it was absolutely unreadable. So I only have two words. At least I think I have two words. The first came from the second 'o' and I'm pretty sure it was '**overlook**'. I think it's '**overlook**', but after combining it with the second word, it didn't make much sense to be '**overlook**', I mean because of the second word." He was looking intently at her face for the slightest change, but Betsy just nodded.

"The second word I could decipher proceeded from the first 'c' in the word **rojocci**. This word was the clearest of all the words on the paper. I know it is the word '**cherished**' and I looked up its meaning in the dictionary."

"What did the dictionary tell you? Did you combine it with the other word?"

At this point, Alan made a mental note that Betsy was actually asking more questions than Alan. So he determined he would quickly turn the conversation around.

"Something about, 'to hold as dear, or to care for fondly, or something like that'. Do you have any idea about all of this, Betsy?"

Betsy smiled and patted Alan's hand once again. "It's getting late, Alan, don't you think?" The tone gave Alan the idea Betsy was using the question to determine how much he really wanted to know.

"It's only a little after seven o'clock, Betsy," he pleaded.

"Alright, Alan, let me see." She shifted on the wooden picnic table bench seat to get comfortable, giving indication this may take a while.

"Number one, I won't be able to tell you everything. However, I think Stanley was trying to help you see something you didn't know was there. And probably, knowing my Stanley," she continued, "he was giving you an indication of where you would have to be, before you could know it was there." She paused trying to emphasize that this was important. "You see, dear, you have to be receptive before you can receive it, or are able to hear it." She raised her voice just as she finished her sentence.

"Receive what?" probed Alan.

"Receive what you really need." She replied frankly.

Alan's eyes darted around the yard as his mind darted around its hidden resources. "I don't understand. What do I really need?" he asked after more than a few seconds passed.

"Look within your heart, Alan. Can you hear the **still** small voice?"[1] she whispered for effect. "It's so quiet, but if you listen real close, you can hear an ever so soft voice." She slowed her speech for emphasis.

Alan's mind raced as he tried to figure out what Betsy was saying, and how it made sense of Stanley's comments. He looked back at Betsy with a most inquisitive expression. It must have been what prompted her next remark.

"Alan, stop trying to figure it out. It's not something to be figured out, at least not mentally anyway. Can you sense a small voice, dear?"

"I'm not sure, maybe I can . . . ." He was almost whispering, thinking if he was quieter, maybe he would hear something.

"Look," she smiled, "when you first met me, did you notice something familiar about me?"

"Yes, ma'am, I did notice something." It was the first question where he felt confident of his answer.

"That's it!" she blurted.

"What's it?" He was close to losing his recently acquired confidence again.

"That's the voice dearie! It's more of a knowing than an audible voice. It's a bit similar to what folks call intuition. It's like an understanding. However, there are times where it is almost audible, not in your ears, but rather in your heart."

Alan still looked perplexed, so she continued. "How did you know that what Stanley mentioned to you had some significance? Even though you may have set it aside as a peculiar statement uttered by an old man, something within you remembered it, right?"

Alan nodded, although his expression hadn't changed.

"And something, I would guess, prompted you, Alan, to search through that little leather pouch, correct? What was that something talking to you? Was it leading you, do you think? Was it helping you to recall certain memories, just at particular moments, to help you along the way you're supposed to go? What do you think, Alan?"

All of Alan's faculties were working at full capacity as he listened closely to the words which were flowing so orderly from Betsy's lips but were creating such perplexity in Alan's mind. He couldn't say anything. He just looked at her, wondering how she could possibly know things hidden deep within him.

"Alan, dear, I think what Stanley meant when he referred to a 'quiet road' was to give indication of what was required of you to receive or hear your own **rojocci**. First, you must take time to find a quiet road, a quiet place, a quiet in your heart, mind, and emotions. It's difficult to hear something quiet amidst all the noise. Do you know what I mean?"

He shook his head as he mumbled, "No, ma'am." Alan was becoming more honest as this astounding, yet revealing, conversation continued.

"Can you recognize how difficult it is to hear from within you, while your mind is so busily trying to figure things out for itself? I would guess there's something, like a super highway speeding through your head right now, and every vehicle is a thought. Is that right, Alan?" He slowly nodded in astonishment that Betsy could somehow see the thoughts running inside his skull.

"Well, first you have to slow the running down to a trot, then to a walk, and finally, all the way down to an easy stroll along a quiet road. Are you following me, dear?"

"Yes, ma'am, I think I know what you're saying now."

"Then, and only then, Alan, along the quiet road, can you began to acquire a **rojocci**— your **rojocci**." Betsy's tone had once again turned serious.

"You need the quietness on the inside, the stillness, before you can distinguish the voice within. Oh, it's always speaking, but you just can't hear it for all the noise in there. It's a choice Alan, a daily choice. If you want to hear it clearly, choose to listen. With practice, over time, you will begin to hear much more distinctly. It is similar to how a man and a woman develop into husband and wife. There is an unspoken intimate knowing of one another. It's absolutely precious, Alan. It's almost like that except closer because it is within you."

"Wow! I'm not sure, but I think I may have an idea of what you are trying to tell me, except my example is kind of negative."

"Tell me what you mean, Alan," urged Betsy.

"Well, uh . . . I have this tendency to say or do things because of my insecure feelings. So it's like I'm listening to the voice of my insecurities and fears of what other people may think of me, and consequently, I'm saying and doing things I end up feeling awful about, which reinforces my insecure feelings. So, if I understand you correctly, there is a different voice, another voice?"

Betsy replied, "Yes, the voice that makes you do things you end up regretting is your own soul. Well, that's one of the sources anyway. There are a few more actually. There's a huge difference between the still voice I'm talking about and those to which you are referring. Those are very natural, appeal to your emotions, and even coerce, to some degree, your reasoning; they urge you to make a decision or an action immediately, and never promote waiting or being patient. They never encourage the development of the good character we all lack. The other voice I am describing is altogether different. It's a spiritual voice. It's quiet, soft, and gentle, appealing to your conscience, your sense of what is right and wrong based on your level of absorption."

"Based on my level of what?" Alan's voice hit a higher octave.

"Based on how much Scripture you have absorbed. Generally, the still small voice will use Scripture you have soaked in or meditated upon in your daily digging in His Word. Occasionally, you will hear a sentence or two you don't recognize, but upon searching the Scriptures, behold, there it is. At least that has been my experience, dear."

Alan slowly nodded, "Then what's this **rojocci** thing have to do with any of what you are explaining to me?"

"Well, now let me see . . . hmmm, okay," Betsy started, "You are correct in your discovery. The word **rojocci** is, in fact, an acronym. Each of those letters in the word **rojocci** represents a word in the **rojocci** mission statement. Furthermore, the two words you have obtained so far are the right words for those two letters in their proper order."

"So is it, '**overlook**' and '**cherished**'?" Am I correct?" Alan pried.

"Yes, dear, those two words are exactly in their proper place. But 'overlook' is actually 'overlooked' and 'cherished' is correct. I cannot give you any more words in the meaning of the acronym. It's not like it's a secret or anything. It's just the way it is. It's a lifetime of searching and discovery that is the rojocci lifestyle, that's all."

"What? Why?" Alan was incredulous. "I don't understand. Why won't you give me the rest of the words Betsy? Would it upset Stanley or something?"

"No, no, heavens, no!" laughed Betsy. "I'm sure where Stanley is, he's as joyful as he can be. I think to explain the why, I better give you a short history lesson."

"But first," she stood up with dirty plates in hand, "how about some homemade banana pudding?"

-eight-

Alan's head was swimming, as he opened the screened door and handed Betsy the rest of the items from the picnic table. He started back for the place where they had been talking, when he heard her voice from inside the kitchen. "Alan, why don't we sit in here? It's getting a little chilly for this old woman."

"But I'm just filthy dirty, Betsy."

"Oh, take off those boots and you'll be fine. Remember, I was married to Stanley for more than a few years. Besides, we'll just sit here at the kitchen table."

After taking off his boots, Alan tried to brush himself off as best he could before entering her always sparkling clean kitchen. Because he was concerned he would spackle the floor with the dirt that was caked on his filthy pants, he gingerly tip toed to the table. Betsy brought over two bowls of fresh banana pudding along with a cup of hot tea for herself and a cold glass of milk for Alan. He wasn't quite finished with the scrumptious dessert when Betsy asked if he would like another helping. Alan wanted some more, but more than the pudding, he wanted to know about the whole **rojocci** thing.

"No, ma'am, thank you anyway. Now, what did you mean by giving me a history lesson?" His curiosity caused his abruptness, and that same curiosity made him a little impatient.

"Well, let me see . . ." Betsy's pause was starting to annoy Alan.

"Are you familiar with our nation's beginnings? I mean, why folks came to our country in the first place?" She looked right at Alan as if she was going to tell him some secret about our nation's founding that wasn't in the history books he studied in school.

"Yes, ma'am, I was a social science major in college. A lot of what I studied was United States History." His impatience was starting to rear its ugly head.

"Oh, good, then we'll be speaking the same language." Betsy grinned as if she was relieved that Alan knew his American History.

"Well . . ." she began, "in the late seventeen hundreds, as you know, there were thirteen colonies here in the New World belonging to England. However, within the colonies there was a growing concern over the dictates from England made upon the colonists. Things like taxation without representation and freedom to worship were at the top of their concerted list of considerations."

Alan interrupted, "Those were just a few of their complaints against the King of England." He wanted her to know there was no need for the elementary history lesson; he was at the undergrad level.

"Yes, you're exactly right, Alan. However, more than that, a small, but growing number of individuals began noticing a strange, yet all too familiar phenomenon among those attending churches on Sunday. This curious spectacle was more of a wave than an event, and it was sweeping over the churches of the colonies. You see, Alan, not unlike today, many of the church goers were forfeiting their great privilege and responsibility of knowing the One who called them personally into an intimate union and were exchanging it for a distant relationship through another person."

"Wait a minute," quipped Alan, "you're saying that the Christian in Colonial America was in relationship with his Lord through another person?" Betsy nodded as Alan continued. "You mean like the Pope or something?"

"Yes, that's right . . . sort of, and some through their minister or pastor. It wasn't every believer, but it was a growing number, if not the majority of folks attending churches. Not too dissimilar from how it is today. Sadly, most would prefer to pay someone to go hear from God and then tell them what He says, rather than putting forth the effort of growing a personal relationship directly with Him. It is a most insidious disease, Alan. Believers actually thought their relationship with God was just fine because they would attend church once, twice, or even three times a week to hear from their professional clergy as to what God was saying to them. They would not recognize the lack of relationship until they would, individually, come upon some great difficulty in their life. Then, in the midst of their trial, just like the Israelites of ancient times, there was no apparent answer from God to their cry for help."

"I'm not sure I understand what you're getting at, Betsy," confessed Alan.

"Okay, let me see . . ." Betsy paused looking up at the ceiling. "Yes, your folks are married correct?"

"Yes, for over twenty-seven years." boasted Alan.

Betsy continued, "In the Scriptures we find that the best example, if not the only living example, of the Lord and His people, is the marriage between a man and a woman.[1] For believers, it is a beautiful living illustration. Now suppose, for your mother to speak with your father or your father to have an intimate conversation with your mother, they had to speak through another person. What kind of a relationship would that be? How close would they feel to one another? How long do you think it would last before their relationship would disintegrate in divorce?"

"Wow, I never thought of that before," Alan resigned. "That would be an awful marriage. Who would want to be married like that?"

"Exactly, Alan!" exclaimed Betsy. "It's a recipe for a disastrous relationship. It would never last. Those were the same thoughts of those early colonists who began the **rojocci** fellowship. It was birthed out of a deep concern for the intimate relationship of the individual believer with his Lord."

"So there's no need for a pastor?" questioned Alan.

"No, no, no, dearie! The pastor is, and always will be, very important. But so are the other gifts and offices of Christ's church. In fact, when the individual members are in right relationship with their God, the gifts are usually in proper order. It's when the many, depend on the one, that things get confused and out of balance. The early colonial believers were very concerned with this delicate situation.

"I mean, think of it, dear," she continued, "they left England so they wouldn't be under the tyranny of the Church of England, who was dictating what, how, when, and where they should or should not worship. Then, after just a few generations removed, they were voluntarily surrendering the exact same rights for which they had left England. Strange . . ." Betsy paused for a moment.

"What's strange?" asked Alan.

"I wonder when the highlight of the Christians' relationship with the Lord, became listening to others talk about their relationship with the Lord?" posed Betsy. "It really shouldn't be that way. Rather, it should be a minute by minute walk of love with Him, not once a week or even once a day, nor done by rote, but out of love for Him. No, my dear Alan, it should be a continual conversation with Him throughout one's day. At least that was the proposal of the ones who started the **rojocci** fellowship; each believer developing his own personal relationship with the Lord. You understand now, dear?"

Alan delayed his answer for what seemed more than a minute and then he asked her, "What is the **rojocci** fellowship anyway, Betsy?"

"Well, it's called a fellowship, but it doesn't have any structure or order. In fact, the title is never even capitalized. It is simply, like the first century church, a lifestyle, a quiet, attentive way of life. There's no membership roll, housed in a building somewhere, to keep record of attendance or how much is given. It's only reason for existence—is the promotion of the personal, intimate relationship of a believer with his Lord, and a knowing that there are others of the fellowship hidden among us."

She looked at Alan, "In fact, you may drive by several of them on your way to work each morning and not even realize it. There's nothing indicating the occupants in the car are of the **rojocci** fellowship. There could be many in your church or perhaps only a small number. You may even work with one, like Stanley, who would never preach at you, but would show you, by his care and concern, his ever growing relationship with the Lord. Most give no outward appearance at all of the Spirit hidden within them. Others, like myself, wear just a faint reminder."

"See." Betsy pulled on the delicate chain hanging around her neck revealing a small golden cross with the tiniest letters engraved vertically upon it. "Can you still read the **rojocci** letters? I've had this since before Stanley and I were married."

"Yes, I can make them out," proclaimed Alan. "But what does it mean?"

"Well, like you guessed, it is an acronym that represents the lifestyle . . . this relationship lasts a lifetime, actually forever. That's the wonder of it all. It's a continual sense of astonishment and discovery in this lifetime here on earth."

"I understand, Betsy." Alan interrupted. "But what do the letters mean? What do they stand for?"

"Now Alan," she countered with a hint of kindness, "if I told you, where would be the wonder of discovery? Where would be the desire to walk further with Him? You would have all your answers and might not advance one more step. Besides, when any of the fellowship of the **rojocci** meet along life's way with a seeker such as yourself, we are bound, by the unspoken code, to give only one answer to a letter in the **rojocci**. You have already received two by accident . . . or was it by Providence? Regardless, you have two, dear. Keep searching, and you will find the rest. Our Lord will lead you. That's the way of the **rojocci** fellowship."

"So, what else can you tell me about the **rojocci** fellowship?" Alan begged.

"Well, there's one more thing, dearie."

Alan leaned forward over the petite kitchen table toward his grandmotherly friend turned profound prognosticator, "Yes, what's that?"

"You're pronouncing it incorrectly Alan. It's not **roe-jock-ee**. It's **roe-joss-see**. I know it's not your fault; Stanley always had trouble pronouncing it himself. It's a minor thing; in fact I know several who pronounce it **roe-jock-ee**. So you can pronounce it whichever way you want, but I thought you should know. Oh my, look at the time."

It was almost ten o'clock and Betsy did look a bit weary. Alan thought he should probably leave, but he sure didn't want to before he had all his questions answered. However, it was late and he did have to work tomorrow.

"Okay, Betsy," he sighed, "I guess I should be going."

"You should have enough to digest for a few days anyway." She was referring to their conversation and not her home cooking.

"Yes, ma'am, thank you for everything. I really mean it Betsy, thank you."

"Oh, you're welcome, sweetie, you know you can come by anytime, and we can visit some more. Just give me a call when you have a minute."

"That would be great, Betsy. But not this weekend, I'm going on a college retreat with my church. We're going up to Western Maryland through Monday."

"Oh, how nice, I hope you have a good time, Alan."

They gave each other a hug and Alan headed for home. His mind was swimming with thoughts of what Betsy had expressed to him over the last few hours. "This is amazing stuff. Could it actually be true?"

His mind wouldn't rest until sometime after two o'clock. When he awoke to his alarm, the topic of last night was his first thought as well. All day long Big Jim thought Alan was distracted by something. Finally, at three o'clock, he told Alan to go home and to come back on Tuesday with his mind on his work. Even though Alan felt guilty, he was really glad to get off early for the Memorial Day weekend.

"Let's see," he told himself on the way home. "I've got enough time for a short nap before I have to be at the church. Oh, yeah, I could really use a nap. I'm whipped and the long drive to Western Maryland will be exhausting."

Alan woke up a mere fifteen minutes before he was supposed to leave for the retreat. He threw a few clothes and some toiletries in a small backpack along with a light jacket, in case it was chilly in the mountains of Western Maryland. He pulled into the church parking lot just as Pastor Fred was parking the church van. Alan parked next to him.

"Here you go, Alan," he said as he tossed him the keys. "I checked the oil and filled up both tanks with gas. She's ready to go!"

"Thanks. I'll be real careful, Fred."

"Oh, I know you will, or I wouldn't have asked you to drive. However, don't let the others distract you while you're on the road. Save the antics for the rest stop, okay?"

"Definitely! Where are we stopping?" probed Alan.

"I'm thinking Cumberland. It's a little more than halfway. Come on inside, and I'll give you the map I marked for you."

As Fred opened the door to his study, Alan couldn't control the urge to ask him a question. "Fred, have you ever heard of the **rojocci**? Or maybe something called the fellowship of the **rojocci**? Uh . . . I mean the **rojocci** fellowship?"

"Hmmm . . . no, can't say that I've ever heard of that, Alan. How do you spell it?"

"r-o-j-o-c-c-i," Alan paused about a second between each letter for clarification.

"No, is it a sports organization?" questioned Fred.

"Well, no . . . I think it has something to do with Christianity. I think it's a spiritual thing," Alan suggested. He was beginning to feel like he shouldn't have broached the subject.

Just then, Fred turned around and looked directly at Alan. "Be careful, Alan. It may be a cult. Don't go getting involved in something like that. You'll be very sorry you did."

"No, no, it's nothing like that. It's sort of a historical kind of Christian fellowship. But they don't have any organization or anything. I'm not sure; I think it's only a set of principles or something. You know what I mean?" Alan's voice trailed off. For now he was certain he shouldn't have brought up the topic.

"Oh, that sounds interesting. Let's talk about it later, okay? The rest of the group should be here shortly, and I need to go over this with you before they get here." Fred gestured toward the map he had unfolded on his desk.

They had just finished reviewing the plan that Pastor Fred had put together when the first of the students showed up. Alan was about to open the church door to head out when it flew open.

"Oh, my jumping track spikes, it's Alan 'Cool Breeze' Browne!" someone yelled from the small crowd of students all trying to get in the door at once.

Alan recognized the voice immediately as belonging to the one and only "Peaknuckle Pete." His nickname was not based upon the size of his finger joints, but rather because he usually lost at locker room card games after track practice. His teammates gave him the "Peaknuckle" moniker simply because it was better than calling him Poker Pete, which carried with it a connotation Peaknuckle didn't like. Besides, even though the track team never played Pinochle, they loved the nickname.

Peaknuckle deserved whatever name he was called because he always looked for any slight imperfection in another for the donning of a new nickname. In fact, that's how Alan had received the "Cool Breeze" nickname. One hot day at track practice several years ago, the sprinters had just finished a few wind sprints on the track. One sprinter, in particular, was bent over beside the finish line in what one might call a "reversal of fortunes." He had no sooner finished his latest heave, when along came Alan. He led the distance runners, charging down the track at almost full speed for yet another lap. He passed the unfortunate, ailing sprinter with a rush of wind.

"Ahhh, that Cool Breeze sure felt nice!" exclaimed the sprinter right on time for another cookie toss. The overdone sprinter was Peaknuckle. Alan had lived with the nickname ever since.

"Hey, Peaknuckle, what's happening, dude?!" Alan barked back with a laugh, "Long time, no see, man!"

"Yeah, what's happening, Cool Breeze?"

"Just like old times, eh, fellas?" Pastor Fred interrupted.

They all laughed as everyone headed to the parking lot. Pastor Fred instructed some of the guys to load the luggage into the church van and the three station wagons. Then he started getting everyone signed up on a list.

"Looks like twelve girls and ten guys," proclaimed Pastor Fred. "Hmmm . . . we're missing a couple of girls though. Anyone seen Rebecca Jones? She's supposed to be bringing a friend too. I better go call them at home and see if they've left yet. You guys finish packing everything, and I'll be right back."

Several minutes later, Pastor Fred emerged from the church building, declaring he was unable to reach anyone at the Jones' home. He decided they would wait a bit longer but would need to get going shortly. After another five minutes, Alan offered to wait ten more minutes, or so, if the rest of the group wanted to go on ahead. Alan assured Pastor

Fred he would catch up to the group at the rest stop in Cumberland.

"Okay, I guess that will work. Let's get going everyone," Pastor Fred declared.

"I'll stay with Cool Breeze!" proclaimed Peaknuckle. "I mean, if it's okay?"

"Me, too?" chimed in Peaknuckle's younger sister, Cindy. She actually hadn't graduated from high school yet. The end of classes was a short two weeks away.

"Alan?" Pastor Fred looked directly at Alan with one of those parental gazes that Alan had seen several times before from his own father.

"I'll keep him in line, Fred, don't worry." laughed Alan. He knew Peaknuckle had always had a soft spot for Rebecca Jones.

The two track teammates started right in with stories of past escapades as they watched the three station wagons, full of students, head out of the parking lot. Alan hopped up behind the wheel and Peaknuckle sat in the front passenger seat. Cindy slid in the back seat since the rest of the van was full of luggage. Laughing at one another's recollections the minutes passed quickly. "Well, it's time, old man," Peaknuckle proclaimed after glancing at his watch.

"Yeppers, let's go," agreed Alan.

Just as they were pulling out of the church parking lot, he saw a car with flashing headlights speeding toward them. Alan stopped halfway onto the street. The car swerved to a stop directly in front of them. It was Rebecca Jones' father with Rebecca and someone else in the back seat. Alan shifted the van into reverse, backed into the church parking lot, and got out.

"Hey, Rebecca Jones!" Alan shouted with his arms wide open. "Wow, it's so good to see you, girl!"

"You too, Alan! Hey, Peaknuckle, I didn't know you were going to be here!?" smirked Rebecca.

"What, you didn't want me to come?" complained Peaknuckle.

"Picking right up where you guys left off eh, Peaknuckle?" laughed Alan. "Here, Rebecca, let me get your luggage. We're really running late."

"Oh, I'm so sorry we're late. We had to pick up my friend at the airport, and her connecting flight from Chicago was delayed. Hey, Alan, I would like you to meet Annalisa Williams. She's an old friend of mine. We went to elementary school together in Arlington before her family moved to Walnut Creek, California, the summer after sixth grade."

"Well, sure! Welcome, Annalisa Williams from Walnut Creek, California," he quipped turning around after throwing the luggage into the back of the church van. "I'm Alan Browne from Oakton, Virginia."

~nine~

Sitting under the giant oak tree, Alan opened his eyes when he noticed a change of the warmth on his face. Turning his head, he gazed out over the beautiful turquoise water of the Santa Rosa Sound. A few miles across he could see the white sand beaches of Santa Rosa Island and Fort Pickens National Seashore Park. Just beyond, to the south, were the glistening waters of the Gulf of Mexico. Since the sun was beginning to set, it looked like it was actually reaching down and touching the Gulf. Having arrived from the arid San Ramon Valley of California a few days previous, the view to Alan was absolutely magnificent.

"Man, I love it here," he exclaimed with delight as he stood up from his favorite spot to ponder life. "But, it's getting late and I better get back."

There was a strange sense in the air, Alan noted while he walked along the sandy shore toward the road that led to where he was staying for a couple of weeks. He had never felt anything like it before. It was an eerie stillness that felt like the calm just before a big thunderstorm back in his home state of Virginia although this was different somehow. Cresting the little hill halfway back to the cottage, he looked south, back over his shoulder. The sun had disappeared to the west, and he could see, through the dusk light, the faint hint of the tops of thunderhead clouds way out on the horizon over the Gulf. He turned around to take in the full view. "I sure wouldn't want to be in a small fishing boat out there tonight," he declared out loud. "I think trouble may be brewing."

He glanced at his watch while he pulled open the screened door to his little rented quarters. "Let's see, two hours difference to the west coast. She should be getting home in just a few minutes. Whoa, don't forget Julie's birthday tomorrow." Alan was referring to his oldest daughter. She would be turning thirteen and at the beginning of what Alan and his wife were dreading . . . the teenage years.

"Wow, I can't believe it's been thirteen years since October 3, 1982. It always amazes me how time flies by. I hate that . . ." his voice trailed off as he thought of his family so far away in California; his dear, sweet wife "the cheerful Mrs. Browne" which he constantly enjoyed calling her, and their two other children, Richard, their second born, along with the youngest, little Emily.

"I just have time to get a quick bite to eat before I call my sweetheart," he pronounced as he entered the tiny kitchen.

It was a small kitchen, indeed, compared to their home in San Ramon. But this was precisely what the doctor had ordered, a quaint cottage with room for one, on a quiet, dead end lane in Gulf Breeze, Florida. It was one of those low country houses set upon a foundation of brick columns, no more than a foot or two high. It was covered with board and batten wood siding run vertically and had a small screened porch on the front. The roof was rusty standing seam metal, which appeared to match the peeling paint of the siding. A petite living room that doubled as a dining room, was just inside the front door. One small bedroom and bathroom were down a short hallway, and the tiny kitchen was in back. Right off the kitchen was a nice, generous screened porch where a rope hammock hung. The hammock had quickly become Alan's favorite spot to take a nap or to contemplate what he should do next.

Alan had come to Gulf Breeze at the command of his physician who, after seeing Alan for the seventh time in two weeks, told him he may need another kind of doctor. When Alan inquired about what kind of specialist he may need, privately convinced he had contracted some terminal disease, his doctor simply replied, "You may need a psychiatrist, Alan." This was no small slap in his face as he suddenly realized the seriousness of his non-medical condition.

"Perhaps you should get away somewhere alone for a week or two. Find a quiet place where you can work things out, Alan. In fact, I'm writing you a prescription for two weeks alone on a quiet island." His doctor wasn't kidding. And to prove it, he handed Alan a signed prescription for two weeks of rest and recovery.

When Alan had arrived home, after the latest in his long line of doctor's appointments, he confessed to the cheerful Mrs. Browne exactly what the doctor had prescribed. At first she thought he was kidding, but eventually she understood the gravity of her husband's condition.

"I feel like an idiot," he confided. "I don't know why I do these things. It is so frustrating and yet it feels so real to me . . . I mean, I'm not making this stuff up you know?! I really feel it!"

"But it's not real, Alan," she pleaded with him. "It's in your mind or heart or something like that, honey. Maybe you should go away for a week or two like the doctor prescribed and see if it would help."

"Why do you want to get rid of me for a couple of weeks?" Alan accused. "What are you going to be doing while I'm away?"

With both arms she reached up around his shoulders, leaning her hips into him, "Praying. I will be praying for you, my wonderful, strong knight in shining armor. I will be praying our Lord gives you the breakthrough you so very much need and deserve." She kissed Alan softly, which turned into a long, deep kiss of love.

"So, you won't miss me then?" he said with a frown.

"Oh, honestly, Alan." she replied as she slapped him on the bottom. "Sometimes, Alan Michael Browne." she laughed, "Sometimes."

He pulled her close to him and whispered, "I love you with all my wretched heart, even if you are a stinker."

"Me, the stinker?" she bellowed. They both laughed out loud as they held each other.

"I'll miss you, my love," he whispered in her ear.

"Me too, honey. But we'll be okay. It's only for a couple of weeks. You'll enjoy some peaceful time. Where are you going to go anyway?"

"Well . . ." they started toward the kitchen, "I'm not sure, maybe Tahoe."

"Oh, no you don't, Alan. You're not going up there again without me." She was referring to a recent trip Alan and a couple of his friends had taken to look at a possible business opportunity.

"Wait a minute," she paused. "Don't the Morgan's have a cottage in Florida? How about going there?"

"Florida?! Are you kidding me? That's too far from home. Suppose something happened, and I needed to get back? No, it's too far away." Alan was using his serious tone to get his point across.

After much cajoling and more than a few bribes only the cheerful Mrs. Browne could give, Alan decided on the Morgan's cottage in Gulf Breeze, Florida. It took a few days of getting the office squared away before he could leave. Then, on September 28, 1995, he boarded the plane and headed for the sunny southern Gulf Coast town with the soft, white sand beaches.

After a dinner of canned beef stew and apple sauce, Alan laid down on the back porch hammock to call home. Richard answered the phone. They spoke of all the things that a father and his ten year old son would normally speak of: the hole he was digging in the back yard, the latest creature he built with Legos toy blocks, and how the family dog, Buster, was doing. Before Alan could ask to speak to his mother, Julie was on the phone inquiring as to how her ailing father was doing, and when he would be better. After much convincing that he wasn't sick, Alan finally asked if he could speak with her mother. Instead, he heard the sweet little voice of Emily, who he affectionately called Emma. This turned out to be the longest of the three conversations he had engaged in up to this point.

"Hello, honey, how are you doing?" This was the voice he was longing to hear. She had rescued him from a most talkative Emma, who was continuing the conversation, even though she was no longer holding the telephone.

"I'm doing fine, my love, how are things there with you?"

"Oh, we're all just fine. We had dinner with Grandma last evening and today has been a blur. The kiddies had the day off from school for teacher's conferences. Other than that, everything is about normal. Are you keeping an eye on the hurricane?" she asked with a bit of trepidation.

"What hurricane?" quizzed Alan.

"There's a hurricane in the Gulf of Mexico, honey, and they are predicting it may head your way. Haven't you seen it on the news?"

"Sweetheart, I don't have a television here. I don't even have a radio. I'm sure it's no big deal anyway. Don't worry about it, okay?" Alan was simultaneously trying to calm both his wife and his own rising fears, as he had never experienced a hurricane before. Rapidly evaluating his situation, he realized he had taken a taxi from the airport and there was no form of transportation here at the cottage, except the bicycle he had brought with him. He had no way to leave and was pretty much stuck come what may. However, he deemed it best not to mention this to his concerned wife just yet.

"Now Alan, you get out of there if the storm heads your way." she demanded. "Remember what that awful Hurricane

Andrew did to Miami just a few years ago, honey. Don't you dare stay."

"Oh, now sweetie, don't worry over something that may never happen." At this point, Alan was trying more to convince himself than the cheerful Mrs. Browne. "One way or another, I'll be just fine. Now, tell me about the dinner with your mother."

Alan knew the potential of the storm hitting Gulf Breeze weighed heavily on his wife because she mentioned it two more times before they said goodbye. He got up from the hammock and plugged his phone into the charger in the kitchen. "I'm really glad I got this new mobile phone. Who knows if the power and phones lines will be down if this storm hits."

He opened the meager refrigerator, pulled out a small container of strawberry yogurt, and headed back to the hammock on the screened porch. With each spoonful his mind began to wander back over the phone conversation he just had with his dear family. "I sure do miss them. I hope they will be okay until I get back next week."

The hammock methodically swayed back and forth with the gentle Gulf breeze. Alan noticed the air had become much heavier. The balmy warmth and the gentle rocking had a wonderfully calming and peaceful effect on Alan. He put the finished tub of yogurt, with his spoon sticking out, down on the floor and closed his eyes. Even though it wasn't quite nine o'clock, his eyelids felt very heavy. He wrapped himself up like a cocoon with the fuzzy blanket. It was as perfect a setting as he had ever been in before, so quiet and peaceful. It had a most soothing effect upon his mind. All his anxious thoughts seemed to dissipate with the soft oscillating roll of the hammock. It was as though peace itself had wafted down from heaven and washed upon the shoreline of his heart. It was a deep pacifying balm, the likes of which he hadn't experienced since he was young. Soon he was sound asleep.

It was the most restful sleep Alan had enjoyed in years. It was interrupted only by the ringing of his phone just before dawn. He fell out of the hammock and, after picking himself up off the wooden porch floor, he rushed to answer the phone in the kitchen.

"Hello?"

"Alan, you okay?" It was the voice of Bill Morgan. "Are the winds bad yet?"

Bill Morgan, Alan's neighbor in San Ramon, owned the cottage Alan was renting for his two week hiatus. "I'm fine, Bill. Isn't it a bit early for you out there?"

"I've been up all night watching this storm. It's headed your way Al. It's called Hurricane Opal. It's a Category 3, and it's headed right for Gulf Breeze. They're predicting it will make landfall sometime tomorrow."

Whatever blissful peace Alan had experienced the night before had just been shattered to pieces with this one phone call. Alan could actually feel his level of anxiety ratcheting upward. It was a terrible feeling, and he felt powerless to do anything about it.

"Category three, Alan! That's a huge storm!" Bill was definitely not helping Alan's desperate struggle to regain some measure of assurance that all would be well.

"Now, before you leave, you need to do a couple of things for me, okay? First, make sure everything is out of the refrigerator and leave the door open. Then, out in the shed there are several pieces of plywood with markings on them stating where they need to be installed on the house. For example, there's one that's marked 'BDW' that means bedroom, west window. So if you would be so kind, please nail each piece of plywood over the windows and doors. You'll find a step ladder, hammer, and plenty of nails in the shed too. Lastly, please shut down the power. It's the big switch by the meter box. Can you do that, Alan?"

"Sure, I'll take care of it, Bill. Don't worry about it."

"Thanks, Al. As soon as you're done, get out of there. This is a big storm and there will be tons of destruction."

"You worried about your house here, Bill?"

"No, hopefully it will be okay. It's been there since the early 1940s, and it's still standing even after all those years of hurricanes. Besides, it's thirty-two feet above sea level, so the storm surge won't get to it."

"Well, don't worry about a thing. I'll make sure it's all secure here." Alan was trying hard to convince Bill that he had everything under control.

"Thanks, Alan, you're a good man. Let me know where you end up fleeing to, okay? I would go east or west, not north though, or you'll just have to keep running from it. Oh, no, I'm watching the news, and it's been upgraded to a Category Four. Get out of there quick, Al, okay?!"

"Okay, I appreciate the advice. I've never been around a hurricane before."

"Be careful. It's a very dangerous situation. And, Alan, leave as soon as possible! The longer you wait, the more the roads get jammed up with traffic, and the less chance you have of getting out of there." With those last words of warning, the two California neighbors said goodbye.

"Well, isn't this a fine kettle of fish? I travel all the way here from California to get a little peace and quiet and here comes a storm. That's just great!" Alan was referring to the storm in his mind every bit as much as the one looming in the Gulf of Mexico.

Sitting down at the table for a bite of breakfast, he decided to use up some of the remaining items in the refrigerator. He ate the last of the yogurt and some milk with cereal. There were still some cheese sticks, three hotdogs, and a small amount of orange juice. While sitting there eating breakfast, he rehearsed his options. Each led him to the same conclusion. Considering his circumstances, it was better to stay and weather the storm. He had determined that the hurricane, if it hit Gulf Breeze at all, wouldn't arrive until tomorrow sometime. So he figured he had plenty of time to prepare the cottage as Bill had requested. After breakfast, to calm his frazzled nerves, Alan decided to go on a bike ride around the area.

Thirty minutes later, donned in his complete cycling regalia, Alan started down the road. At first, he just took it slow and easy. He observed how most of the folks he passed were boarding up their windows or bringing in patio furniture. As he meandered through several streets of what the locals called "Proper", which Alan later discovered meant within the actual city limits of Gulf Breeze, he eventually found himself at the foot of the bridge that crossed the Santa Rosa Sound, leading to the beach. He started up the long hill that is the bridge itself. Halfway to the top, he heard voices approaching from behind him. "It could only be other cyclists," he concluded. "Runners could not be moving fast enough to catch me, nor did I hear a motor indicating a vehicle."

"On your left!" called out the first cyclist in what would be a long line of riders passing him. About two-thirds of the way down the column of cyclists Alan heard,

"Come on, man, hop on."

Then another call, "Latch onto the train, dude, we're rolling."

Alan smiled as he shifted a couple of gears to accelerate to the same pace as the long line of bike riders. Over the top of the bridge and flying down the other side the group went. Alan tucked into the huge draft the peloton provided and noticed that although his speed had more than doubled, it actually required less effort. The front of the long line of about twenty riders turned right at the sole traffic light on Santa Rosa Island. The group now headed west on Fort Pickens Road, which runs parallel to the Gulf and the Sound on the sliver of land that is the Santa Rosa Island. The way was quite breezy and the water looked like, as his daughter Emma would say, "It had on its angry eyes today."

"This is just what the doctor ordered." Alan declared to himself as he tucked into the pack of riders heading for the Fort at the end of the road. There was very little communication as everyone seemed bent on getting to the end of the ride. However, at the rest stop by the Civil War era, red brick Fort Pickens, there was no lack of conversation.

"Looks like a nasty headwind on the way back," expressed one middle aged male rider to Alan. "It'll be a Sufferfest."

Some of the riders were very friendly, while several others stood more aloof. It didn't really bother Alan. He was used to the way cyclists tended to be around one another. Some were just out for the exercise and fresh air, while others, to be sure, were continually sizing everyone up. Alan was shaking hands, smiling, and introducing himself as a visitor from California. His eyes glanced around at all the different clothes and machines. He loved the variety of bright colors and especially the racing bicycles.

Most of the conversation surrounded the impending storm that was evident from the foreboding sky and Gulf. One of the riders must have had some experience as a meteorologist because he was explaining, to those that would listen, how the clouds and the way they were moving indicated where the hurricane was located. Alan found it all very fascinating. Gazing up at the sky, he heard someone shout,

"Let's roll!" and the group was off again.

As they started back toward the east, Alan noticed the brand name on a particular bicycle that happened to be passing him on his left. "What in the world?" he thought as he chased after the rider. He had almost pulled up next to him when someone in the back yelled, "Flat!"

The word was repeated several times throughout the entire group. About half of the riders continued on down the road, however some, including the rider Alan wanted to question, stopped for the unfortunate one with the flat tire.

"Hey, I'm Alan Browne." He thrust his hand forward to greet the rider next to him on the bike with the curious name. Alan had noticed he was tall and quite thin, almost skinny, except quite muscular. He had a weathered face with grey hair protruding from the sides and back of his cycling helmet.

"Joseph, Joseph Hinote, although everyone around here calls me Joey. How you doing, Alan?" he smiled.

"Good, man. Hey, I gotta ask you, what kind of bike is that?" Alan smiled, more out of curiosity, than because he was feeling friendly.

"Oh, I built it myself," replied Joey.

"Really? Well, I'm interested in the brand name. Where did you get it?"

"Oh that? It's a long story. What did you want to know?"

"What it means?" responded Alan. "I have a little leather pouch with that word stamped on it, but I don't fully understand what it means."

"Well," started Joey, "we don't really have the time right now to discuss it. However, if you are truly interested in the **rojocci,** I would be more than happy to meet you somewhere. I think it will have to be after this storm passes though." Joey turned to face the Gulf and noticed it was starting to churn up some rather large waves.

"I'd give you my phone number, but I don't have anything to write with," apologized Alan.

"Yeah, me either," replied Joey.

"Hey, tell you what, Alan, we ride every Saturday from the foot of the Three Mile Bridge in Pensacola. Now, I'm sure we won't be riding this Saturday because of the storm, but I can meet you there the following Saturday. We ride at seven a.m. How's that sound to you?"

"No, that won't work. I leave that day to head back to California. Do you have any time before then?" Alan pleaded.

"Well," Joey looked up at the sky, "if this isn't too bad of a storm, I have that Friday off. I had planned to go fishing, but I'm pretty sure that won't be the case now. This is going to be a bad one I'm afraid. One of the guys told me it was upgraded to a Cat Four."

"A week from this Friday works for me, Joey. Where can we meet? You name the time and the place and I'll be there."

"Okay, meet me at Bayview Park in Pensacola at eight a.m., one week from this Friday. Bring your bike, and we'll get in some miles. Do you know where Bayview is, Alan?"

"Nope, but don't worry. I'll find it somehow. I really want to know more about the **rojocci** thing. I haven't seen or heard anything about it in several years. I think I have some ideas as to the meanings, but I'm not positive. So don't worry about me Joey. I'll be there."

"That's great, Alan, I'll look forward to our visit, uh . . . assuming we make it through this hurricane." Joey looked up at the clouds and back out toward the Gulf. "This may be a nasty one . . ."

Just then a National Park Ranger pulled up and rolled down the window of his patrol car, "You guys need to leave the park right now. This is a mandatory evacuation."

"Yes, sir," replied one of the cyclists. "We're just fixing this flat, and then we'll be out of here." The ranger waved as he drove away.

Alan arrived back at the cottage before lunch and started right in on the storm preparation. He stopped about halfway through his work to eat a couple of the hotdogs still left in the refrigerator. Then he went back to covering the windows and doors with the plywood he had found in the little shed in the backyard. He finished up everything about midafternoon. After sitting in the dreary, darkened cottage for twenty minutes or so, he decided he would soon be spending plenty of time sequestered inside because of the storm. "How about a stroll down to the old oak tree by the Sound?" he thought. And with a slam of the wooden screened door, he was off.

The wind had definitely increased, but Alan didn't believe it was anything to be concerned about. It felt like a balmy sea breeze. The clouds overhead were moving in fast off the Gulf, and the waves on the Sound had increased significantly since yesterday. Alan sat down in his favorite spot under the massive oak. He reclined back and looked straight up through the huge branches.

"Well, old friend, looks like you have a challenge just on the horizon. Remember when I asked you how you get through storms? I wasn't exactly meaning a hurricane. Now it appears that we both must weather a storm . . . you on the outside and me on the inside."

Turning his gaze back out over the Sound, his eyes drifted to the tiny strip of sand that is called Santa Rosa Island and to the Gulf of Mexico beyond. The skies were getting very dark to the south, a deep charcoal shade of grey, almost black. He enjoyed the damp breeze blowing upon his face. He leaned his head back upon his giant, stalwart friend and closed his eyes. His mind drifted back to a more peaceful time. A simpler season of life, the one where he first laid eyes on her.

"Hmmm . . ." he smiled, "She sure was a cutie, wasn't she?"

~ten~

While keeping his eyes on the road, Alan shouted, "Peaknuckle, you goofball! What in the world are you doing? Get back in the van, man!" The three girls in the backseat screamed as Peaknuckle hung more than half of his body out the front passenger side window. In fact, he was sitting on the door slapping the roof of the church van with his hands while singing his unique version of Cindi Lauper's, "Girls Just Want to Have Fun."

Alan still had one hand on the steering wheel and the other holding Peaknuckle's foot. Rebecca, who still had feelings for Peaknuckle, was reaching over the front seat with both hands grasping the side of his belt. She and Peaknuckle had dated for almost a year when they were seniors in high school, but she had ended it stating he was just too immature. In reality, she had hoped her ultimatum would cause Peaknuckle to grow up, and they would get together again. However, her plan hadn't worked, and she regretted her ploy to mature him. Now here she was, loving his craziness and immaturity while tightly holding onto him, as the church van rolled down Highway 15 toward Fredrick, Maryland.

Glancing in the rearview mirror, Alan saw a look of terror on the face of Peaknuckle's sister, as her brother's fate seemed to, literally, hang in the balance. Then, he caught a glimpse of Annalisa, who was smiling back at him. Their eyes were almost transfixed as if both knew something about the other, yet neither wanted to reveal the secret, at least not yet. It was one of those moments that Alan would never forget. He swung his head around to view her face to face.

"You okay, Annalisa?" he asked using his caring voice.

She smiled back at Alan as if to say, thank you for your concern, "Yes, I'm fine, Alan."

That was all it took. He definitely wanted to get to know her and the sooner the better. At that moment, Alan's plans for the weekend began to look much brighter as they gained a new and promising focus.

He yanked on Peaknuckle's leg and barked out an order to get back in the van. To everyone's surprise, this time it worked. Peaknuckle wiggled back through the window and dropped into his seat while he continued tapping out the tune with his hands on the dashboard.

"Now, fasten your seatbelt, man!" Alan barked. "And stay put."

After checking the road in front of him, Alan glanced back at his new found interest seated in the middle of the back seat. She was talking and laughing with Rebecca about Peaknuckle's latest antics. He alternated his eyes from the road in front of him, to Annalisa, and back to the road. He was trying to be discreet, but frankly he was having a great deal of difficulty taking his eyes off her smiling face, which he thought was framed quite nicely with her shoulder length, auburn hair. He had noticed, as they were loading the van back at the church, that she was a petite girl of perhaps five foot-four inches tall. She had expressive dark brown eyes and a smile, which if it were possible to tap into its brightness could light up a small city. Alan already loved the way she laughed and how her hair fell gently across her forehead. He hadn't really noticed before now, but she was wearing jeans and one of those soft cotton shirts with some embroidery around the neck and a little drawstring at the top. "I don't know why they make those shirts with a drawstring," he thought as he again caught a glimpse of her in the rear view mirror, "girls never tie it." He also favorably took note of the necklace with the small gold cross that she wore around her neck.

"Yes," he thought, "she is cute and beautiful all at the same time."

Alan reached over and slapped Peaknuckle on the arm as he quipped, "What in the world is the matter with you?! You could have gotten killed, man!"

"Nah, I knew you wouldn't let me fall, dude. I knew I was safe with Cool Breeze driving."

"Cool Breeze and Peaknuckle?" laughed Annalisa, "What kind of names are those?"

"Well," started Rebecca, "It all began when these two characters were on the same track team back in high school."

"Track team?" questioned Annalisa, "I ran track in high school too."

Alan glanced in the rear view mirror to see Annalisa grinning at him once again. Without saying anything, Peaknuckle slapped Alan on the arm with the back of his hand. He didn't have to say it; both of them knew exactly what it meant.

Explaining the whole "track-team-nickname-thing", as she called it, Rebecca talked all the way to the rest stop at the Burger King in Cumberland. She offered all kinds of details that neither Peaknuckle nor Alan had any idea she knew. It was particularly humorous as she mixed the descriptions with a hint of her unique flavor of sarcasm and had all in the van laughing so hard their stomachs ached.

Although it was well after midnight, they all arrived safe and sound at the retreat center. Everyone received their room assignments then headed off to find them. Peaknuckle and Alan shared a room as did Rebecca and Annalisa. It wasn't until the next morning, while standing on the balcony outside his room in the early morning light, that Alan could get a good look at the scenery, including the lodge itself.

It was located part way up the side of a heavily wooded mountain covered with pine and fir trees as well as a smattering of oaks and maples. The occasional blooming dogwood added some delightful splashes of color. Alan peered across the small valley to the ridge on the other side, which was about a mile or so away. Below the fieldstone and red cedar plank sided lodge, was a beautiful, grassy field approximately four hundred yards wide by half a mile long. Just below the grassy area were a few trees shading a small river, which splashed and crashed over rocks and boulders as it sought its way toward the Atlantic Ocean some three hundred and fifty miles to the east.

The air was crisp and full of early spring fragrances. Alan breathed them in deeply as he leaned his head back and closed his eyes. He took a second breath as he arched his back even farther, causing him to lose his balance. He tried to catch himself on one of the two wooden chairs on the balcony, but it snapped to pieces under his weight, and he tumbled to the floor in a heap of wood and chair cushions.

"Well, that was graceful," he laughed as he pushed the second chair aside. He looked around and turned to peer through the closed sliding glass door that led to his room and the sleeping Peaknuckle.

"Glad he didn't see that or I would never hear the end of it," he said softly.

Just then he heard the faint sound of what resembled a giggle. Alan looked around but saw nothing, yet the sound continued. In fact, it was getting a bit louder. From the prone position on his back he glanced upward to catch a glimpse of what appeared to be an eye looking down at him through a crack in the deck boards on the balcony above.

"You okay, Alan?" came the question framed between giggles. It was the unmistakable, sing song voice of his new found interest, Annalisa.

"Yes, I'm fine," Alan replied with a bit of disgust mixed with some sarcasm. "I always get up early to smash patio furniture. Yep, nothing like watching the sunrise from the floor of your balcony. You should try it." Alan's sarcasm was getting right up to the point of no return where he knew he would regret any further comments.

Just then Annalisa laughed right out loud, "Alan, you are too much! You've made my day and it isn't even seven o'clock yet."

She walked over to the railing and stretched way out, so she could see him face to face. She smiled that gorgeous smile right at Alan, who was still lying in a pile on the floor, and cooed, "You hungry, Alan?"

Alan picked himself up off the destroyed chair trying not to look too excited about his potential breakfast invitation. "Yeah, uh . . . sure. You hungry?" he quipped.

"I'm starving." Annalisa lifted her face toward the rising sun. "Mmmm . . . that sun sure feels marvelous, don't you think, Alan?"

Alan, who was back on his feet and standing directly below Annalisa, answered, "Yea, I really have learned to enjoy mornings this past year."

While still drinking in the sunshine with her eyes closed, Annalisa asked, "What do you mean by that?"

"Oh, it's a long story," acknowledged Alan. "Maybe I'll bore you with it some other time. You want to meet me in the dining room in ten minutes?"

She leaned over the rail once again and, looking directly into his eyes, replied, "Absolutely! Better make it fifteen though," and off she ran.

Breakfast seemed way too short, but Pastor Fred had asked Alan if he would open the first meeting at eight o'clock sharp with prayer and a reading from the Gospel of John. Before Alan left the table, he made certain he asked Annalisa if she would enjoy a hike during the afternoon break. They agreed on a meeting place and time. Alan assured her he would research the trail map to determine which loop would work best for their limited time stating,

"Dinner is at six."

At ten minutes to three, Alan was sitting on the huge leather sofa in front of the enormous stone fireplace, in the grand hall just off the lodge's main lobby, waiting for her. He didn't want to be late for this meeting. A few minutes later, Annalisa came bounding down the curved staircase and ran over, right next to Alan.

Alan looked up at her, "Afraid of elevators?" he jabbed.

"No, I actually like using the stairs. Always have." She bantered back as she plopped down on the sofa not six inches from Alan.

"It's as if she actually likes challenging me," Alan pondered.

"Well, here's what I've got," Alan declared as he unfolded the trail map on the giant coffee table between the sofa and the fireplace. "This trail leaves from the east side of the parking lot and, mainly using switchbacks, ascends to the top of the mountain behind the lodge. It looks pretty tough though . . ."

"Let's do that one!" blurted Annalisa before Alan could finish.

"But you don't know how long it is. Maybe you would like one of these other two I picked out?" retorted Alan.

"I don't think so," she smiled. "I like being up high where you can see a long way. In fact, I've climbed in Yosemite." There was no small amount of delight in Annalisa's voice with this last revelation.

"Uh . . . where's that?" asked Alan.

"It's in the Sierras, in California, where I'm from." Her tone of glee was nearing a crescendo.

Alan was starting to feel more than a little insecure. "Uh, so no hike along the river, skipping stones, and putting our feet in the water?"

"No, if it's okay with you, Alan, I would love to climb to the summit."

"Hey, it's no Mount Everest or anything. It's just a hike in the Blue Ridge," he snapped back sarcastically. "Oh no, I'm blowing it here," he thought. "Just shut up, Alan, you idiot. Shut up and get hiking." He was fearful he was going to offend Annalisa, and he had hardly had the chance to get to know her yet.

"Oh, I know that, silly. Mount Everest is in the Himalayas. But, if it's okay with you, Alan, I really would like to hike to the top of the mountain. We have time don't we?"

With this last question she put on her semi-serious face. It was the first time Alan had seen it, and it made him chuckle a little.

"What?" giggled Annalisa.

"Nothing," teased Alan with a smile. "We better get going if we're going to summit Mount Everest before sunset."

The trail led upward from the east end of the parking lot and was marked with a small brown sign with white lettering. The words "Summit Trail" were written in block letters above the words "Summit 3.6 miles."

"I think we can do it in about an hour and a half, Annalisa," assured Alan. "That will give us about thirty minutes on the summit before we need to head back for dinner. We should be much faster on the way down. Sound good to you?"

"Perfect," breathed Annalisa. The steepness of the trail was already taking its toll.

"Pace okay?" Alan asked.

"Sure, just fine," she responded.

The trail was marked with a white paint stroke measuring approximately 2" by 6" on a tree or rock every five hundred yards or so. It kept heading upward though, always upward, through many switchbacks, across slabs of rock, and around large boulders. Alan and Annalisa made good progress passing the "One mile to the summit" sign less than one hour after leaving the lodge. Every time Alan thought he might be going too fast, he glanced behind to find Annalisa right on his heels.

"Still doing okay?" questioned Alan.

"Just fine," came the reply directly behind him. "This is so beautiful. It's so lush here. Much different than California."

Annalisa used short sentences to keep from becoming winded. Alan noticed a break in the trees just ahead where they would have a view of the valley below. As he stepped aside to stop, so she could rest a minute and take in the view, he began to tell her a story about himself.

"Yea, I went to school south of here in Virginia. In the Shenandoah Valley in this small town called . . ."

Annalisa strode right past him. Within seconds she was yards up the trail. "Hey, wait a minute . . . don't you want to look at the view or something?" Alan's voice hit a high pitch that usually meant he couldn't believe what he was seeing.

"Tired, Alan?" mocked Annalisa as she smiled back at him. "I'll lead for a while if it's too exhausting for you." Then she laughed that beautiful laugh that Alan was quickly becoming very fond of.

"No, no, you go on ahead and put the hammer down!" quipped Alan smiling at her.

"Hammer what?"

"Hammer down. It's a cycling term that my friend down at the shop told me about. He used to race in Europe. It means, go as hard as you can." Alan used a matter-of-fact tone indicating he was knowledgeable about such things.

"Do you like to ride bikes?" Annalisa quizzed as she gulped in more air.

Alan noticed she had picked up the pace in no small degree. He was actually starting to breathe a bit heavy himself. "Well, yeah, kinda. I still like to run more than ride bikes. But I just accepted a job at a new bicycle shop in Arlington. So I'm thinking I may be riding more in the near future. How about you? You ride any?"

"Yes, in California I ride to and from work when the weather is nice. Sometimes on the weekends," she replied. "What kind of bike do you have, Alan?"

"Well, it's an old Raleigh Record ten speed. It's a clunker, but I get around on it. Sometimes I ride from my house all the way down to the Mall and sit on the steps of the Lincoln Memorial. I love to listen to all the different languages the touri speak as they walk by. I would guess there is someone in Washington from every country on earth."

"What's touri?" asked Annalisa.

"What?"

"You said touri. What's touri?" Her voice raised an octave with this last inquiry.

"Oh that. It's plural for the word tourist. You know, like cacti or fungi . . . touri. We locals call tourists, touri." Alan presumed Annalisa would think he was very clever for his creative use of the English language.

She quipped, "Clever. By the way my bike is a Cannondale. It's one of those new aluminum frames. It's lavender with bright silver highlights. I love it."

"Cannondale?!" exclaimed Alan. "Where did you get it?"

"I purchased it from a little shop in Roslyn, just across Key Bridge from Georgetown. But sadly, they closed a short time ago."

"Wait a minute Annalisa," reasoned Alan. "Do you know the names of the owners? Was it Frank and Carol?"

"Yes, that's them. I'm so sorry they closed the shop. I really enjoyed getting to know them. They are such nice people. Besides, I wanted to buy some little packs for my bike."

"They didn't close up the shop." explained Alan. "They moved to Cherrydale. It's just a couple of miles up Lee Highway. In fact, I built their new store. Well, kinda . . . I mean I helped build it. And next Thursday is my first day of work. I have a part time job there selling bikes."

"Wow! Now we're just going to have to ride bikes together, Alan." She looked back at him with a smile as they stepped onto the summit.

"How come I'm the one out of breath?" asked Alan as he slowed to a stop to take in the panoramic view from on top of the mountain.

"Because I asked all the questions." chuckled Annalisa. "It's a little trick I learned from running with my teammates on the track team in high school. I keep my questions short so I can breathe. They have to give long answers so they are hindered from catching their breath and I win." Annalisa pointed her finger at Alan and laughed, "I needed an equalizer, Alan. You were so strong churning up that trail."

"No, you were the strong one," argued Alan.

"Nope," she smiled. "I just kept asking questions."

Alan nodded his head and pointed a finger back in her direction. Then they both laughed together.

"Well, let's sign in," she stated matter of factly.

"What?" asked Alan.

"Here, it's over here." She opened a small metal box, which she pulled out from under a few rocks piled up in a cairn adjacent to the summit clearing. She removed a worn pencil on a short string and wrote upon the little book in the case.

"What's today's date, Alan? Do you have the time?"

"Uh . . . May twenty-ninth and its four-seventeen p.m. What are you doing?"

"Signing us in. Every mountain in the Sierras has a log like this at the summit. Well, kind of like this one. In the Sierras, it's placed and maintained by the Sierra Club. This looks like it may have something to do with the lodge where we're staying. Regardless, we summited, so we'll sign in."

Alan responded, "Let me see that."

She handed the little logbook with the pencil attached by the string to Alan stating, "Make sure you close the case tight or rain will get in and ruin it, okay?"

"Sure."

Alan looked down and flipped through the pages of the little book. The first entry was from back in August 1962. There were hundreds of names and dates all through the years. He turned the pages of 1962, then 1963, and on into the 1970s. He noticed a couple of years where an entry had been made on his birthday. There was an entry on the date he graduated high school too. He thumbed on through to 1977 and then right up to the last entry.

His eyes fell on that handwritten date. Then, he looked around to see what had happened to Annalisa. She had climbed up on a large boulder just off the summit and was sitting there crossed legged. She was looking past him in the direction of the sun and the mountains in the west.

"What are you doing?" he asked.

"Oh, just praying a little prayer."

"She is such a breath of fresh air. Or, is it just this fresh mountain air having an effect on me?" he wondered.

He looked back down at the logbook and her handwriting. He glanced back up at her. She was still sitting crossed legged but was now leaning back on her hands with her face fully lifted up toward the sun. Her soft wavy hair, which she had released from the ponytail, was now cascading down from her shoulders as she arched to the source of warmth.

Just as he was becoming lost in this vision, she opened her eyes and looked in Alan's direction. "Come on up," she coaxed, "It's so beautiful, Alan."

"Yes, it is." replied Alan. Then he repeated in a whisper, "Oh, yes, it is."

Annalisa turned her face upward again. Alan gazed at her for what seemed like a long time, yet not quite long enough. He finally turned his attention back to the little logbook. A smile broke across his face as he read, ever so slowly, Annalisa's entry. First, he read the date and time. Then, his eyes moved very attentively across the final words, savoring the entry written by her very hand:

"Alan Browne & Annalisa Williams"

-eleven-

Replacing the logbook in its tiny case, Alan tucked it inside the cairn of rocks that protected it from the elements. He then climbed up on the boulder and sat down next to Annalisa, who was still enjoying the sunshine. They talked together so easily. Alan thought the two of them floated from one topic to another with "nary a pause" of silence. He had never felt this comfortable around a girl before and especially one he found so attractive. He wanted to know everything about her. Where did she live? What did she do for fun? Did she have any close friends? What did she hope the future would hold?

But it was getting late in the afternoon, and Alan knew they really should be leaving if they had any hope of making it to the dining room for dinner. The conversation continued to flow easily, however, and there didn't appear to be any stopping point. So they decided they would skip dinner and leave with enough time to attend the evening meeting, which was scheduled to start at seven thirty p.m. in the Banquet Room just off the Grand Hall.

Alan was really enjoying getting to know Annalisa, and it appeared to him that she delighted in their time together as well. He had discovered she was from a small suburb outside of San Francisco called Walnut Creek. It was in the East Bay, about twenty minutes from Oakland and Berkeley. She attended the University of California at Berkeley through the first semester of her sophomore year. She explained it just wasn't for her. She wasn't happy there. However, she had a friend from high school who was attending a college nearby. She had invited Annalisa to sit in on a couple of classes one day.

"I just loved it!" she blurted as her eyes lit up. "It's the California College of Arts and Crafts, and it's so awesome. The classes are small compared with Cal, and there are so many hands on learning opportunities. I hardly go a day or two without designing or building something. I mean, I've only attended for one semester, but I just love it."

"That doesn't sound like any college I've ever heard of before. Are you sure it's really a college?" Alan was trying very hard not to sound sarcastic and was thinking he would actually love a school like that. "What's your major?" he asked.

"Design," she replied. "It's a broad major I can narrow down in the next year or so. I'm thinking interior design might be where I'm headed. I love being creative."

"Well, what are you doing in DC? I mean, if you love it there, what are you doing here?" Alan's tone sounded more like he was annoyed rather than sincerely wanting to know why she was in Washington.

"That's a long story, Alan. I had agreed to do an internship for Congressman Leo Ryan. Leo represents our district in California. With my major at Cal being political science, I thought, at the time, it would be a feather in my cap to intern for a Congressman on Capitol Hill. But that was almost a year ago. So here I am doing what I committed to do." She glanced at Alan as if to convey this is something crucial in a relationship too.

Alan nodded his head but said nothing. However, he did make a special note in the back of his mind that commitment is important to her. "Hey, it's getting late. We better start heading down or Pastor Fred will be upset with me."

"Why would he be upset with you, Alan?"

"Because he asked me to lead a couple of songs and open the meeting with prayer tonight, so I really need to be on time. It's almost a quarter of seven. The meeting starts in forty-five minutes. We need to scoot."

Alan jumped down first. Then, he turned to help Annalisa. She slid down the boulder and put her hands on Alan's shoulders as they came face to face, only inches apart. They looked into one another's eyes for more than a few seconds. They both sensed it . . . no question about it.

Suddenly, something caught Annalisa's attention. "What's that?" she asked as she peered around Alan's shoulder toward another boulder just behind him.

"Looks like a walking stick someone left behind," replied Alan, who now let loose of her waist to turn more fully in the direction of their discovery.

"Wow, that's a nice one," expressed Alan, as he picked it up grasping the big knob at one end. Nice smooth resting place for your hand, feels good. I wonder . . ."

Just then Annalisa interrupted, "Look there's some writing carved into the staff. Maybe it's the owner's name."

Picking up the walking stick to examine it more closely, Alan felt the carving on the opposite side. There, hand crafted by what appeared to be a knife or chisel, along the length on one side of the stick, were the letters r-o-j-o-c-c-i. Alan's eyes widened. He couldn't believe what he was reading.

"Whaaat?!" The pitch of his voice matched his astonishment at their discovery.

His mind began racing. He ran back through his memory banks trying to remember everything Betsy had told him regarding the fellowship and its history. His mind was in disbelief and belief all at the same time. He just stood there, stone still, as his internal mechanisms were in high speed overdrive.

"Whaaat?! This can't be so. Can it?" Whaaat?!"

This third, "Whaaat?!" caused Annalisa to finally cry out. "What? What's wrong? What does it mean Alan? What does that word mean?"

He slowly handed her the walking stick as if to say, "Here examine it for yourself because I can't believe what I'm seeing."

Placing his hand on his forehead, he arched back looking to the sky for answers. Then, he bent forward looking straight down at the ground. "Wow," he exclaimed. "Wow!"

Annalisa crouched down still holding the object of their curiosity. Then, craning her neck she looked right up into Alan's face.

"What does it mean, Alan? Come on, tell me what it means. Please?"

Standing up slowly, Alan shook his head from side to side.

"It means, my dear one . . ." He was using his very gentlemanly southern drawl voice. "That most assuredly everything Betsy told me about the **rojocci** fellowship is, most likely, absolutely true. And furthermore, my little sugarplum, I need to talk to whoever owns this stick!"

"Why?" Her voice sounded almost anxious. "Why do you want to find the owner? So you can give it back? Aren't you going to keep it?"

"Only if we can't find the owner. Oh no, look at the time. You okay to run back to the lodge, Annalisa? We no longer have time to walk back."

"Let's do it!" she challenged with a smile. "But you'll need to tell me more about the walking stick and about the word that's carved on it."

"Oh, you can bet on that." he chuckled, and off they scurried down the trail, Alan, with the new found piece of evidence and Annalisa right on his heels.

Both Alan and Annalisa were strong runners, so the three and a half miles on the downhill trail did not pose a problem for either of them. In fact, they arrived in the lobby of the lodge with about ten minutes to spare. It was just enough time to get cleaned up, change clothes, and for Alan to find a hiding place for the new treasure.

During the meeting, his mind kept running through all that the new discovery meant to him. Who was the owner of the stick and how much would he actually know about the word carved down the side? Maybe he wouldn't know anything. Maybe he found it himself and just used it because he couldn't find the original owner. Regardless, he had to find this person who had left it on the summit of the mountain, one way or another. He determined to ask Pastor Fred what he thought, right after the meeting.

When the gathering was over, most everyone headed to the snack bar for popcorn, chips, and sodas. Alan made a beeline for Pastor Fred.

"Hey Fred, do you have a minute?"

"Yes, Alan, I need to talk to you. Where were you and the new girl at dinner this evening?"

"You mean Annalisa?"

"Yes, Alan. Where were you two, and what were you doing?" Pastor Fred was looking over the top of his reading glasses, which he hadn't yet removed.

"Oh that, we were just, uh . . . on the summit. I mean, uh, nothing happened or anything. We were going for a hike and stopped on this boulder and talked and stuff, that's all." Alan wasn't sure why he felt guilty, but he undeniably did.

"Young lady is that true?" Fred questioned, using a softer tone.

Alan swung around to see Annalisa standing directly behind him. "Uh, hi! How long have you been standing there?"

"Oh, I don't know, why?" She cranked her neck to the side like she was eating a taco. "What's up, Alan?"

She straightened back up and looked at Pastor Fred. "Yes, your honor, that's true. We were just talking and the time got away from us. I'm sorry, it won't happen again, sir."

Pastor Fred looked away at the snack bar and chuckled, "Oh, okay. See that it doesn't."

At that moment, Alan glanced at Annalisa who was looking back at him with one of those are-you-kidding- me expressions.

"Alright, you two, I'll talk to you later."

"Pastor Fred seemed more interested in the snack bar than what you were about to ask him," she smirked.

"Now, Annalisa, how do you know what I was going to ask him, huh?"

"Well, my guess is it had something to do with that walking stick. Let's go ask at the front desk. Maybe somebody reported a lost stick," she laughed as she turned toward the lobby area. Alan stood there watching her walk across the Banquet Room.

"Lord, so far I haven't discovered anything I don't just absolutely adore about that gal."

He continued to watch her as she turned to go out the double doors leading to the Grand Hall. She stopped, glanced back at Alan, and with a big smile waved, "Come on!"

Running past her, Alan bounded up the stairs to his room and the hidden walking stick. At the landing he called back that he would meet her at the front desk.

The man behind the front desk was cordial, but not at all helpful, simply stating that no one had reported a lost walking stick. When Alan continued to press him, he picked up the phone and began talking with someone on the other end. Evidently, the person on the other end of the phone showed some interest because the man at the front desk hung up the phone and impatiently declared,

"The manager will be here momentarily."

As if on cue, a door opened along the Grand Hall, and a short, stocky man lumbered in their direction. He had a dark, curly wisp of hair and was wearing a plaid flannel shirt under a dark grey cardigan sweater. While he approached, Alan thought he must be an amiable man as he had a kind face.

"Hi," he said extending his hand forward in Alan's direction. "My name is George Cotton. I'm the General Manager. How may I assist you?"

"Hi, Mr. Cotton, I'm Alan and this is Annalisa. We found this walking stick up on the summit behind the lodge. Would you know if anyone has reported it lost?" Alan reached forward, presenting the stick to Mr. Cotton.

"Why, yes, I believe that's old Archibald Whitaker's walking stick. He carved it himself. Now, let me see here." Mr. Cotton held it within a few inches of his face. "Yep, here are his initials, AW. It's Archie's alright. I'll see that it's returned to him as soon as possible. Thank you so much for bringing it in." Mr. Cotton turned to retreat back to his office.

"Wait, I would like to return it to him personally. That would be okay, wouldn't it? I mean, is he close by?" Alan had one hand on the opposite end of the stick from Mr. Cotton.

"Oh, I guess he wouldn't mind. He lives just across the valley. Come over here and I'll show you."

Mr. Cotton led Alan and Annalisa out the front entrance and to the railing, overlooking the large grassy field sloping down to the river. It was late, so they couldn't see much from where they were standing by the lodge's front canopy, although they could make out a few lights on the dark mountain across the valley.

"See the small light directly across from us, the one about halfway up the mountain? That's Archibald Whitaker's house. Do you see it?"

"Yes, I see it," replied Alan. "But how do I get there?"

Just then, Annalisa slapped him on the arm. Alan turned to see what her problem was.

"How do we . . ." she opened her eyes wide for emphasis when she said, "we".

Alan turned back to Mr. Cotton. "Uh, yeah, how do we get there?"

"It's not too far, just a bit arduous. But you're young folks, so it shouldn't be too difficult. Archie walks the distance three or four times every week and in the winter too. Nice guy that Archie."

Mr. Cotton looked away then continued, "Anyway, walk down our entrance road to the road which runs along the river. Turn left and in about a half mile or so you'll see a single lane bridge that crosses the river. Go across the bridge and turn right onto a gravel road. The county was going to pave it several years ago, but the river floods on that side just about every springtime, sometimes destroying the road. So they decided it was better to leave it gravel because it's cheaper to repair than asphalt."

Alan glanced at Annalisa as if to say, "You sure you want in on this?"

"Anyway," resumed Mr. Cotton with his somewhat lengthy directions, "Turn right and follow the gravel road along the river for about a half mile or so, and you'll see a dirt and gravel lane leading up the mountain on your left. There's one small mailbox right there at the beginning of the lane. The mailbox doesn't have any numbers on it, just two letters like these." Mr. Cotton turned the walking stick so Alan and Annalisa could see the letters "AW".

"In fact, most of the folks down at the church call him, A Dub, because he signs everything with the initials AW. And, A Dub is short for AW, get it?" Alan glanced at Annalisa and smiled as Mr. Cotton continued, "Tomorrow being Sunday, you won't find him at home until after church services are over. I'd try him maybe sometime after two o'clock. Good luck, you two." With that, Mr. Cotton shook Alan's hand then turned and tipped his head in Annalisa's direction.

"So are we leaving right at the afternoon break tomorrow?" Alan spun around to see a smiling Annalisa as she continued, "That's about three o'clock. I'd guess it will take us an hour to get over there. What do you think?"

"I think you're not going, that's what I think. It's way too dangerous. We know nothing about this A Dub character. He could be a serial killer or something. Besides, you heard Pastor Fred giving me a hard time about you and me. He wanted to know what we were doing this afternoon." Alan was using a firm tone that Annalisa thought was most inconsiderate.

"Now, wait just a minute, Alan Browne!" Annalisa interrupted as she pointed her finger right in his face. "I found the stick first, and I had the idea to talk to the front desk people, or you would still be back there trying to explain to Pastor Fred what we were doing up on the summit. Besides, two is always safer than one. So it's settled.

Let's go get a snack." She snatched the stick out of his hand and turned to leave.

Alan's stern face broke into a soft smile as he wagged his head acknowledging that she was going tomorrow, whether he wanted her to or not. He laughed out loud as he allowed himself to recognize that he really did want her to go on this adventure with him.

"Alright," he conceded. "Let's get some popcorn."

Sunday afternoon was bright and sunny without a cloud in the sky. The afternoon meeting let out early, so Alan and Annalisa eagerly started from the lodge down the entrance road at about quarter to three. Within thirty-five minutes, they were at the mailbox with the initials AW on it. Without missing a stride, they turned and headed up the dirt and gravel lane. It was steep with several switchbacks that were even steeper.

After nearly fifteen minutes of uphill hiking, they turned a corner, and there, in full view, stood a small white clapboard sided house with a porch that spanned completely across the front. Because of the sharp incline upon which the structure sat, the floor of the porch was some seven to eight feet above the ground in front of it. From the left side of the porch, wide stairs led down to the sloped yard, though it wasn't much of a yard at all. The front door was just above the stairs at the left end of the home, which also displayed two windows with three modest dormers on the gabled roof.

As the two explorers continued hiking up the gravel lane, they could hear a dog barking from inside the home. It sounded like a big, burly dog. Just as they rounded the final switchback, the front door opened and out stepped an older, white haired man with a neatly trimmed beard, which was every bit as white as the hair on top of his head. He was wearing denim overalls and a bright red flannel shirt. Even though they appeared to be work clothes, he was dressed as neat as a pin. Alan thought he very much looked and sounded like the actor James Earl Jones, only older.

Commanding the dog to, "Quiet down!" he closed the door behind him. Alan noticed he had a deep, booming voice that sounded a bit intimidating.

"You folks lost?" he called across the distance of about fifty yards.

"Uh, no sir. We're looking for Mr. Archibald Whitaker," Alan shouted back.

"What you want him for?" barked back the deep voice.

"We have his walking stick!" yelled Annalisa. "Do you know him? Is this his home?"

"Where'd you find that stick?"

And with that, the large man started down the stairs and toward the couple. Alan and Annalisa stopped in their tracks, not quite sure of the precariousness of their situation. Here they were a mile or two from the lodge and close to a half mile up a winding gravel lane, which appeared as though no car had driven on it in quite some time. However, it was too late to avoid a conversation as the man was within a few feet of them.

"May I see that?" his voice was strong and almost dreadful. Yet his face and eyes had a conspicuous tenderness about them. Alan reached out and handed him the walking stick.

"Yep, that sure enough is my old walking stick. I never thought I'd see it again. Where y'all find it?"

"Up on the summit across the valley. So you're Archibald Whitaker?" Alan was starting to feel a bit more relaxed with the situation.

"Yes sir, that's me. But nobody has called me that in years. Everyone around here calls me A Dub or just Archie. I prefer A Dub though. Mind me asking where you folks from?"

"We both live in the Washington, DC Area, but we're up here on a church retreat over at the lodge," Alan explained.

"I'm actually from California," Annalisa added.

"Hmmm . . . California. Now, that's a long way. Yes sir, a mighty long way away," A Dub replied, as he glanced at Annalisa then back to Alan.

"Uh, Mr. Whitaker," Alan interrupted, "do you have a minute for me to ask you a few questions?"

"Well, no sir, not if you're going to insist on calling me Mister, I don't." Mr. Whitaker was smiling but that deep voice made Alan feel as though he was serious. "Just call me A Dub. I feel most comfortable being called A Dub. Now, what can I help you with?"

"Hi, uh . . . A Dub, I'm Alan and this is Annalisa. It's about those letters on the side of your walking stick." Alan was pointing in the direction of the stick, which was now in its proper place, upright, with one end on the ground, and the other in the palm of its rightful owner. "I have a couple of questions about the word there."

"What would you like to know?" A Dub's big, strong voice suddenly grew much softer.

157

"Uh . . . well, I'm not quite sure where to start. Ummm, would you happen to know Stanley and Betsy Taft? They live in Arlington. It's in Virginia," probed Alan.

"No, I don't recall ever knowing any Taft family. How might I'd have known them?"

"They're a part of that same fellowship. The **rojocci** fellowship, I mean. Betsy told me all about it seeing that Stanley had passed on and all." Alan's confidence was starting to return as A Dub seemed very interested in Alan's inquiries. "I mean, would you have a few minutes to tell me more about it? Maybe you could tell me how you got involved?" Alan was really testing the waters with this last question.

"Now, Alan, Annalisa, that would take more time than just standing in this here drive. You'd have to come up on the porch for some lemonade and sit a spell. But if you got questions and are willing to listen, I'd be more than happy to accommodate."

-twelve-

racious and kind, A Dub took the time to answer all of Alan's questions. He told Alan a great deal more than Betsy had the time to tell him. The most fascinating part of A Dub's story was how he came into the **rojocci** fellowship, and how that brought him to the mountains of Western Maryland, his home of more than fifty years. Alan guessed A Dub was in his late seventies or maybe even early eighties. He was a soft spoken man, who used the tone and volume of his voice to emphasize a point better than anyone Alan had ever heard. He and Annalisa were literally on the edge of their seats listening to A Dub.

He related to them that his ancestors were brought to America as slaves. When they were taken off the ship at Charleston, South Carolina, in 1807, less than a year before the United Kingdom banned the slave trade, they were immediately sold at auction. However, his great, great, great-grandfather was sold to a kind Christian man who granted his recently acquired slaves their freedom once they arrived at his plantation. Most of them chose to stay under his protection because he was a compassionate and charitable man, willing to teach them the language and how to manage crops.

"It was a rice growing planation," stated A Dub plainly. "He fed, clothed, and paid them for their labor. He also shared with some of them the **rojocci** fellowship way. My ancestor, Adoniram Whitaker, decided at the end of the Civil War to move north. Hitching a ride on the Underground Railroad, he arrived at a tiny crossroads in Ohio named Pfeiffer Station. Over the next several months, he made his way east into the mountains of Western Maryland because he heard its nickname was the 'Free State'."

Taking a long gulp of his lemonade, Alan shifted forward and exclaimed, "That's an amazing story. You must be very proud of him. May I ask, what you mean when you say the '**rojocci** way'?"

"The way is a lifestyle really," answered A Dub. "It's a way of living your life. If you call yourself a Christian, meaning you call yourself a disciple of Christ, then you ought to live like one. Or, like me, at least be trying to live like you mean it, you know. That's what's most important."

Right then, at the end of the last sentence, A Dub's voice increased in its deep tone and volume. It had a very sobering effect on Alan. As he glanced at Annalisa, he could tell it was speaking to her as well.

"So your spiritual part of life is the most important, right?" probed Alan.

"No! No sir, it's not," retorted A Dub. "There ain't no part to it. It's not your spiritual part or you're physical part or your intellectual part. No, sir." At this A Dub leaned forward in Alan's direction and pointed two huge fingers right at Alan's heart.

"It's life. There ain't no part to it. You're either a spiritual man or," A Dub again glanced in Annalisa's direction and softened his tone, "a woman," he smiled, "or, you are a carnal man, an intellectual man, a physical man, or any other type of man. You're headed some place. Ask yourself, where you going?"

With this last question those two meaty fingers poked Alan right in the chest exactly where his heart was. A Dub reclined back in his porch chair, picked up his glass of lemonade, and took a long drink. He placed it back down on the exact spot where the glass had left a wet ring on the arm of his chair. Alan noticed the ice had all but melted.

"Yes, sir," continued A Dub, "that's the question everyone has got to ask themselves. But especially every Christian got to ask themselves, 'Where am I going?'"

"Now, that's the way," A Dub was nodding his head. "That's what the **rojocci** fellowship is all about. Right there, yes sir, that's it." A Dub did the thing with his voice again and Alan was beginning to understand why he did it. It really was most effective in emphasizing his point.

There was a long pause of silence. Alan was staring out over the porch railing into the tree tops and across the valley. He was trying to bring some sense to what he had just heard, to recall some experience in his past he could latch upon to help him identify anything this insightful gentleman was trying to explain to him. After what seemed like several minutes, Alan mustered up the courage to ask his next question.

"So, you're saying, I should be reading my Bible and praying and going to church and stuff like that, right?"

"Well, sure," responded A Dub, "that's a good start. But, there's so much more to this than that. Yes, sir, that's sure enough a good start, but why stop? It's like, how do you say . . . a carpenter or a builder who starts building a house. He ain't finished until he finished. You know what I'm sayin'? You understanding me?" At this point A Dub leaned forward again to assure Alan and Annalisa were hearing him. Alan was more than a little intimated though, so he tried to change the subject.

"Yeah, I'm a carpenter too, well kinda."

"Me, too." smiled A Dub. "I built this here house with my own hands, and it took me pert near two year to finish it off. But, that's not the point. It really don't matter what you do on the outside, you know, if you do carpenter work or teaching or businessman or whatever. It's what you do on the inside that matters. Oh, you building a house alright. You building a spiritual house, and it takes your entire lifetime, no matter how many years that be, to complete it; yes, sir, right down to your very last breath." A Dub's voice became so soft and quiet, Alan and Annalisa could barely hear it. It was something Alan would remember the rest of his life.

Once again, there was a long silence with Alan staring out across the horizon. Considering how many questions his mind was pondering, it was no wonder he was struggling to put them in order, to narrow them all down to just one, the next question. At the same moment a question formed on his lips, A Dub broke the silence.

"Look," he started. "You two seem like a nice couple. How long y'all been married?"

"Oh, we're not married," snapped Alan who took a quick glance in Annalisa's direction. He was surprised that she didn't turn toward him but rather remained facing and smiling in A Dub's direction. "I mean, we're not, you know a couple or anything." Alan's response was bordering on sounding more like an apology than a factual statement.

"Oh, you will be," retorted A Dub. "You two are most definitely going to be married. And I'd dare say, what the Lord has brought together let no man put asunder."[1]

"Well," replied Alan as he began feeling very uncomfortable with the situation, "it's getting late, and we need to be going so we're not tardy to our meeting, right, Annalisa?"

"Let me just finish this one thing. Then I'll let y'all head on back. If you're running behind, I can drive you there. It's only a few minutes to the lodge."

"I don't know," dickered Alan.

"Oh, let him finish Alan," interrupted Annalisa. "I think this may be something very important that we both need to hear."

"Thank you kindly," nodded A Dub to Annalisa. "The point I was trying to make is that the way, the **rojocci** way, is like a marriage. When you first start out on this journey, you don't really know each other well. But as the years go on by and you get to know one another and go through them difficult times and through them easy times too, you get real close. It's like she knows what you thinking and you know what she be thinking. There's this trust, this knowing that she going to be there no matter what trouble come your way. You know what I'm saying to you?"

"You don't ever stop," continued A Dub with a smile. "It's always there and no matter where you go or what you do, she thinking about you and you thinking about her. It's not a part of you. It **is** you!" At this A Dub leaned forward and pushed those two enormous digits into Alan's chest again. "You have got to take responsibility for this relationship. You hear what I'm saying to you?"

Alan nodded his head slowly and said, "I think so."

"I'm only using marriage as one of them metaphors, as an analogy to this invisible relationship between you and the Lord. Most church going folks don't even realize they **have** a responsibility, much less that they need to **take** some responsibility in this relationship. A Dub was smiling, but his tone made Alan and Annalisa know that this was something he considered very important.

"We go to a Presbyterian church," Alan confirmed. "Uh, at least I do, kinda. Actually, I've missed a few services lately." Alan was surprised at his own transparency with someone he hardly knew.

"I attend a non-denominational church in Pleasant Hill," contributed Annalisa with a smile.

"That's real nice," replied A Dub. "But that's not what I'm talking about. Going to Sunday service is a real good thing. Reading them Scriptures and praying is essential. Don't get me wrong. All that is real good. What I'm trying to tell you is this . . ." A Dub paused for a second or two.

"Uh, why do you go to that Sunday service? Why do you open up that Holy Word and read it, memorize it, meditate on it? Why do you pray? Why do you fast or why do you give? It don't matter what church you go to. It don't matter if it be a Presbyterian or Baptist or Pentecostal or Catholic," then turning his eyes toward Annalisa, "or even one of them non-denominational churches. The question is why you doing what you doing?" And pausing for just a few seconds he added, "Where you going, Alan?" Shifting in his seat, so he was now facing Annalisa, "And, Annalisa, where you going? Decide what's important in life, and then you got a purpose, a reason for what you doing."

Glancing down at his watch A Dub questioned, "What time did you folks say you need to be back at the lodge?"

"Oh no, not again, two days in a row. This isn't good," complained Alan.

"Ah, it's my fault. Let me drive y'all back. It takes less than ten minutes, okay?"

Alan looked over at Annalisa as he jumped to his feet. She nodded back to him acknowledging that it was okay with her if they let A Dub drive them back to the lodge.

"Well, okay, I guess if it's the only way to avoid being late again."

Rising to his feet A Dub replied, "Let me get my keys, only be a second."

Alan and Annalisa proceeded down the porch steps and started across to the pickup truck parked on the side of A Dub's home.

"Wow, what did you think of that?" whispered Alan.

"Which part?" Annalisa whispered back.

"All of it. I mean, what did you think of all of that? I thought it was incredible. I've never heard anything like that before." Alan was staring at the ground trying to put into words the ideas in his mind.

"It was pretty amazing," replied Annalisa, her voice almost back to its regular volume. I've never heard a message like that before, and I've been going to church all my life. I think A Dub has walked with God for a long time. I sure would like to know God like that. You know what I mean Alan?"

"Yeah, me, too," Alan whispered. Then reaching across, he softly took hold of her arm, guiding her across the slope and repeated, "Me, too."

Hearing the door to the house slam shut, Alan quickly moved his hand away from Annalisa. A Dub was making his way down the stairs when he called out, "Y'all go on ahead and get in."

The drive back across the valley to the lodge only took a few minutes. Alan was relieved that it was such a quick trip. A Dub pulled right up under the front entrance canopy just as George Cotton, the General Manager, was walking in the door.

"Archie, how you been doing?" he called from the open door.

"Just fine, Mr. Cotton, just fine sir. And better now that these folks found my walking stick. I need that stick to make it up to the summit."

"Good to see you. Don't be a stranger," with that Mr. Cotton went inside.

Alan and Annalisa were standing outside A Dub's pickup truck resting against the closed passenger door. "Just one other thing, please, Mr. A Dub," begged Alan.

"It's just, A Dub. Like I told you when we first met, no mister, just A Dub be fine."

"Okay, sorry, A Dub. Do you know the meaning of each of the letters?"

"What letters?" A Dub scrunched up his face.

"The letters on your walking stick, the **rojocci** letters?"

"Yes sir, I sure enough do," replied A Dub.

"Please, can you tell me what each one means?" Alan pleaded.

"Do you know any of them?" asked A Dub.

"Yes sir, I know the second "o" and the first "c". Can you tell me the rest of them please?"

"How did you find out about those two?" asked A Dub.

"Well, kind of by accident. Betsy told me that I was right about it being an acronym. Then she gave me this kind of history lesson and all. But I still only have the words to those two letters."

"Did she tell you that anyone in the fellowship can only explain one word from one letter at a time? I'm sure she must have told you that."

"Yes, yes sir, she did. But I would really like to know more than one. Can you tell me two? Please?" Alan's beseeching tone was bordering on becoming whiny.

"No, sir, I can't. Just one, Alan. You see it is the whole spirit of the **rojocci** fellowship. It is a lifelong continual journey of discovery and of understanding the mysteries of our Lord and Savior. The word is just a reminder to keep going, to never quit. Look you two, I'm eighty-eight year old. I was born in 1890, and I didn't discover the last word of the last letter until I was nearly seventy. Be patient. Remember, it's a lifestyle, not a job. It's like one of them marathons, not a sprint. Now, which letter can I help you with?"

167

Alan's mouth gaped open, "That's just what Stanley used to tell me."

As they were speaking, the front door to the lodge swung open and Pastor Fred called to Alan, "Hey Alan, are you still opening our meeting? We're starting in less than five minutes."

"Yes, sir," Alan called back. Then turning his attention back to A Dub, "I don't know, maybe the "j" or how about the first letter. What do you think Annalisa? Maybe I should do the other "o" or perhaps the other "c" then I'll at least have both of one of those letters." Swinging around to look her in the eyes, he asked, "What do you think?"

Annalisa looked up and then back to Alan. "I think I'd find out what the first one means. You might be able to figure the rest out for yourself, if you know the first one."

"Nah," replied Alan. I want the first "o", and then I'll know all the "o" letters." Facing A Dub once again, he requested, "What's the first "o" mean? Uh, what does the letter stand for?

"**Of**, "A Dub stated frankly. "It means 'of'."

"Whaaat?!" groaned Alan, "Of? Are you serious?"

Annalisa bent over with quiet laughter. She covered her mouth with her hand so as not to be too obvious in her glee. But she could barely contain herself and finally gave in to a full blown holler.

"I'm so sorry, Alan, but when you think about it that's just too funny. Oh my, I think I'm going to hurt myself laughing!"

"Sorry, Alan, really enjoyed the afternoon though," said A Dub. "You two drop by anytime you want. It was real nice visiting with you."

With that A Dub put his pickup truck in gear, and waved his huge hand as he headed back down the entrance road. Alan just stood there in disbelief. The first two words were so deep and had such strong potential. Even the way he found them late that night in his father's garage just as the clock struck midnight. It seemed to him that "**overlooked**" and "**cherished**" were so mysterious and had beckoned to him of further meaning and discovery. But now this "**of**", he was quite dumbfounded as to what step to take next in this new adventure of his.

He hadn't quite noticed her tugging on his shirt sleeve, but when Annalisa blurted, "Come on, Alan, we're going to be late!" he awoke from his daytime stupor and headed for the meeting alongside her.

It was around ten o'clock in the evening when the meeting finally dismissed. Most everyone wandered over to the snack bar, but Alan told Annalisa he was exhausted and was going to head back to his room. Once in bed, however, he laid there until almost one o'clock in the morning. He finally decided to go out on the balcony because Peaknuckle was snoring up a storm.

It was still and, oh, so quiet outside. There was a chilly dampness in the air. The night sky was absolutely devoid of clouds, yet he could still vaguely see the faint outline of the mountain across the small valley. Alan thought it was incredibly peaceful, providing a sharp contrast to the extreme agitation of his mind. The questions were continually running, never stopping. As soon as one would slow down enough for him to try and answer it, another one would pop up, each equally as perplexing as the previous one.

Looking down to the blackness of the field below the lodge, his eyes scanned across to what he was sure must be the river. He listened very carefully and could just barely hear the water falling upon the rocks as it made its way ever lower to the valley below. Just then, he heard a very quiet whisper.

"Alan, is that you?"

He swung around but couldn't see anyone. He leaned out over the rail again, listening for the voice. A few seconds passed.

Then again, "Alan, is that you?"

This time he craned his neck around and peered upward to the deck above. He could see the nearly imperceptible outline of a face with shoulder length hair peering out over the railing above.

"Alan?" the soft tone was unmistakably that of Annalisa. "Can't you sleep?"

"No. I can't get my mind to slow down. How about you?" Alan whispered.

"Me either," she replied softly. "You hungry?"

Now, Alan wasn't hungry, but he recognized this was not actually a question regarding food. No, what she really meant, he determined, was, "You want to talk for a while?"

"Sure," he whispered back. "I'll meet you on the big sofa in the Grand Hall in five minutes."

Alan threw on some clothes, splashed on a little after shave, and was seated on the sofa inside of four minutes, waiting for her entrance down the stairs. As the five minute mark went by, he glanced up the stairway again. "Where is she?" he thought. He suddenly swung around to see her parked on the sofa right next to him.

"How'd you get here? he questioned.

"Elevator," she replied frankly.

"I thought you always used the stairs?" he quipped with a hint of sarcasm.

"I do," she smiled. "But I don't like to be predictable, so on occasion I take the elevator." She shrugged her shoulders and giggled.

"You're too funny," he laughed. "Hey, want me to get you some popcorn?"

"Nope. Not hungry," she chirped.

"Wait a minute," griped Alan. He wasn't actually bellyaching, but wanted to appear as though he was. "I thought you said you were hungry?"

"No, I asked if you were hungry. I'm not hungry. Are you?"

At this point, Alan was just about to absolutely bust over her cute, sweet ways. He swung around to face her and started to say something very personal. She turned around to face him as well. Alan had one leg cocked up on the sofa while the foot of his other leg was flat on the floor. Annalisa sat crossed legged and was looking as pretty as anyone Alan had ever seen.

Alan scooched slightly forward with his arm high on the back of the sofa, "Annalisa?" he quietly said her name.

"Yes, Alan," she whispered as she teasingly fluttered her eyelids. Then she couldn't help it and began to break out in a giggle.

"Hey, come on. I'm trying to be serious here," he feigned a grumbling tone again.

"Oh, I'm sorry, Alan, what is it?"

"Nah, it's nothing. I mean, uh . . . what did you think about today? Awesome, right?"

"Yes, it was a pretty day Alan, nice and sunny." Knowing he really wanted to have more of a heartfelt conversation, a huge smile appeared on her face.

"No, no, I mean . . . well, yes, it was a beautiful sunny day. But what did you think about the time we had with A Dub?

"I was thinking about that too, Alan." Her tone became more sincere once she was confident the conversation would be about their time with A Dub. "How do you suppose he gained such a depth with God? Everything he said just seemed to flow from his lips, like he didn't even have to think about it. You know what I mean?"

"Great hearts have seen great hardships, or at least that's what Betsy told me. I would guess he has experienced more than his share of struggles. He has such a unique gentleness about him, and that voice. He got me to doing a lot of thinking," conceded Alan. "He has a remarkable walk with God. He even . . ." Alan stopped mid-sentence and looked over at the dwindling fire in the huge stone fireplace.

"He even what?" probed Annalisa, "He what?"

"You know . . . that thing he said. Do you suppose that was like a prophecy or something?"

"Was what a prophecy? What do you . . ." she gasped. Annalisa's hand clamped tightly over her mouth. She shook her head and then looked straight into Alan's eyes for just a second to determine if he was somehow thinking this was a joke. She turned her gaze toward the fire and then back to Alan's face. They sat quietly on the sofa pondering the amazing day they had just enjoyed together.

Now, here it was, well after one o'clock in the morning. They were leaving later today to head back to the Washington, DC, area. The room was comfortably quiet, just the occasional crackle of the fire in the fireplace broke the silence. Alan was wondering if he would ever see her again. If she could sense what he was feeling for her? Did she have the same attraction for him as he had for her?

Several minutes must have passed before Alan broke the silence. After shifting around a bit in his seat on the sofa, he reached across and gently took ahold of Annalisa's hand. "Umm," he whispered. "Since we are leaving in a few hours, and I don't know where you live in DC, or if I'll ever see you again after today, would you be open to maybe going out sometime? I mean, for dinner or something, even a lunch or snack . . . I mean, coffee or something? Do you already have a boyfriend in California or one around here?" Alan was feeling very insecure and not at all sure of the next words that would proceed from Annalisa's lips.

"Well, Alan," she smiled, "in terms of never seeing each other again, in a few hours you will be driving the van I am riding in back to DC. So I'm sure we'll see each other again. In regards to dinner, lunch, a snack, or something, well, I think that would be nice. However, I start my congressional internship on Tuesday, so I'm not sure what my schedule will be."

"Now, on to the topic of a boyfriend; I don't have one in California. Well, I did, but when he heard I had decided to fulfill my commitment for the internship this summer, he broke up with me."

"Oh, I'm sorry, was it recent?" Alan asked quietly, hoping to hide his delight.

"About three and a half months ago. He was an okay guy. But he wasn't a spiritual leader and not at all romantic."

Alan took special note of this last sentence.

"So, I no longer have a boyfriend in California." She was using a very soft tone which Alan particularly liked.

"And do you have a boyfriend here?" he coaxed with slight smile.

Annalisa sniggled back, "Maybe."

-thirteen-

Still grinning when he opened his eyes, Alan glanced to the south, noticing the dark clouds over the Gulf of Mexico had grown quite large. Or were they just closer? Regardless, his blissful smile, as his memory was replaying that wondrous video from 1978, had turned into a look of semi-controlled anxiety. He had never been in a hurricane before and wasn't sure what to expect. The color of the clouds, and the strong breeze that was bordering on being a stiff wind was starting to have an adverse effect on his much needed peaceful retreat.

Glancing at his watch, he declared out loud, "Well, guess I better head back to the cottage and begin hunkering down. It's getting late; time for dinner and a phone call to the cheerful Mrs. Browne."

With that, he stood, using the trunk of his old massive friend to wedge himself upward. "Not sure I'll be out this way tomorrow. You take care of yourself, okay?" He paused, as if expecting a reply from the giant confidant. Then, Alan turned and walked slowly toward the road that led to his little storm shelter, more commonly known as the Morgan's cottage. Dusk was moving in quickly, exaggerated by the thick black clouds. It was nearly dark when Alan trotted around to the back porch, up the rickety stairs, and pulled open the old wooden screened door.

"Sure is getting windy," he acknowledged aloud. Alan usually talked to himself when alone, and almost always when he was getting stressed about something. And he was most certainly getting stressed about something: his situation.

Turning on the kitchen light as he entered through the back door, he immediately felt claustrophobic. With all of the windows and the front door covered with the storm plywood, the little cottage was quite dim inside. The only hint of light peeking in from outside came through the kitchen door that led to the back porch. Alan had decided, since he couldn't flee the hurricane, his best choice of an exit was this door, so he left it uncovered. He had painstakingly nailed each sheet of plywood over each of the five windows and the front door. At first, he hadn't been sure how many nails would be needed to secure each opening. But drawing from his carpentry background, he used twelve nails each, reasoning, "It's better to have too many than not enough."

The little cottage was way too quiet, terribly quiet, ominously quiet. The only noise he could hear was the wind rustling through the trees, as well as the occasional scratching of the branches on the wood siding and metal roofing. The whole effect was very disconcerting to Alan. Not eerie or scary, but it induced a very uneasy feeling within him, like something unsuspected could happen at any moment.

"I think I'll turn on more lights," he proclaimed. "That may cheer the mood in this dreary old place."

He walked across the room to the lamp on the little table next to the deteriorating drab green sofa. After several clicks of the tiny knob, the light finally illuminated part of the room. Passing the front door he decided to flip on the front porch light too, in case someone would wonder if any one was home. Then, peering into the dark bedroom, he switched on the small globe ceiling light. Finally, as he passed the modest rectangular kitchen table with two chairs, he pulled the chain that turned on the lamp at the back end of the table.

"There, that's, uh . . . better. Well, kind of anyway." Alan could hear his own voice and determined that it didn't sound very hopeful. He could actually feel himself beginning to sink into the dark despondency. It could be extremely difficult to extract himself, once he started down that slippery slope into what he called the black hole.

"No! No! NO!!! I'm not going there again!"

Getting louder with each word, his voice sounded almost panicked. Then, with a calmer tone, as if trying to convince himself, he assured, "Look, you're just visiting. It's not like you live here. This storm will be over soon, right? It won't be that bad. Things will turn out okay. I mean, how bad can a hurricane named Opal be anyway?"

Alan was trying very hard to persuade himself that the storm was outside, in the Gulf of Mexico. Way out there, that was the real concern, the real potential for trouble. However, he was becoming overwhelmed as he wrestled the burgeoning tempest within his soul that was threatening to become a full blown typhoon. His emotions were shoving their way into his thoughts like bullies on a neighborhood playground. And those thoughts were starting to run at more than a casual trot. Yes, this was beginning to look like a full scale battle, one he knew he had lost so many times before.

After Alan finished his daily call home, he tried to get some sleep. However, he had a troublesome night's rest, if it could even be called rest. Refusing to look at his watch, he was certain that it must have been the wee hours of the morning before he dozed off, only to be awakened by yet another gust of wind or the sound of a tree limb beating against the cottage.

At some point, he got up from the bed and stumbled out to the sofa in the murky darkness of the living room. He couldn't drop off to sleep there either, so he staggered across the room and sat at the kitchen table. He tried leaning back in the uncomfortable chair resting his feet upon the table top, with the hope that this position would help him sleep. After what must have been more than an hour, he decided to try the bed again, resigning, "At least it has a mattress."

Sometime around dawn, he must have dozed off to sleep because at eight o'clock sharp he was startled out of his slumber by the ringing of his mobile phone.

"Alan, where'd you end up going?" It was the excited voice of his neighbor in San Ramon, Bill Morgan.

"Uh, hi, Bill, and good morning," came the reply from an incredibly groggy Alan. He glanced at his watch as his mind began to register the noise of the storm outside. It was much louder and more violent.

"Where are you?" was the urgent reply. "You okay, Al?"

"Yeah, I'm fine. It sounds like it's getting pretty windy though, and the rain, well . . . it's coming down in sheets."

Bill interrupted, "You still in Gulf Breeze? Are you in the cottage Al? Man, are you nuts?! That's a bad storm. You need to get out of there now!" Bill's voice was near panic in both decibels and cadence.

"Well, I can't Bill. I don't have a way out of here. Besides, where would I go?" Alan's own voice was beginning to match Bill's. While still holding the phone to his ear, Alan started down the short hall and into the living room flipping on the first light switch his probing hands found.

"Power's out, Bill. That's not good. It's almost pitch black in here with the windows boarded and all. The only hint of light radiates in from the back door window. It's such a minute amount that I can hardly see anything at all."

"You didn't board up the back door?" Bill's voice was entering a new octave range that Alan had never heard come out of his neighbor before. "You need to get that boarded up quick, Al, before this storm gets any worse."

"Bill," retorted Alan. "If I board it up now, how will I get out? Or better yet, how can I get back in if I nail boards over the door. You're not making any sense Bill."

Pausing for a response from Bill, Alan was formulating his own side of this pointless argument. After all, he was stuck here in this dingy cottage in the middle of what sounded like a terrible storm raging just inches away outside these walls. Bill, was, no doubt, enjoying a beautifully sunny morning a couple thousand miles away in San Ramon. It appeared to Alan, that if anyone should be worried here, it should definitely be him, not Bill.

"Bill?" The pause was certainly long enough for Bill to respond to Alan's logical side of this discussion. "Bill, you there? Can you hear me?" Alan moved the phone from his ear and looked intently at the tiny screen.

"Uh, oh, no signal. And look, hardly any charge left on the battery. He realized he must have forgotten to plug it into the charger last night. Upon pondering the way he was awakened a few minutes ago, he remembered unplugging the charger from the phone just before he answered Bill's unwelcome morning wake-up call.

"It's because the power went out sometime last night," he exclaimed aloud. "Oh, no, how will I be able to make a call for help if my phone battery is dead?" A cold, deep fear began creeping into his fragile emotional state of mind. "How can I call home? How will they know how I'm doing?"

With this last protest, his mind drifted to their home in San Ramon. It was early morning, he imagined, as he meandered through each room of his lovely California hacienda style home. He checked each door to assure it was still locked and peeked in on the children he so adored, as he walked by each bedroom. He then ambled along the buff adobe tiled floors to the kitchen where he poured himself a hot cup of coffee. In his imagination, he moved slowly across the kitchen through the archway and into the dining room stopping at the French doors, which led to the small courtyard, where he and the cheerful Mrs. Browne spent their early mornings together.

As he peered through one of the window panes in the door, he saw her there, the love of his life, the most wonderful person he had ever known. She sat where she always sat, in her chair at the little round table with her cup of coffee placed on top of a napkin next to her open Bible.

Across the quiet courtyard, looking northeast, he could see the top half of Mt. Diablo framed in the archway leading to their drive and detached garage. The scene was perfect and she looked beautiful sitting there, his life partner, as he was accustomed to calling her. He truly loved her with all his heart.

A huge, "Crack!" pierced the air and startled him back to reality as he stood stone still in the dark, stuffy cottage. The raging of the storm outside was almost deafening. Every so often he would hear yet another loud crack or pop and wonder if this was his end.

"Was that noise the house or another tree limb?" he questioned out loud because, he reasoned, it was nice to hear a voice, even if it was just his own. His long sigh broke into soft weeping. He dropped to his knees in a heap as his shoulders began shaking. Within seconds, he was sobbing uncontrollably.

"Oh, I miss her so bad, dear Lord." he silently mouthed through the sobs. "Oh, please help her, God. Keep her safe and watch over her and our precious little ones," he lamented aloud. "Oh, how I ache, dear God. I really hurt. Please help. Please help me I pray! Please . . ." His cries tapered off as if resigning himself to the obvious; "I'm going to die in this shabby cottage. They'll probably never even find my body."

He crawled the few feet across the small room and pulled himself up so he could kneel at the sofa. Burying his face in the cushions he pleaded with all his might, "Oh, God, help me! Please help!"

Compared to the constant noise of the storm, he could hardly hear his own entreaty for help. "Quiet!" he shouted at the storm. "Oh, quiet, please be quiet," his appeal for peace now softer this second time. "Oh, dear God, where is the quiet?"

With this last inquiry to the only One who is able to calm the storm, he looked up from his makeshift altar of drab green cushions. "Quiet, I need quiet, but not on the outside . . . I need quiet on the inside, dear Lord. It's just like Stanley said all those years ago on the second floor of that house we were building in Great Falls. Yes, I remember it was snowing and Big Jim was ragging on me good that day. I recall that Stanley put his hand on my shoulder and told me I needed to find a quiet road. I needed to find my own **rojocci**."

His amazement at how simple the words seemed to him now was matched only by how stupid he felt that he never understood them. He swung himself around and sat down on the sofa, the tears still falling. He strained to pull himself together.

"Okay," he conceded, "if the quiet is really on the inside, like Betsy explained right after Stanley died, then I need to find that quiet place on the inside, in my heart, no matter the noise outside. Afterwards, I can hear from God and maybe discover my own **rojocci**, whatever that may mean, or . . ."

Alan tried diligently to convince his already overloaded mind that maybe he had just made some sort of discovery. "Hmmm . . ." he breathed.

Just then, a small quiet voice entered his thoughts. "Where did you get that discovery from?"[1]

Alan opened his eyes. They darted around the dim room looking for who had spoken to him. He wasn't actually convinced it was a voice. It was more of a thought than a voice. "No," he reasoned aloud, "It was more than a thought; it was a knowing."

"Be still," continued the next thought. "Quiet your heart. **Be still and know that I AM.**"[2]

Startled, Alan jumped off the sofa and ran across the room to the back door yanking it open. He literally leaped halfway across the porch before realizing there was a horrendous storm raging around him. The screening on the porch had all but been destroyed, and the hammock was nowhere to be found. One porch chair was across the yard, laying broken in pieces, having smashed into the shed. He couldn't find the other chair. In the timespan of a few seconds, he decided it would be safer inside the cottage than standing ever so close to what he deemed was certain death outside.

Therefore, with trepidation, he stepped through the open back door. It slammed shut behind him as a result of the hurricane strength winds rushing past the cottage. The abrupt motion rattled him even further. He cautiously peered into the ill-lighted room, swinging his head from side to side, searching with his eyes through the dark, half expecting to see the form or figure of the one who had spoken to him. Alan found his way to the chair at the kitchen table. He slowly took his seat and listened. He reasoned within himself, if he listened closely he would be able to hear if someone was moving in the hallway, or if the person he heard was now in the bedroom.

He wasn't scared, at least not real scared, like the time, a few years ago, when he went backpacking in the high country of Yosemite. Then, he had climbed out of the tent in the middle of the night for the call of nature. Although it had been extremely dark, there was no doubt he had almost run into an ill-mannered bear, who was grousing for some grubs. The deep, threatening growl that had rent the starry night air had made it perfectly clear to him. "That was scary." he whispered, acknowledging this situation was not as intense.

After several minutes had passed, he mustered up enough courage and decided to break his silence. "Lord, was that you?" he whispered. He waited for several more minutes trying to quiet his anxious thoughts. He realized he wasn't quite sure which answer he really wanted to hear. He raised his elbows to the surface of the kitchen table and bowed his head into his hands.

"Lord, if that was you, I'm sorry I ran out. I'll quiet myself if you want to speak again, okay?"

Alan glanced up from his hands just to be sure there was no one there ready to tap him on the shoulder. A few more minutes went by, but all he heard was the constant commotion of the storm outside. Alan glanced down at his watch.

"Wow, it's after eleven o'clock already," he allowed himself to say out loud although it wasn't really much more than a whisper. He settled back in his chair, closing his eyes once more.

"Why not read the Scriptures?"[3] came a thought.

But quickly another thought followed it, "Man, I'm getting hungry. I wonder if there's anything left to eat?"

He stood up from the kitchen table and began moving across the floor toward the refrigerator. "Oh, yeah, Bill told me to make sure there wasn't any food left in the fridge just in case the power went out." He swung open the refrigerator door revealing one lone cheese stick, which he quickly unwrapped and devoured.

"Hey, wait a minute," he declared aloud as he rested back on the countertop. "Wait-a-minute!"

"Lord, was that you just a minute ago when I was sitting right over there in the chair at the table. Was that you Lord? Do you want me to read my Bible?"

Alan listened closely as if he expected to hear a voice telling him, "Of course, I want you to read your Bible." After a few seconds of waiting, Alan broke into a quiet laugh stating, "Of course, He would want me to read my Bible. It is His Word, His message of love to me."

He made his way down the hallway slowly, partly because he couldn't see clearly through the darkness, and partly because he still wasn't quite sure some "being" wasn't hiding in the bedroom.

As he turned the corner, he found nothing in the bedroom except the creaky, old bed and the nightstand. His hands groped along the nightstand for his Bible and notebook. Picking them up, he headed to the dim light coming from the glass panes in the door leading to the

R. J. Graves, Jr.

porch. He decided he definitely wouldn't open the closet
door in the bedroom. Instead, before he left the room, he
pushed the bed over a few feet, wedging the door to the
closet tightly shut, just in case.

Sitting down at the kitchen table once again, he quietly,
respectfully resigned, "Okay, dear Father, I'm here. I'll quiet
my soul. Then if you would be so kind, please speak to me
again. I mean, if that was You? Uh . . . at least, I think it was
You."

He discontinued his monologue realizing that he was
not doing what he had just committed to do, which was to
be quiet. After a few minutes, Alan thought he heard a
whisper, not in his ears, but in his heart. "Start in Hebrews,
there's an answer for you in the Book of Hebrews."

Alan opened his eyes as if to assure himself that no one
was in the cottage. After peering around the continually
dusk room, he closed his eyes and started to ask again, "Was
that you, Father?"

"Of course, it must be Him," he interrupted his own
thought. "Why would anyone else tell me to read the
Scriptures?" Picking up his Bible, he started flipping the
pages, looking for Hebrews, stating in his matter of fact
voice, "Of course it was You, Lord."

He held up the pages so he could maximize the faint
light. He squinted at the words of the first verse of the first
chapter. He read them slowly, deliberately, pausing several
times to ponder if this was the answer he thought he had
been promised.

"Hmmm . . ." he whispered, "maybe verse two."

His eyes moved purposefully across the letters that formed the words of each sentence. Quietly, reflectively, he drank it all in as though he was savoring a delicious meal for the first time after being released from a prison cell. Gradually, he made his way through each word of the second verse. Then, on to the third verse his eyes deliberately moved, absorbing every vowel and consonant of the magnificent phrase:

> "And He is the radiance of His glory and the exact representation of His nature, and upholds all things by the word of His power . . ."

These words seemed to jump off the page. It was as if they had been somehow raised above the rest of the words and had some bright light illuminating them from behind.

"But who is the 'He' in this verse?" questioned Alan aloud. His eyes moved back up to the previous verse. "It's His Son," Alan whispered. "It's His Son; it's Jesus." His eyes returned to dissecting the words below.

> "and, upholds all things by the word of His power . . ."

Stopping right there, Alan read no further. Instead, with his eyes closed, he listened to the winds raging outside the walls of his now, almost welcoming sanctuary. "Now, there's power. Who can stand against this storm?"

Simultaneously, he heard the quiet voice in his thoughts. This time it was unmistakably the same voice he heard while seated on the sofa.

"I can still the storm within you 'by the Word of My power.'"

Alan's mouth gaped open. He could hardly believe what he had just heard. He actually gasped deeply as he now knew this most assuredly was the Lord. He was afraid to open his eyes because of what he might see. Instead, with eyes shut, he tried to remain as quiet as he could . . . as still on the inside as he could. After what seemed to Alan to be more than a few minutes, and just as he was about to open his eyes, that same soft, quiet, gracious voice of Love came once again into his thoughts.

"Keep searching, never give up and you will find Me when you search for me with all your heart."[4]

Then another thought, "Alan, it is line upon line, here a little and there a little."[5]

Sitting perfectly still in the darkness of the little cottage, Alan could hear the intense storm raging all around him. He was trapped inside those four walls, yet he felt freer than ever before. In his heart, there was a lightness, an absolutely new sensation he had never experienced before. It was like peace, deep, sweet, overflowing peace, but more than peace. It was a knowing, an understanding.

The sensation was starting to bubble up within him, like the carbonation in a soda bottle after just being opened. He lifted his hands upward to heaven, opened his mouth, and began to thank the Lord for this wonderful sense he was experiencing. Tears, like streams in his desert, flowed unhindered as he praised his God for this new found freedom and joy deep within his now unbelievably, untroubled soul.

After what must have been more than an hour of singing, praising, thanking, and praying, Alan fell to the floor, laying there face up, exhausted, with his arms still lifted toward heaven. Soon however, they dropped to his sides and he fell fast asleep.

It was a deep, heavy, sound sleep like he hadn't experienced in years. He dreamt a most vivid marvel. Near the conclusion of this majestic interactive scene, he found himself in what appeared to be a church service. It was being held in a small building, with everyone standing, sitting, or kneeling in a circle. Alan couldn't see a preacher, a choir, or any musicians, yet the entire congregation was singing with all its heart. Everyone knew the words and all were singing and worshipping the Lord. Although Alan couldn't see Him, he very much sensed the Lord was there in that place.

Joining right in with those singing, Alan took a spot in the group about halfway around the circle to the right. He raised his hands as high as they would stretch, singing with all his heart, completely unconcerned as to how he sounded to the others. Alan sang several songs with this wonderful gathering. When the singing paused, someone read a passage from the Scriptures loud enough for all to hear. Then, they sang another song or two. After the song, another of the group prayed aloud. It appeared to Alan that each one had sensed his or her own role in the gathering, but there was no one visible directing them. It continued on unhindered for quite some time.

As they sang the old hymn, "His Eye is on the Sparrow," Alan awoke from his vibrantly life-like dream. He found himself still lying on the floor in the kitchen of the Morgan's cottage, and curiously his arms were still lifted heavenward. He decided he should write down the entire dream in his notebook so he would always remember it.

Sitting up, he pulled himself onto the chair at the kitchen table. As he rested upon his seat, he noticed two very distinct differences compared to when he had fallen asleep. The first, the noise outside had diminished to a point where it was only heard occasionally. The other difference, the sun was shining.

Glancing down at his Bible, he noticed it was still open to the Book of Hebrews. He held his watch up to the light coming in through the back door so he could see the time.

"Twenty after ten?!" he declared in disbelief. There's no way it could be after ten."

His eyes darted to the miniscule square where the numbers on the face of his watch indicated the date.

"What?" he exclaimed out loud. "It's tomorrow!"

-fourteen-

Moving down and across the page of his open Bible, Alan finished chapter one of Hebrews. Yesterday he was certain the Lord had indicated there was something more, if he would only keep searching for it. So after splashing some lukewarm water on his face, the same water he had saved two days ago before the storm hit, he changed his shirt then sat down to quiet his heart.

"As soon as I find this answer in Hebrews, I want to call home, see how everyone is doing, and let the family know I'm okay." Afterwards, he planned to start removing the boards from the windows and the front door. "That should really brighten this place up," he reasoned.

Soaking in chapter one of Hebrews slowly, as one savors a bath after a long distance run, he took copious notes as he continued on to chapter two and three. He noticed how much of what he read seemed to sink deep into the open petals of his thirsty soul. He grazed slowly upon this new found source of nourishment. He didn't realize how hungry he was for the solid food he discovered within the pages of Scripture. It was nearing noon when he came upon the words in chapter four. It was close to the end of the chapter in verse twelve:

> **"For the word of God is living and active and sharper than any two edged sword, and piercing as far as the division of soul and spirit, of both joints and marrow, and able to judge the thoughts and intentions of the heart."**

Alan's eyes widened as if trying to take the words deeper within his being. He read them over and over, slowly, deliberately, sensing there was something special the Lord was trying to tell him. Closing his eyes, he quieted his heart. He listened earnestly for the "still small voice" as Betsy had called it so many years ago when they sat at the picnic table in her backyard. He realized it was the same voice he had heard just yesterday deep within himself. A few seconds turned into a few minutes as Alan, seated at the kitchen table, patiently waited, perfectly hushed, and precisely still. He was learning how to listen.

"There is an answer here if you will search for it. Look deeper still. Remember, 'the kingdom of God is within you.'"[1]

It was the ever so soft voice. He knew it was the Lord Jesus, and he was beginning to recognize Him.

Deciding to memorize this verse, he wrote it down on a sheet in his notebook, tore it out, and folded it in half. He then slid it into his shirt pocket.

"Okay, now, let's call home." he smiled. Finding his phone on the kitchen countertop, he pressed the tiny power button. After several minutes, there still was no signal.

"Maybe all the towers were blown over during the storm. I hope they get them fixed soon. I really need to hear her sweet voice," Alan sighed. "Well, let's get some light in this place." He turned toward the back door, swung it open, and walked out into another world, like Dorothy stepped out of her house into the land of Oz. Except this Oz was not one of make-believe beauty. It was one of very real destruction.

"Wow, this place has been obliterated. I've never seen anything as terrible as this before!"

Walking over to the shed, which surprisingly had survived the storm, he pulled out a few carpenter tools and a step ladder to remove the plywood covering the windows. Alan crossed the gravel drive. Once he did, something out by the street caught his eye. There was a huge pine tree lying completely across the drive that led from the Morgan's cottage to the street. The tree had been snapped off approximately thirty feet above the ground, and he estimated the diameter of the trunk to be sixteen to eighteen inches.

In fact, while Alan walked forward to get a closer view of this curious sight, he noticed several pine trees in the front yard in the same condition. The two large oak trees had some limbs broken off too. He came to the conclusion that he should complete a thorough reconnaissance of the property before doing anything further on the cottage.

"Hey," he reasoned, "this is a very dangerous situation and seeing as I am the only one here, I better be extra careful."

He leaned the step ladder against the side of the cottage by the plywood covered living room window. With hammer and flatbar in hand he, like so many others along the Gulf Coast, began the emotional task of surveying the destruction caused by Hurricane Opal. He was amazed at the number of damaged and fallen trees on the Morgan's property. Making his way out to the street, he discovered many homes had been ravaged as well.

He noticed a man, across the street, who obviously was accomplishing a similar task on his home as Alan was for the Morgan's property. Upon seeing Alan, he waved and called out, "Everyone okay at your place?"

Jogging across the street, Alan walked up the concrete driveway, so they wouldn't have to shout back and forth across the distance. The skies were filled with more sun than clouds now, and the wind was no more than a breeze. Alan appreciated the drop in humidity also.

"Yes, it's just me, but I'm fine," answered Alan, stretching out his hand to greet his fellow survivor.

"That was a bad one," came the reply from the bald man, who, Alan guessed, was in his seventies.

"I'm Alan Browne from San Ramon, California. I just arrived here last week for a quiet retreat, and wow . . . I sure didn't expect this."

"Come on?!" was the reply with the deep, Southern accent mixed with a bit of Louisiana Cajun. "I guess they don't report them storms out west now."

"No, I didn't even think to look at the weather forecast before buying my airline ticket. I guess I didn't realize something like this could happen." Alan felt a bit foolish confessing this to someone who evidently had survived a few of these storms over the years.

"Come on?!" With these words the man was shaking his head.

"Your name, sir?" asked Alan.

"Oh sorry . . . uh, name's Way, Jimmy Way, and that there is Molly." Using his chin, Jimmy pointed in the direction of the grey haired lady coming out of the garage with two glasses of ice tea, one in each hand.

"Ice tea, you two?" she called as she walked in the direction of the two standing on the neatly manicured, although branch strewn, lawn in front of their brick, ranch style home.

"Yep, lived here near fifty year now." His matter of fact tone had more than a hint of pride in it.

"Ah, don't bore the poor man Jimmy," said Mollie. Then turning to Alan, "Y'all get through that storm okay?"

"Yes, ma'am, and thank you for this."

Alan, in an acknowledgement of thanks, raised up the cold glass of iced tea before draining the entire glass of its sweet, tasty goodness. They all three swung around simultaneously to see what was creating the low rumbling noise slowly approaching from down the street.

"It's a firetruck!" cheered Mollie.

"Come on Mollie, sure enough is." added Jimmy.

The three survivors walked toward the street as the large red machine came to a halt in front of them.

"You folks okay?" called out the uniformed driver from behind the steering wheel. Two firefighters, a man and a woman, hopped off the back and walked over to Jimmy, Mollie, and Alan who now stood in the street.

"Sure enough are." replied Jimmy. Alan and Mollie nodded in agreement.

"Well, there's a Red Cross truck just behind us with some water and food if y'all need anything." Pointing with his thumb he added, "And further back are two pickup truckloads of men and chainsaws. By the way, the road is open to town now. Bruno's market says they'll be open in the morning. I don't have any information as to when the power will be back on though."

"Got a generator," replied Jimmy. "But this here fella is visiting from California."

The female firefighter responded, "Wow, really? Sorry to hear that. You need anything?"

"Some food and water would be nice. But if the store will be open tomorrow, I'll be fine until then. Thanks." Alan's tone sounded more tentative than appreciative although he was very grateful for their concern.

The man behind the wheel announced, "We're going to check on others now. Y'all have a good day, and let us know if you need anything."

Letting off the airbrake, the big diesel started lumbering on down the road. As it was leaving, the Red Cross truck pulled into its vacated spot right in front of the three neighbors.

The Red Cross volunteers were generous with food and water as well as helpful advice on how to get through the next few days, until the basics of life would be somewhat back to normal. Alan thanked them, then headed back down the gravel drive laden with bottles of water, Meals Ready to Eat, (MREs), and a blanket. Even though he told them he didn't need this last item, they insisted he accept it.

Depositing his bounty on the back porch, he returned to the task of removing the plywood storm panels from the windows. Each one came off the trim around the windows with relative ease. However, two in particular required more than a little strain. He pulled them off the wall with the use of the flatbar and hammer, letting the panels fall to the ground. After removing the nails, he leaned each piece of plywood back against the wall, adjacent to the window or door where it had just been removed. As he replaced the final panel in the rack in the shed, he heard voices quickly followed by the unmistakable sound of chainsaws coming from in front of the cottage.

Jogging around the side of the cottage to the front, he found, to his amazement, more than a dozen men cutting branches from the fallen trees and dragging the limbs out to the street. One worker wrapped a large chain around the trunk of the huge pine tree that had blocked the gravel drive and then proceeded to clip it to the back of one of the two pickups. Two other woodsmen were cutting the tree, one on each side of the drive, to remove the trunk from barring the way to the cottage.

Alan approached one of the men, who was cutting the giant oak tree closest to the cottage. Noticing Alan out of the corner of his eye, he shut down his chainsaw.

"Hey, what are you fellas doing?" asked Alan with a smile.

"Oh, just trying to get you access to the road. We're not going to take all of this out of here, but enough to make sure you can get in and out," answered the workman. He was wearing a visor, sunglasses, tank top, shorts, and flip flops.

Alan decided he looked more like a surfer, than a lumberjack. "Well, I can't pay you anything. I don't have my checkbook, and all I have is a little cash, unless you take credit cards?"

"Nah, man, we're just helping folks out. We don't want any money or nothing." The man replied with a laugh, while slapping Alan on the back. "We're simply a bunch of rednecks out helping our neighbors." With that, he smiled, yanked on the cord of his chainsaw, and went back to work.

Surveying the entire group as they were busily working, Alan reached over to tap the man he had been speaking with on the shoulder. He glanced up at Alan without changing his focus on his cutting. Alan mouthed, "Thank you!"

Twisting around, the worker stretched out his gloved hand and shouted above the noise of the saw, "You're welcome!" The two smiled at each other. Then Alan picked up one large branch with each hand and started dragging them to the road.

As quick as they had arrived, the group departed, chainsaws, pickup trucks, and all. A few of the men sat in the cab while the rest clambered into the back of the trucks. Alan waved and called out, "Thank you, so much!" He continued to move the rest of the branches to the road. When he finished, his watch read sometime after five o'clock. Observing all that had been accomplished brought Alan a sense of accomplishment. Now, he would be able get in and out of the cottage using the gravel drive instead of scrambling over, under, and around all the branches of the fallen trees.

As he rounded the back corner of the cottage and headed toward the porch stairs, he discovered the hammock resting up in the branches of the oak tree.

"There you are!" he exclaimed with delight, "Let's get you out of there and put you to good use."

Although it took no small amount of effort and time, once extricated from being entangled within the branches of the oak, Alan replaced it on the hooks on the back porch.

"Now, if we only had the screening. Man, that storm really tore that up. And the leaves, where did all the leaves go?" he wondered as he plopped down in the rescued hammock. "There are hardly any leaves left on the trees. That storm blasted the trees clean."

From his peaceful repose in the hammock, he noticed the Red Cross box on the floor of the porch. "Hmmm . . . I wonder what an MRE tastes like? Might be an adventure, but I'm hungry, so let's find out."
Falling out of the hammock he carried the box inside and removed the contents, placing them onto the kitchen countertop. He selected a pouch, tore it open, and devoured every morsel of the meal, saving the candy bar for last. "Either I was famished, or that was really quite good," he smiled as he leaned back against the kitchen countertop.

Glancing around the main area, the kitchen, dining, and living room, he decided he liked the cozy cottage. The sunlight was streaming in through the open windows and a gentle breeze was flowing through what, just a day ago, had been a very stuffy atmosphere. He still didn't care for the stained knotty pine walls and the dingy white ceiling, but somehow it all seemed much more pleasant to him after the events of the last few days. His eyes roamed around the room and stopped at the kitchen table where his Bible was still lying open upon it.

He thought, "With all the busyness of the day, I totally forgot the Bible verse I wrote down and slipped into my shirt pocket." He pulled it out of his pocket. After unfolding it, he read slowly the twelfth verse of the fourth chapter of the Book of Hebrews:

> **"For the word of God is living and active and sharper than any two-edged sword, and piercing as far as the division of soul and spirit, of both joints and marrow, and able to judge the thoughts and intentions of the heart."**

Alan read the words three times out loud. Then, he read them a fourth time and a fifth. He tried to memorize every word by emphasizing, individually, each one as he read it aloud. When he spoke the word, **"division"**, he stopped immediately. He waited silently as if trying to hear what the words on his unfolded paper were attempting to declare to him.

"**Division**," he whispered, "**division**," this time his voice was a bit louder, "**division**." Alan looked up at the ceiling and then slowly back down to his paper lying on the kitchen table. "Wait a minute . . ." he breathed softly.

"division of the soul and spirit . . ."

"There must be a difference between the soul and the spirit. And," he paused, "the word of God divides the two from one another. The word of God shows? Or, maybe, declares the difference?" Alan's eyes were wide open as if trying to attain more insight, like one groping in a dark room trying to gain more light.

"Lord, why is this important?"

Reclining back in his chair, Alan listened. He had a thought to search the small concordance in the back of his Bible, but it was quickly followed by a different thought of how much he missed his wife and children. His mind quickly ran upon those well-worn emotional grooves in his memory. He missed them terribly. If only he could talk to them for a few minutes. He picked up his phone and pressed the power button. As he waited for the phone to acquire a signal, he formulated all he wanted to report to them and imagined their responses.

Just then, the phone made that almost imperceptible chirp Alan recognized as the no-signal-available indicator. He quickly turned it off and tossed it onto the kitchen table. He bent forward resting his head in his hands as his eyes drifted downward to the unfolded paper. He sat, once again, silent.

"What in the world just happened?" he questioned quietly. "What on earth was that? Whoa, wait just a minute!" he barked with more fervor.

It dawned on Alan that he had totally ignored a thought which might very well have been influenced by the Lord. The very same thought, about doing a little searching in the concordance in the back of his Bible, was curiously and immediately followed by emotional thoughts of his wife and children. Thus, the second thought, wherever it may have come from, completely blocked the first thought from becoming an action. Alan wrote these things down in detail, acknowledging them as lessons from the Lord Himself. Then, he turned to the concordance.

"Let's see, there are a few verses on, '**division**,' but they don't seem appropriate. How about, '**soul**'."

Beginning a record in his notebook, he wrote down the many listings of the word "**soul**" and also the word "**spirit**". Flipping back and forth in his Bible, he jotted down every word of the verses he found interesting, determining to do some digging into what the Lord might be saying to him.

There were two verses that seemed most curious to Alan. The first one, found in First Thessalonians, chapter five and verse twenty-three, gave indication that humans are made up of a physical body, a soul, and a spirit. However, the next verse, found in Isaiah, appeared to jump off the page. Isaiah, chapter twenty-six, verse nine:

> "At night, my soul longs for thee, indeed my spirit within me seeks Thee diligently..."

Alan ruminated upon these words for quite some time. To him, there was a significant implication of a very unique difference between the two components.

"Let's see," mused Alan, "my *soul longs* for God. My *spirit seeks* God."

Deciding the two key words were, "**longs**" and "**seeks**", he noted how they were tied to "**soul**" and "**spirit**" respectively. He leaned back again in his chair, pondering the potential of what this could mean in his own life. Determining to investigate these terms further, he began again to turn the pages of his Bible, from one verse to another, in search of further clarification. A thought entered his mind,

"...here a little, there a little."[2]

Searching, he flipped from the Book of Proverbs to the Epistles then to Jeremiah, when his eyes fell upon Psalms, the first verse of the forty-second chapter:

"As the deer pants for the water brooks, so my soul longs for Thee, O God."

Then, in the fourth chapter of the Gospel of John, verses twenty-three and twenty-four:

"But an hour is coming and now is, when the true worshippers shall worship the Father in spirit and truth; for such people the Father seeks to be His

worshippers. God is spirit; and those who worship
Him must worship Him in spirit and truth."

Having read these words so many times before, he could
almost quote them from memory. In ninth grade, he and
several others in the youth group, had accepted a challenge
from Pastor Fred to read through the Bible in a year. Later,
while in his thirties, he had spent years reading almost
nothing but the Psalms and the Gospels. In fact, John was
his favorite Gospel. However, he had never before
comprehended these verses like this.

"Whoa, what are the implications here?!" he questioned
aloud. "My spirit has an immensely significant role in my
relationship to my Father in Heaven. I never knew that
before. Yet, from what I can determine from my searching in
the Scriptures, my soul has an entirely different function or
role."

Rising from the table, Alan paced around inside the
cottage. First, he clasped his hands behind his back as he
walked and thought. He then rubbed one hand across his
scruffy, unshaven chin, as if to indicate something was
dawning within his strained thinking. "There's something
really important here," he acknowledged with a grunt.

He moved slowly around the room creating a figure
eight pattern for each lap. "But what is it? Well, the light is
getting too dim to read, so let's head out to the hammock
and see if that helps."

Alan accepted the fact that the hammock was much
more of a help for his weariness from the day's activities,
than an aid to finding the answers to his life's most difficult

questions. Nonetheless, it was deeply relaxing, so he rolled into the springy webbing and settled into its gentle swaying as he stretched out, interlocking his fingers behind his head.

"I wonder what the cheerful Mrs. Browne is doing now? Maybe she's fixing dinner for the kiddos or maybe scurrying about from soccer practice to the grocery market to the gas station and back home. I sure hope my phone works tomorrow. If it doesn't, I'm riding my bike to town and finding a pay phone or something."

A smile broke across his face as he recalled the first time he heard her voice on the phone. In fact, it was the first time they rode bicycles together. Alan pondered aloud, "Man, I love that gal. I have loved her since way back then. Now let's see, when exactly was that?"

-fifteen-

It was the summer of 1978, and, oh, what a summer it was, thought Alan as his face stretched to accommodate a smile. His mind began to drift among those wonderful, pleasant memories. He enjoyed going there and returned to those places again and again in his frequent daydreams, but none more often, than the summer and autumn of 1978.

"That was a good year," he stated frankly, as if discussing with close friends his favorite Napa Valley wine.

"I remember just getting back from the church retreat in the mountains of Western Maryland. We kept glancing at each other in the rearview mirror. I was in the front, driving the old church van, and she sat in the back. Man, I loved that gal. I think I loved her before I ever met her."

Laughing aloud, Alan remembered his first date with Annalisa. He had waited until Wednesday evening to telephone her at her apartment. Her new phone had just been connected. She later defended, "Being an unpaid congressional intern and all, I couldn't really afford it, but my parents insisted I have one."

He had suggested Friday night for dinner and a movie. She didn't seem to think it was a good idea. So he asked about meeting someplace for lunch on Sunday. She wasn't keen on that plan either. Therefore, Alan asked if she wanted to get together at all.

Annalisa quickly blurted out, "How about a bicycle ride Saturday morning?

"Uh, I can't," grumbled Alan, "I start my new part time job at the bike shop this Saturday."

The phone went silent.

After several seconds, which to Alan, seemed like several minutes, he asked, "You still there, Annalisa?" He was hesitant to break the silence, fearing there wouldn't be a response to his question.

"Yes, I'm just thinking," came her reply, "Okay, didn't you tell me the bike shop where you work is the same one where I purchased my new bike? I mean, the one I thought had closed, but it had just moved into the new store you built. Isn't that right? Didn't you mention it's in Cherrydale, on Lee Highway?"

Alan tried to answer each question, but before he could reply to one question, she posed another one. This went on for more than a couple of minutes. When a pause finally came, he started to respond to the first question, but before his answer was halfway finished, she concluded by asking,

"So maybe I could drop by around lunch time with my bicycle, and we could get a sandwich or something while they're fixing my wobbly front wheel. Would that work for you Alan?"

"Uh, sure . . . yeah, that works."

He was much less confident in this arrangement than he was with the suggestions he had made at the beginning of the conversation. The plan that she came up with would only give them a few minutes alone at best. He had been hoping to spend a lot time together, so they could start to become acquainted with more than just what each other's favorite dessert or color might be. Alan wanted to get to know her on an intimate level, not just learning what her preferences were. He wanted to know why she liked what she liked, or disliked what she disliked. He wanted to understand how she thought, what she enjoyed most, as well as what made her angry and brought her happiness. He wanted to know where she was from and where she was headed. This short, thirty minute lunch break they had just planned wasn't going to provide enough time to accomplish his goals.

"Okay, then what time do you take your lunch? I mean, what time should I plan to be there?" Her voice sounded like she was smiling. This slightly bolstered Alan's weakened self-esteem.

"Plan to be there at quarter to twelve. We can get your bike on the repair stand before we drive down the street to the little Italian deli, okay?"

"Oh, that sounds nice, Alan. What's the name of the deli?" she asked.

"Uh, it's called, The Little Italian Deli," he replied in monotone with a hint of sarcasm.

Annalisa laughed, "That's a funny name for a little Italian deli."

Alan chuckled, "Well, that's the name. You can see for yourself when we go there on Saturday."

"I'll look forward to it." she snickered. "And while we're there, maybe we can talk about where we're going bike riding on Sunday afternoon."

"Oh, really?!" bantered Alan, with a bit of hopeful sneer in his voice.

"Yes, really!" laughed Annalisa, with an equal amount of friskiness in her response. "I haven't seen but a few of the monuments in DC. Nor have I seen George Washington's home in Monticello."

Alan interrupted, "Mount Vernon. You mean Mount Vernon. Monticello is Thomas Jefferson's home in Charlottesville. It's about a two hour ride, I mean, in a car. Mount Vernon is where George Washington lived, and it's maybe forty five minutes by bicycle."

"Oops," giggled Annalisa.

Using a fake southern belle voice, the same one she tried a couple of times on the retreat, the one Alan just loved, she pined, "You see, kind sir, I'm in need of a tour guide. A Southern gentlemen who can navigate these harsh, crocodile infested waters, they call Washington, DC. Would you happen to know anyone who could help little ol' me with this problem?"

"Oh, why, yes, Miss Annalisa, I sure enough do." Alan was laying on his Southern drawl with a soft, warm tone. "May I recommend a handsome, suave, yet quite humble, Virginian who may guide you through the treacherous waters of the monument maze with the utmost of care and Southern hospitality?"

"And, who, may I ask, is this debonair gentleman?" Annalisa continued her role in this impromptu skit of a bygone era.

"Why, I do declare, Miss Annalisa Michelle Williams, I am referring to yours truly."

"How did you know my whole name?!" Her voice no longer held the teasing, Southern belle lilt, but now sounded rather serious.

"Uh . . . I asked around I guess. Well, actually Rebecca and I were talking at the retreat, and she kind of told me. I hope that's okay?" Alan sounded apologetic, timid, and unsure of himself all at the same time.

"Oh, sure, that's fine. I was just wondering how you knew my middle name. I should have known it was Rebecca. I mean, who else would have known, right? Oh, Alan, sometimes you crack me up." The smiling sound had come back into her voice once again.

"I do?" balked Alan.

"Yes, you sure do, Alan Browne. Hey, wait a minute, what's your middle name?"

"Uh . . . it's, I mean, it's no big deal . . . ."

"Well, what is it, Alan?"

"Michael," he confessed. "It's Michael. Alan Michael Browne."

"Hey, we have the same initials, at least kind of the same. They both start with AM. It's like an upside down AW, like A Dub. Remember him? What a kind man. I sure did like him. Didn't you, Alan?"

"I thought he was awesome. I really liked the way he talked. It was like a mix of Darth Vader, Santa Claus, and my dear old grandfather Browne. Plus, his knowledge of the whole **rojocci** fellowship thing I thought was fascinating. Didn't you?"

"Yes, it was amazing, but he was even more amazing. Maybe . . ." Her side of the phone went silent for a few seconds, then she continued, "Oh, Alan, look at the time. I have to get going. I leave the house at quarter of seven to get to work by eight. I'm sorry, I really need to get going. But I'll see you at the bike shop on Saturday, okay?"

"Yep, I'll be there," he was trying to sound lighthearted through his disappointment with the brevity of the phone call. "I'll look forward to it. See you there at eleven forty-five."

"Okay. Me too, Alan. See you then. Bye bye."

The phone clicked and silence returned. Alan hung up his phone. "Me, too," he said. Then those same habitual thoughts crept into his mind, like a cheetah stalking its prey.

"I wonder why she hung up so quickly? I'm guessing it was something I said. I probably offended her again, or maybe someone was there with her, and she had to hang up quick. Man, I hate these thoughts. Hate them! Hate them! HATE them!"

The rest of the week seemed to fly by. Alan was very busy at the Great Falls house helping with everything from touch up paint to landscaping to cleaning countertops and sinks. As was his habit, Dan the Man stopped by Friday afternoon to drop off the paychecks, go over the week's progress, and check the schedule for the upcoming week. After finishing up with Big Jim, he called Alan aside and told him some unsettling news.

"Alan, we've got a lull in the action coming up in a week or two. I'm going to have to lay off some of the fellas. I usually start with the most recent hire, which would be you. Big Jim says you've really improved since coming back from Tiny's job, so I'll do my best to keep you on, okay? I mean, that and the fact you're my cousin and all. But listen, seriously, if I can keep you employed, you'll be running around for a few weeks, and some of those weeks will be part time. I most likely won't be able to find you forty hours each week. You understand me, Alan? I'll do the best I can, but I can't guarantee anything. Ever since the crazy gas crisis a few years ago, it's been difficult, at best, to forecast these projects. Everything is so unstable. You would think President Carter would do something about this mess. Anyway, I wanted you to know I'll do what I can for you, okay?"

"Thanks, Dan, I really appreciate it. I do have a part time job down at the bike shop we built, but it's only about ten hours a week. Plus, it doesn't pay much, so I really appreciate anything you can give me."

"Sure thing," Dan reassured Alan and patted him on the shoulder. Then he got in his truck and drove off.

Alan's insecurities had been on high alert ever since the minute Dan asked to speak privately with him. That last comment and pat on the shoulder felt more like a "Nice knowing you" than an, "I'll do what I can for you," to Alan.

The rest of the day, as well as that evening and the next day, Alan had a dark cloud hanging over him. It was more of a dread, than a cloud. He was convinced that at some point next week he was going to be unemployed. In fact, the only bright ray of sunshine that entire Saturday was when Annalisa walked through the bike shop door rolling her bicycle with the wobbly front wheel. Wearing a large smile, he jogged across the showroom floor. He took the bike from her hand and quickly mounted it on the repair stand.

"Wow, how'd you do this?" he laughed, while checking the wheel on the truing stand. "Your wheel is way out of true. This is a bit past my level of ability; let me see if Bruce or Frank can take care of it."

"I got it, Alan," Frank called from across the showroom. "You kids go get some lunch. I'll have it fixed by the time y'all get back."

"Thanks, Frank. We'll be back in thirty minutes."

"Oh, take your time, you two. It isn't like we're swamped with customers today," replied Frank. With that, the two were out the door.

Alan noticed the forest green car with California plates in the parking lot.

"Is that your Datsun B-210?"

"Yep," replied Annalisa proudly. "My Uncle George bought it for me when I graduated from high school. It wasn't new, but it was new to me and I love it. You want to drive it?"

"Sure! You have an uncle who bought you a car?"

"Yes. And he's the best uncle ever!" she declared as she sat down in the passenger seat and shut the door. Alan started up the small four-door sedan and down Lee Highway they went, toward the Little Italian Deli.

All the way there they talked and laughed, and laughed and talked some more. It was the same while they ordered their sandwiches at the counter and sat down at one of the tiny round tables covered with a red and white checkered cloth. It was the fastest thirty minutes Alan had ever experienced. Before he knew it, they were in Annalisa's car heading back to the bike shop, talking and laughing all the more.

Alan opened the glass door to the bike shop allowing Annalisa to enter first. No sooner had the door shut, than they heard a call from behind the repair counter.

"Sorry guys, I'm not quite done with this wheel. It was really out of true. Alan, maybe you can show her around the store." Frank was smiling, but Alan knew his comment really meant, "Maybe you could sell her something."

"Yes, sir, will do." Alan had noticed her bike didn't have any water bottle cages, so he suggested maybe she should purchase one along with a water bottle for their bike trip the next day.

"Oh, man, that reminds me," Alan slapped his hand to his forehead, "I have everything planned out for tomorrow except where to meet. I thought we could head across Key Bridge into Georgetown, then over to the Mall and the monuments. If there's time, we could cross back into Arlington on the Memorial Bridge, ride up through the cemetery, and stop to take in the view at the Iwo Jima Memorial. How's that sound?"

"That sounds great, Alan, but I thought we were trying to go to Monticello . . . uh, wait a minute, I mean Mount Vernon?"

"Well, yeah, sure, but we don't have enough time tomorrow. I mean, all we would be doing is riding. Uh, there wouldn't be time for anything else. I mean, for talking and stuff." He was trying to make his voice sound confident even if his words weren't.

"Oh, I guess that's okay. I mean, it sounds like a nice time," she replied with a smile.

"Okay. Great. Now where do we meet and what time?" he coaxed.

"Well, I live just off Spout Run Parkway close to Key Bridge, so how about at the foot of the bridge. Would that work for you?"

"Sure, let's meet in front of the Key Bridge Marriott, okay?"

Just then, Frank called from across the showroom that her wheel was ready. Alan quickly picked up a black bottle cage and a clear water bottle with the bike shop logo stamped on it.

"Here," he said to Annalisa, "you're going to need these."

After she paid for the wheel truing, and Alan paid for the water bottle and cage, he installed it on her bike, and walked her to her car. He removed the wheels enabling the bike to fit in her back seat. After Alan closed her door for her, he waved goodbye. She rolled down her window and with a wave of her hand confirmed, "See you tomorrow!"

"Oh, no, wait a minute," called Alan, "what time? We never set a time?"

"Noon?" returned Annalisa.

"Perfect. See you tomorrow at noon." He watched her as she turned onto Lee Highway, headed around the curve and out of sight.

"Oh, you're in big time trouble, Alan Michael Browne," big time trouble," he thought aloud. "Did you see how stinking cute she looked today? Man! Jeans and flip flops. Good gravy, I'm a dead man."

The next morning, Alan was up early and made sure he had everything ready for their bicycle trip together. Before closing the bike shop yesterday, he had purchased a couple of spare tubes and a miniature repair kit, as well as one of those little tire pumps that mounts on the bicycle frame. After throwing his cycling clothes, shoes, deodorant, and a change of clothes in the cab, he put everything else in the back of his truck. He had decided to attend the church service this morning, since he had had such a nice time at the retreat the weekend before.

Pulling into the parking lot, Alan saw Annalisa walking in the church doors with Rebecca and her entire family. He quickly found a parking spot, then ran for the door. As he peered through the small glass window in one of the doors leading to the sanctuary, he felt a tap on his shoulder. He turned around to find a smiling Peaknuckle, not two feet away.

"Hey, man, what on earth are you doing here Alan?"

"You're not the only one that attends church here, Peaknuckle."

"Ah, come on, man, you haven't been here in like, forever. Que pasta?"

"What?!" Alan's voice hit a higher octave. "First of all, it's not 'Que pasta' it's 'Que pasa'. And second, I thought it was a nice retreat and Pastor Fred had invited me, uh . . . several times, that's all."

"Sure, Alan," replied Peaknuckle with a hint of sarcasm.

He leaned closer to Alan and whispered, "And I'm sure it has nothing to do with Rebecca's friend from California, right? She's sitting right over there, dude, with Rebecca's family. Why don't you go on in and have a seat next to her?"

"Ah, shut up, man! I think she's a nice gal that's all, but . . ."

At that moment, Pastor Fred approached the two from behind and yanking the sanctuary door open smiled, "So, you guys coming in or are you going to stand out here arguing all morning?"

"Uh, yes, sir. But I'm sitting in the back row because I have to leave right after the service ends," appeased Alan.

"That's okay, Alan. It's really nice to see you. And thanks again for driving the van for the retreat."

Slipping into the back pew, Alan settled in, trying to get a view of a certain someone. He obtained just the right position where she was in his line of sight although it was somewhat obstructed. After a few minutes, precisely as the senior pastor rose to walk up to the pulpit, Peaknuckle slid in next to Alan.

"So I heard you fixed her bike or something?! Yeah, and you bought her lunch yesterday and you bought her a water bottle and you're going on a bike ride this afternoon. What gives, man, you guys getting married or something?"

This whispered line of questions and statements made Alan feel as if he was being interrogated by a detective at the local police station. However, the timing of Peaknuckle's final question had come at the exact moment in the church service when the senior pastor asked the congregation to stand for prayer.

In response to Peaknuckle's questions, Alan barked out, "No!"

More than a few in the congregation that morning turned around to see who had negatively responded to the simple request from the pastor. Fortunately, with most of the people standing, they couldn't see who it was, toward the rear of the sanctuary that had called out, "No!"

Thankfully, the remainder of the service was uneventful although both Peaknuckle and, yes, Alan too, were having no small amount of difficulty holding back the snickers. Before the singing of the final hymn was over the two friends had quickly slipped out the back sanctuary doors and into the parking lot.

"I'm gonna kill you, man!" Alan laughed. "I can't go in there again."

"Nah, man, nobody knew it was you. Don't worry about it. Nobody saw you or anything."

Peaknuckle paused, then laughed out loud, "You sure have impeccable timing though. That was like, perfect. I mean, it was like, right on cue."

They both laughed aloud as Alan hopped in his pickup truck. "I mean it," Alan laughed, "you're deceased, buddy boy. Your tombstone will say, 'Here lies Peaknuckle a genuine knucklehead.'"

They both had a good laugh again. Then Peaknuckle leaned into the open passenger window, "Hey seriously man, have a great time today, okay? Rebecca says she's a really nice girl and kind of likes you too."

"Really?!" Alan's voice hit that high note again.

"Yep, no kidding. Well, have fun, Alan, man. Maybe next time we can double date or something?"

"Ha!" Alan laughed. "Not in this lifetime." He shifted his truck into gear and quickly drove out of the parking lot heading for the bike shop and then Key Bridge.

He parked in the bike shop parking lot thinking that since it was always closed on Sundays, Frank and Carol wouldn't mind. "I'll need about fifteen minutes to ride down Lee Highway to Key Bridge," he thought as he unloaded his bike and gear from the truck. After checking the tire pressure, he stuffed the saddle bag with two inner tubes and the small tool kit.

"Okay, now where can I change my clothes?" Deciding the cab of his truck was as good a place as any, he emerged a few minutes later ready to ride.

Annalisa was bent over her bicycle, elbows resting on the handlebars, waiting at the entrance to the Key Bridge Marriott parking lot when Alan arrived. He pulled right up next to her and stopped.

"How'd you get here so fast?" he snorted.

"I told you. I just live around the corner, so it only took a couple of minutes to ride down here."

"Wow, I didn't even have a chance to get a bite of lunch, did you?" he asked hoping she hadn't eaten.

"No, I haven't either. Maybe we could stop somewhere and grab something, if that's okay?"

"Sure!" he smiled. "I think that's a great idea."

Then, they mounted their bicycles and started across the Potomac River on Key Bridge toward Georgetown. Once they crossed the bridge, they turned right on M Street and rode it all the way to Rock Creek Parkway. From there, they meandered over to the Mall and the monuments. They continued riding along the river at a leisurely pace down to Haines Point in East Potomac Park. Stopping there, he pulled the water bottle from its cage on his bike and took a long drink as he pointed out National Airport across the river in Virginia.

"It sure is beautiful here, Alan. It's not like this in Walnut Creek. I mean, we get blooms and flowers, but nothing like this. This is so gorgeous."

"Yeah, it sure is pretty. And the weather is nice too. Although, I'm keeping my eye on those clouds to the south. You never know in the DC Area when a thunderstorm could pop up out of nowhere. Are you getting hungry? There's a snack bar up by the clubhouse at the golf course. It's only a five minute bike ride. We could get a bite there."

"Sounds perfect," she smiled.

Having both ordered cheeseburgers with fries and a soda, they talked mostly about their families. Alan discovered she has an older sister named Abigail who aspires to follow in their father's footsteps and become an attorney. Her mother taught school in a town called Pleasanton. However, when they moved to Walnut Creek, about seven years ago, the commute became too much for her. So after two years, she decided to stay home and now does some substitute teaching nearby. Her father had some political aspirations, but after an unsuccessful campaign for a local city council position, he decided to become involved with Congressman Leo Ryan's bid for another term in office. Her father and Leo had become quick friends. That was how Annalisa got the summer internship in his office on Capitol Hill.

"Wow, so that's how it works?" Alan jeered with a hint of sarcasm. "But I thought you mentioned you're attending some artsy craftsy school?"

"Well, yes, that's really my mom's fault. I'm much more like her than my dad. She's from Sausalito in Marin County. She's very creative, and I just love doing crafts and things with her. Sometimes we'll spend a whole weekend mainly doing crafts and stuff. It's awesome."

Alan was taking detailed mental notes of all these particulars about her as she talked. He loved how she almost always smiled, and when she did, her whole face smiled. Even her eyes arched upward. He was convinced she actually smiled more with her eyes than with her mouth, if that was possible

After finishing lunch, they rode over to the Thomas Jefferson Memorial. Alan locked their bikes together at the bike rack. Then, they walked up the stairs on the Tidal Basin side. Annalisa took it all in. She had never seen anything so majestic before. After about thirty minutes, they made their way over to the Reflecting Pool and right up to the bottom of the almost regal, Abraham Lincoln Memorial. Again, Alan locked their bikes together, attaching them to the bike rack, and they started the climb up the stairs together.

"There are one hundred and forty-five steps," he stated proudly.

Reaching over, he slipped his hand in hers as they stepped on the first one. She lightly squeezed his hand as she glanced up at him with a smile. They walked each one of the steps together in unison. Upon reaching the top, the portico where Lincoln sits, they turned around to take in the view. They stood there side by side, hand in hand, for several minutes without saying a word. A gentle rain began to fall. Alan moved them to the far side of one of the enormous pillars where they could still take in the view but were protected from the rain.

After several more minutes spent gazing at the beautiful reflection of the Washington Monument with the Capital Building in the distance, Alan turned and faced Annalisa.

"Would it be okay if I kissed you?"

She smiled, nodding her head slowly. Turning to face him and placing one hand on his shoulder, she leaned her head slightly to the side. She glanced up at him for just a moment and then closed her eyes.

~sixteen~

The remainder of the month of June was a blur to Alan. He worked for his cousin at least forty hours every week because several projects that Dan had assumed he had lost were successfully renegotiated. This, coupled with his commitment at the bike shop, made it no easy task to spend time where he really wanted to . . . with Annalisa. However, they both made it work, as she evidently had similar feelings for him as he had for her. If he was able to get off work early, they would arrange to meet at a restaurant, or sometimes he would just come to her apartment, and she would make them dinner. Then, they would talk of their hopes and dreams well into the night.

June ran into July, and July into August. The fleeting summer was speeding by way too fast and with each day a burden weighed heavier on Alan's mind. They hardly talked of it because it usually ended with them having an argument or at least departing yet again with the conversation unfinished. Friday, September first, was the last day of Annalisa's internship and signaled the first day of her trip back to California. Indeed, this was no easy topic of discussion as summer neared its end.

As the August days ticked off, Alan and Annalisa spent every moment they could steal away together. On several occasions, Alan's insecure thoughts of what would happen to their relationship spilled over into his words, creating angst between them. It often began with a harmless question of what Annalisa would be doing once back in California, or perhaps how she would be spending her weekends. But she was learning these questions, almost without exception, ended in an argument of some sort. And Alan was discovering this was having the exact opposite effect on Annalisa than what he intended.

Alan thought the month of August was driving them apart. Annalisa later confessed it was Alan's insecurities that were driving them apart. They would be having a wonderful time at a museum, at dinner, or while stopping for a break on one of their many bicycle rides together, but after a few minutes, Alan would ask one of his, "It's just a harmless question", questions. Then, depending on Annalisa's response, the two would head down the slippery trail of "what if this" or "what if that". This didn't happen every time they saw each other. However, it was often enough that Annalisa was thinking of spending less time with Alan, the very thing he desperately wanted to avoid.

One Sunday afternoon, Alan asked her to please consider staying in Washington, DC, after her internship was over. Annalisa gave him a number of very valid reasons why that would be impossible, including the fact that her parents had been supporting her financially while she was an intern. She explained that her father had already purchased his airline ticket to fly out and drive back with her to Walnut Creek.

She had also given her notice to her landlord and therefore, would no longer have a place to live. Plus, she was due to start classes a week after she arrived back home.

"Alan," she assured very sincerely, "I have strong feelings for you, as I know you have for me, right?" Alan nodded his head, although he said nothing.

She took his head in her hands, forcing him to look directly into her eyes. "Then please, oh please, believe me when I say that nothing on this earth, at this point in my life, would make me happier than to stay here with you in Washington, DC. But Alan, I can't. It would take a miracle of God for that to happen. Now, He can do anything, but He hasn't yet. Do you understand?"

"Uh, yes, I know, but today is the twentieth of August, and you leave in less than two weeks. I'm sad, and I'm worried about what will happen to us. This isn't just a summer fling to me, my dear. I really care for you. You know what I mean?" Alan's eyes were welling up with unshed tears. He softly said, "I mean, who knows where this may lead if we were able to give it, to give us a chance."

"I know, Alan. I've had the same thoughts too. But at this point, it would have to be God doing some sort of miracle."

Realizing the impossibility of their circumstances, they held each other in their arms and quietly wept. There was such a strong chemistry between them that they could hardly muster the courage to acknowledge it. This was something neither had ever felt before. There was a deep intimacy, yet without the physical side of things. There was intense desire there as well. But also a mutual respect, a friendship, a oneness that was so precious, so valued, neither would allow the other too much territory before they would jointly agree to a change of topic.

"Maybe if you would pray for us," she whispered in his ear while they held each other. "Pray that God would do a miracle if He wants us to be together, okay?"

He whispered a prayer in her ear that God would grant their request. It seemed to Alan she held him even tighter as he continued to pray, asking their Father in heaven if, it be His will, they could be together. It was one of those absolutely cherished moments in the grand scale of time that would forever be recorded as a monumental intersection in their shared memories.

The week that followed was a very difficult one for Alan. Try as he might, he couldn't get off work in time to spend an evening with Annalisa. On Monday, there was a special custom beam Dan the Man had asked him to fetch from Lexington. He was to be sure it was delivered to the job before Tuesday morning. He didn't arrive home that evening until after ten thirty.

Tuesday was no better, as he helped the carpenters on a job in Winchester. The drive home was nearly two hours. This was compounded by the fact that they had to get the roof buttoned up because the forecast for Wednesday was rain.

And Wednesday evening, Pastor Fred had asked him to lead a youth group discussion on how to be a Christian couple in today's society. Alan had no desire to accommodate Fred's request, but knowing he would see Annalisa there, he had agreed to lead the discussion.

However, she didn't show up at the meeting. This caused a great deal of concern to his already heightened insecurities. It wasn't until after he had arrived home that his phone rang.

"Alan, I'm so sorry I couldn't be there tonight." It was that same sweet, gentle voice he so longed to hear.

"A group of us had to work late on mailers for Leo's re-election bid. We didn't finish up until after nine o'clock. I just got in the door, and I'm headed to bed. I'm exhausted."

"Yeah, I understand Annalisa. I'm beat too. I guess all of these emotions about you leaving in less than two weeks are draining me."

"Yes, me too, Alan, so let's not talk about it, okay? We prayed about it, and there's really nothing else we can do. Besides, I am very tired. Let's just talk tomorrow, okay? We have an early staff meeting in the morning, and I really should get to bed."

"Okay. I'll talk with you tomorrow. Good night, my dear." Alan's voice tapered off as he started to hang up, but he decided to wait just a second more.

"Good night, sweetheart," she said softly.

Her last little word brought such buoyancy to his heavy heart that he determined he wanted to do something for her that would cheer her up as well. So the next morning, on his way to take care of a construction warranty issue at the bike store in Cherrydale, he dropped by a florist shop and ordered a bouquet of red roses to be delivered to her office on Capitol Hill. The florist confirmed they would be able to deliver the flowers that day right after lunch. Alan was certain, if he wasn't able to see her, he would receive a phone call from her sometime in the evening. This would be a special treat because it was Thursday. He worked late at the bike shop on Thursdays and usually didn't get to see her at all.

After he finished the warranty repair on the door hardware at the bike shop, he hopped in his truck. He started to complain about all the driving he had been doing lately: down to Arlington, out to Winchester, over to Leesburg, and to the one project Big Jim had started way down in Woodbridge.

"Man, all I do is spend time behind this windshield," he groused. "It would be nice to have a job where I just stayed in one place for a while." But then a grateful smile broke across his face. "Well, at least Dan is keeping me employed. I could be sitting at home, so I guess better this than that."

Before he could drive away, he noticed Frank flagging him down from the front door of the bike shop. "Yeah, Frank?" Alan shouted from his truck.

"Hey, Alan, it's your boss, Dan, on the phone. He wants to talk to you."

Having backed his truck into a parking spot, Alan jumped out and jogged to the door. "Thanks, Frank!" he acknowledged, then put the phone to his ear.

"Yes, sir?"

"Hey, Alan, you got the warranty issue done there yet?"

Before Alan could get the words, "Yes, sir," out of his mouth, Dan barked out his next order.

"Look, I need you to run down to Woodbridge and get the payroll timesheets from Big Jim, then drive them out here to the office as quick as possible. See you shortly. Thanks." The phone clicked dead.

As Alan hung up the bike shop phone, he muttered, "Good stinking grief, all I do is run, run, run. I'm ready to just work on one job for a couple of months, I'm sick of this."

"My offer is still good, Alan!" Frank shouted from across the showroom. I could use someone like you during the daytime hours. We're getting a lot of sales traffic in here, especially from about eleven until one or two in the afternoon."

"I may take you up on that, Frank," Alan laughed. "I mean it, if Dan wasn't a close relative, I probably would already be working here. But, as it is . . ."

"Food for thought, Alan. See you at six," interrupted Frank.

"Yep, see you then," he called back as he headed through the door toward his truck.

"Man, how am I ever going to make it back here by six today?"

Alan drove the hour and twenty minutes from the bike shop to the Woodbridge project. Then, the one hour and forty-five minute drive out to Dan's office in Leesburg, arriving just before two in the afternoon.

Cousin Dan's office was in an arched roof, turn-of-the-century wooden barn on several acres of land it shared with his beautiful two-story, brick colonial he had built on the property shortly after he bought it in 1972. It was situated on a grassy knoll with several large oak and maple trees just north of Leesburg off Highway 15. The original home had burned down sometime in the 1960s. However, the enormous barn had survived.

A few months ago, when Alan was assigned to do some busy work at the office, Dan had confided in him that the old barn was entirely what had attracted him to purchase the property.

"In fact," he concluded, "it was the only thing I actually liked about the property."

Walking through the big wood door, Alan strode into the office with its stark contemporary finishes. He loved the clean lines and the minimalist trim and woodwork, but thought it looked a bit strange inside such an old structure. In some of the rooms, as well as in the entrance, lobby, and conference room, rustic dark brown wood beams, with nail holes and grooves worn from decades of use, could be seen coupled alongside smooth-finished sheetrock painted a flat creamy white. All the doors and trim were painted a stark high gloss white, which gave the illusion the trim actually stood aloof from the surface of the wall. It was a gorgeous office, and Alan thought he would like to have one like it if he ever owned a business someday.

Alan handed the timesheets to Dan's wife, Nancy, who always calculated payroll and paid the company's bills. Before Alan could leave, Dan shouted from his office, "Where you going, Alan?"

Striding past a smiling Nancy, Alan entered Dan's office. "I guess to Winchester to finish out the day."

"No, no, don't do that. Have you had lunch yet?"

"No, sir, I thought I would grab something on my way there."

"No, look, why don't you run into town and get a bite to eat. Then, come back out here and pick up the payroll for tomorrow. Nancy, will you have it ready by the time Alan gets back from lunch?" Dan was still looking at Alan but calling past him to his wife in the adjacent office.

"If he takes an hour or so for lunch, I will."

"Okay, thanks, honey." He turned to Alan and explained, "Nancy and I are trying to get up to the mountains for the weekend, so I need someone to deliver the payroll checks to the jobs tomorrow morning. I can handle Winchester. That's on the way to the cabin, but I need you to take them to the rest of the jobs. You understand, Alan?"

Dan's tone sounded much more serious than Alan required for he knew how important this task was, not just to Dan, but to himself, and the rest of the men as well.

Dan continued, "So after you get the payroll from Nancy, you can call it a day, but get those checks out early in the morning to the jobs. I want to be sure everyone has been paid before we leave on our trip tomorrow."

"Don't worry, Dan, I got it."

"Okay then, go get some lunch. We'll see you back here in a few."

It was shortly after four in the afternoon when Alan arrived home, paychecks and all. Looking at his alarm clock as he entered his room, he figured he had just enough time to clean up and change his clothes before driving down to the bike shop to work.

"I think I'll stop by and see how Betsy is doing," he thought.

He made it his habit to do his best to drop by, if only for a few minutes, at least once a week. He usually visited with her on Thursday evenings or sometime on Saturdays, as the bike shop was near where she lived.

When Alan arrived about twenty minutes after five, Betsy was in the front yard trimming her bushes with a small hand clipper. She smiled and waved as she made her way up from the kitchen stool by the roses. She often brought the stool out to the yard to sit on while she worked.

"How are you, Betsy?" he called from beside his truck as he slammed the door. Jumping the white picket fence, he walked up to her and gave her a gentle hug.

"Oh, I'm fine, Alan, just trying to tidy up this mess."

Alan laughed, "This is the most meticulously manicured lawn I have ever seen . . . what mess are you referring to?"

"Oh, now, stop that, dearie. You know what I mean," she squawked with a smile. "Now, how's that sweet girlfriend of yours?"

"She's still super sweet!"

"When are you going to bring her by again? I sure hope I get to see her before she moves back to California."

"Me too, Betsy. I hope I get to see her too." he scoffed. "Between all my hours at work and her having to help her boss get re-elected this fall, it's been difficult to get a few minutes alone this week." Alan was starting to depress himself.

"Oh, not to worry, sweetie, God has everything in control. And, if I know Him, He's already got it all worked out. He loves you, Alan, and He loves Annalisa every bit as much. In fact, He loves her more than you do." With that she stopped and looked up at him with a very serious look upon her face. "Have you told her?"

"Have I told her what?" quipped Alan.

"Have you told her you love her?"

"Well . . . uh, no I haven't told her. I mean we care for each other and all, but I haven't told her. I mean you just don't come out and say something like that today. You know, today we don't just blurt things like that out."

He was trying not to let his sarcastic side take over the inflections in his voice, but it was beginning to win the fight.

"Now, Alan, listen to me," Betsy took his two hands in hers, "I want you to hear me good. Do not, under any circumstance, allow your sweet, precious Annalisa to leave for California without telling her your true feelings, or you may regret it for the rest of your life."

Pausing so as to let those words sink in a bit, she then concluded, "Now you hear me, dearie?" Although she was smiling, her tone was very serious.

"Yes, ma'am."

"Good. Now let me get you a bite to eat. I have some ham, peas, and mashed potatoes left over from last evening's dinner. How's that sound?"

"Sounds wonderful, Betsy, and thank you so much for your kindness. While you're getting dinner, I'll run these clippings to the pile out back."

"Oh, you're very welcome, Alan. Thank you for the help." Then with a smile and a wink she said, "We have to stick together. There aren't many like us left anymore."

"Betsy, what makes you so sweet? Did you have a nice upbringing or something?

"Oh, good gracious, no. In fact, our early years in Germany were really tough. My parents were friends with Dietrich Bonhoeffer just before World War II. He was imprisoned and later murdered by the Nazis. Those were very hard days. My father sold our house and all our belongings, so we could flee to the United States through Southern France. It was a frightening time. Christians were being persecuted by those who claimed to be Christians. At the time, you couldn't tell them apart, like the Lord's parable of the wheat and the tares.

My parents would tell us accounts of what I thought must have been the most difficult years of their lives. However, it wasn't much better when we first arrived in New York, being German and all. My folks didn't have jobs or a place for us to live. They didn't even speak much English. Those were real tough years. But, as my father always told us, "Great hardships make great hearts." Let's save that story for another time though, dear. Now, how about some dinner?"

On the way to the bike shop, Alan had more than enough to think about. He always did after visiting with Betsy. She had the perfect manner of expressing herself to him, a combination of gentle firmness along with borderline bossiness, which so reminded him of the perfect grandmother he wished he had known.

Usually they would talk of the **rojocci** fellowship and Christian insights along with answers to more of his questions regarding its history, and how it mysteriously flourished without any apparent leader or structure. But tonight was different. She hadn't been interested in talking of the past, but mainly of Annalisa. She was the chief topic before, during, and after their short dinner together. He helped Betsy clean up a bit before giving her a hug as he ran out the door headed for the bike shop.

Spying them through the front window from the parking lot, Alan noticed Frank, Carol, and what appeared to be a very excited female customer talking at the sales counter. Upon entering the front door, he discovered the female was actually Annalisa. As soon as she saw Alan, she ran toward him throwing her arms around him.

"It's an absolute miracle Alan! God did an absolute miracle! I can't believe it, but He did it!"

Carol called from across the showroom, "I think it's a miracle too."

"Me, too," agreed Frank. "But we'll let Annalisa tell you."

Annalisa was so excited she hardly knew where to start. "You're not going to believe this, honey! You're just not going to believe this!"

"No, no, you can't tell him something like this in a bike shop," cajoled Carol. "You guys go get an ice cream or something. It's okay; this is special."

"Alan," added Frank, "take the evening off. We can manage here without you for one night. Go ahead, you kids have fun. Things like this only happen a few times over the course of your lifetime."

"Uh, okay . . . thanks, y'all. I guess I'll see you Saturday morning."

The young couple walked out to Alan's truck. Actually, Alan was walking, and Annalisa was jumping up and down

while hanging onto his shoulders from behind. No sooner
had they sat down in his truck, than Annalisa blurted out,

"Let's just find a park, okay? I don't think I could sit still
in a restaurant."

"What is going on?" Alan snapped back with a laugh.
"Why on earth are you so hyper?"

"Oh, Alan . . . you're not going to believe . . . hey, what
park are you going to anyway?"

"I know this little park down off Military Road. There's
a path that leads out to a small overlook on the Potomac
River. Hardly anyone knows about it, so it will be quiet
there. Now, what's going on?"

She slid across the torn, vinyl bench seat in his truck so
she was right up against him. She grasped his arm at the
bicep and gave him a kiss on his cheek.

"Alan, God heard your prayer. I mean, our prayer!"

"Uh, what prayer, which prayer?"

"Well, this morning Joe called me into his office. When I
got to his door, Jackie was there seated across from his desk.
They asked me if I had a few minutes to talk. I wasn't sure if
I was in trouble or something, so I was really nervous. They
told me with the election coming up in November, several of
the current staff would have to be traveling more than
normal with Leo on the campaign trail. Therefore, they
determined they were going to be short staffed this fall."

She paused as they stopped at the park on Military
Road. "So," she continued, "they asked me if I would be
willing to stay on in a paid position until Christmas!"

At this Annalisa started yanking and pulling on Alan's arm and simultaneously stomping her feet on his truck's rusty floorboard.

"What? yelped Alan, "Say that again? What did they say?"

"They want me to stay on as a paid employee until Christmas!"

"What? Really?!" Alan was incredulous.

Here he had been dreading every day for the last two weeks knowing her departure was imminent. This news was "un-be-stinking-lievable!"

"I told them I would have to talk with my parents and see what they thought about it. They let me use the phone to call dad at his office in Walnut Creek. He thought it was a great opportunity for me and advised me to take it. Ha! I started laughing out loud right in my office. I mean, I was cracking up!" At this point Annalisa's infectious glee overflowed onto Alan, who joined in her merriment.

"He even told me not to worry about the finances. He explained how with me getting paid to work now, instead of the unpaid internship, there would be less out of pocket expenses for he and Mom. I was in shock." She laughed as she opened her mouth and eyes real wide to animate a shocked look.

"Then Dad told me to check with the apartment manager when I got home to determine if I could stay in the same unit until Christmas. He said it's better to do that kind of thing in person. So I checked with the manager, and guess what?" she giggled.

"What?" smiled Alan.

"They hadn't found another tenant yet and would be happy for me to rent it until the end of December!" Then she laughed out loud again.

Alan turned toward her so he could hold her with both arms. They both rejoiced together, holding each other tightly. Once their laughs subsided, tears began to fill their eyes, as they held one another smiling and weeping those ever so sweet tears of absolute joy. They gazed into one another's eyes and softly kissed, then again, and a third time. Alan pulled her close again and whispered in her ear, "I just can't believe what God has done for us. It is truly a miracle."

Annalisa gently pulled away from Alan so she could look him in the eyes. "Alan, I have to tell you something, or I will absolutely burst. I have wanted to tell you this for almost two weeks now, but I just couldn't bring myself to say it because of our situation and all."

"Can I say it first?" he gently volunteered.

She nodded her head and waited quietly, with a partial smile that revealed her heart.

"Annalisa, I am more certain of this than I have been of anything in my whole life. I absolutely love spending time with you. I love the way you talk, and how you almost always smile when you speak, and how when you smile, your eyes arch upward. I love the silly little things you do. Even how you almost always sit crossed legged. I even love the way you read a book, and the way you cook, and how you hold a glass and how . . . I don't know how else to say it, "I love you. I am so in love with you Annalisa. I really and truly love you!"

She leaned forward hugging him tightly as she softly spoke in his ear those words he was so hoping to hear, "I love you too, Alan. I am so very much in love with you, darling."

~seventeen~

The autumn weather was exceptionally pleasant that year motivating Alan and Annalisa to take advantage of it whenever they could. They went hiking at Great Falls National Park, rode their bikes on the C & O Canal Towpath, or sat on the steps of the Lincoln Memorial talking for hours: talking of nothing, talking of everything, talking of their future together. Neither wanted those days to end. The love they had for one another was blossoming into something precious, something beautiful, and both of them did everything they could to cultivate it.

Although Annalisa's work was very busy with the re-election efforts, Alan's construction job had slowed dramatically, allowing him to work more hours at the bike shop. The owners, Frank and Carol, had become good friends with Alan and Annalisa. In fact, they had gone on a few bike rides together, as the older couple had much more experience riding than did Alan and Annalisa. One Sunday, for example, the foursome rode the C & O Canal Towpath from Glen Echo, Maryland, all the way to Harper's Ferry, West Virginia, and back. It was a feat of nearly one hundred miles accomplished in one day.

In October, they traveled twice to Shenandoah National Park to see the fall colors along Skyline Drive. They had to go back the second time, because the leaves hadn't fully changed the first time they drove the ridgetop road, so Alan had insisted on trying it again. Annalisa was grateful for his persistence. Then, on Halloween, they had Rebecca and Peaknuckle over to Annalisa's apartment for dinner. They all dressed up in costumes, answering the door with a roar or a shout that delighted all but the youngest of trick-or-treaters. However, the very next day, with the election just one week away, Annalisa was back to working long hours at the office.

Throughout that fall, Alan, on more than a few occasions, was able to get to her apartment before Annalisa got home from work. Even though he was a terrible cook, he attempted to make spaghetti or a soup and sandwich combo for her. She was most grateful for his thoughtfulness, no matter how unappetizing the meal may have tasted.

Fortunately, on Election Day, Leo Ryan was re-elected to the United States Congress by the voters in his California district. There was much celebration in the office that day, and Annalisa was then given a much needed, lighter work schedule with fewer hours. However, it was short lived. For just over one week later, while in Guyana investigating an organization named People's Temple and their peculiar leader, Jim Jones, Leo Ryan was murdered by members of the group as he was getting ready to board his flight home. The date was November 18, 1978. It was a Saturday.

Annalisa didn't have a television, nor did she subscribe to the Washington Post newspaper. Alan had slept in that Sunday morning, then went down to Annalisa's apartment to spend the day with her. They had planned to drive to Carderock, a park on the Potomac River in Maryland. But after packing their picnic lunch, Annalisa suggested they just stay close by. So they simply walked from her apartment to Spout Run and down to a quiet spot overlooking the river.

It was a chilly day made warm by the bright sunshine. The two spent the entire day talking of their future and of the upcoming Thanksgiving holiday weekend trip. They had purchased airline tickets for the flight back to Annalisa's home in Walnut Creek, and more importantly, to her family. Things had become much more serious between the couple since September, when she was offered the full time position. They had shared their true feelings for one another as well as their hopes, dreams, and fears. Their relationship was deepening, and they enjoyed spending most of their free time together.

"It was so easy to love her," Alan would confess years later. "She was such a breath of fresh air, like when you have lived in a hot and humid Southern climate all summer long and then are suddenly transported to the cool, crisp air of the Northern autumn. She's like that, so fresh and light."

Monday morning Alan was working at the bike shop. Dan had given him Thanksgiving week off from his construction job because, as Dan put it, "Nothing ever happens on the construction sites the week of Thanksgiving. All those guys are off hunting in the mountains." It was ten thirty-five when the phone rang. Alan had just finished repairing a bottom bracket on a bicycle. Glancing at the clock, he answered the phone.

"Hello, Cycle Sports Pro Shop, may I help you?"

The voice on the other end of the phone was unmistakably that of Annalisa, and it sounded as though she was in a complete panic.

"Alan, it's absolutely horrible! Leo, Joe, and Jackie were killed in Guyana, Saturday. Well, Jackie may still be alive, but Leo and Joe are dead! It's the most terrible thing ever; the whole office is in complete chaos, everybody's crying, and as of this morning, I don't have a job anymore. Oh, Alan, this is absolutely awful, what am I going to do?"

"Wait, wait . . . hold on a second. Did you say they were killed? Weren't they down there checking out that church group?"

"Yes, they were on a fact finding mission. Nobody ever thought something horrific like this would happen though. Oh, Alan, I can't believe this! They just told us they won't need us anymore because the governor of California will appoint a new interim congressman. This is just so terrible. I can't stand it."

"Wait a minute, Annalisa, who said you don't have a job?"

"The new congressman will hire all his own people, so none of us have a job starting tomorrow morning. I think some of the others, who have been here longer, may get some extra pay or something, but I don't. My pay stops today. What am I going to do, Alan?"

"Well, the day after tomorrow we're flying to California. You can last until we get there. In fact, you already paid the rent for December, so you don't have to worry about that. I'll tell you what, let me see if Frank will allow me to leave early when he gets to the shop. Then, I'll drive right over, and we can work things out, okay? However, as soon as you get home, you should call your parents and let them know."

"My dad already called here at the office."

"Really?! What did he say?"

"Well, he mainly wanted to know if I was okay. After we spoke for a few minutes, he said that we'll discuss what to do next when we get back to Walnut Creek."

"That's good. And you're okay now, Annalisa?"

"Yes, I'm okay. Uh, I'm really shaken to my core though. This is such a horrible situation here. Everyone is crying and hugging and is worried about what's going to happen. It's awful, Alan, really awful."

"I'm sure it is, honey. Just hang in there, okay? When do you think you'll be home?"

"They told me I could leave whenever I want, but I thought I would stay until lunch, so I'll probably arrive home sometime after one o'clock."

"Okay, Frank gets in at two o'clock, so I'll drive down as soon as he lets me leave. Call me if you need anything, okay?"

"I will, Alan, Thanks so much. I love you, bye bye."

"I love you too, honey. See you soon, bye bye."

Alan was beginning to learn an important lesson at a young age that would stick with him for the rest of his life. "I never know what is going on at the other end of the phone line, so when the phone rings I should pray before I answer. It may announce good news, or it may be bad, but whoever is calling has a reason, and I need God's help when answering."

All that afternoon and evening they discussed the options, the possibilities, and how they would handle the uncertain future. Alan had to work the next day at the bike shop. As soon as he got off work, he was at Annalisa's having another conversation about what they should or could do. Honestly, they were both frustrated with the prospect of Annalisa being on the West Coast, while Alan was on the East Coast. They had grown so close over the last few months and both wanted their relationship to continue. Neither was ready to even consider calling it quits.

The following day, the Wednesday before Thanksgiving, they flew non-stop from Washington Dulles International Airport to San Francisco International Airport. Annalisa's family met them at the gate. It was a joyous reunion for Annalisa. But it was awkward for Alan. Her mother and her sister did most of the talking in the car on the drive to Walnut Creek. Alan found them warm and friendly as they continually made an effort to include him in the conversation. Her father, however, said very little. In fact, Alan was sure her father was listening intently so he could prepare his case against him. It all made Alan very insecure and cautious in how he worded any response he made to questions from Annalisa's mother and sister.

The town of Walnut Creek was beautiful, and Alan fell in love with it immediately. The weather, although it was late November, was a pleasant mix of cool air and warm sunshine. The William's home was an attractive stucco and beam, single story ranch. It was decorated with warm earthy tones that gave it a very homey feel. The lawn, though small compared to Alan's home in Oakton, was nicely manicured with lovely trees for shade during the hot California summers, as well as a couple of palm trees, two orange trees, and one lemon tree. Alan thought it idyllic. The backyard had a swimming pool with a pebbled finish concrete pool deck surrounding it, along with several lounge chairs and an umbrella table. The yard was fenced with a six foot high, redwood privacy fence. Backing up to Mt. Diablo State Park, the whole setting was absolutely gorgeous.

Once Alan was settled in the spare bedroom, he headed out to the family room to visit with Annalisa's family. They were laughing and making random comments about things Alan knew nothing about. Topics were brought up such as Annalisa's high school, which friend was doing what, and who was going to be in town for the Thanksgiving weekend. This all made Alan feel significantly insecure. Then Mr. Williams announced,

"Hey, Alan, why don't you and I leave these cackling hens to their gossip while we go out by the pool and talk?"

"Uh . . . sure, Mr. Williams, that sounds great."

Now, Alan's insecurity increased to full blown, anxious fear. They sat down at the umbrella table, each with a glass of fresh squeezed lemonade. Alan caught a glimpse of three female faces peering out the kitchen window.

"Where're you from, Alan?" Mr. William's voice sounded friendly, but Alan felt like he was on the witness stand in a court of law, being cross examined by a cunning attorney.

"My family and I live in Oakton, Virginia," replied Alan, trying to sound confident.

"Oh, that's just outside of the beltway, isn't it?"

"Yes, sir, in Fairfax County."

"What does your father do for work?"

"He's an architect."

"Do I know any of his designs?"

"No, sir, I don't think so. He's designed a couple of Smithsonian projects and several things at Georgetown University. He's also done a number of private undertakings, but nothing major. He's a project architect, so he mainly does one part of a project and not the whole building or anything."

"I see. Does your mother work?"

"No, sir, not really. I mean, she would say its work and all, but not anything big you know. Well, on occasion she substitute teaches."

"Hmmm, do you have any brothers or sisters?"

"Yes, sir, I have two brothers and one sister. They all live at home with mom and dad."

"And where do you live, Alan?"

"Well, I, uh . . . live at home with them. I live at my parent's house. I mean, I have my own bedroom and all. Uh, I really can't afford my own apartment or anything, you know."

"Really?"

"Uh, yes, sir. I mean, no, sir. I mean, yes, sir. I can't afford my own apartment or anything."

"Are you working, Alan?"

"Yes sir, I work full time at a construction company and part time at a bike shop."

"Oh, Harley Davidson? They make a nice bike."

"Uh, no, sir. I work at a bicycle shop. I fix and sell bicycles. I mean, when I'm not working as a carpenter."

"So you're a carpenter?"

"Well, yes sir . . . kind of anyway. I'm still learning and all."

"Where did you go to school? Did you go to college?"

"Yes, sir. I attended Bridgewater College through my sophomore year. Actually, I applied for and received my Associates in Arts degree."

"Really? Did you have a major, Alan?"

"Yes, sir. I majored in social sciences."

"What does that mean?"

"Well, I guess it means I like history and geography."

"What were you planning to do with that major?"

"I was thinking of maybe teaching, but really only so I could be a coach."

Just then, Annalisa and her mother came out the French doors and walked over to the table where Alan was being grilled. Mrs. Williams chirped, "You men want to talk about where you're taking us out for dinner?"

Alan thought she must be an angel sent directly from God in Heaven because her friendly tone was a welcome reprieve after the interrogation he had recently endured.

"Sure, sure, Alan and I were simply having a friendly conversation. Weren't we Alan?"

"Uh . . . yes, sir."

Alan was nodding but glanced at Annalisa to see if she could determine from the look on his face that he was more than ready to do something else.

"Look, you ladies head on in and get ready. Alan and I were just finishing up. We'll be right in."

Mr. William's tone sounded friendly, but Alan guessed the ladies knew he was serious because they turned around and went back in the house.

"So Alan, do you have any plans for the future? What would you like to do with your life?"

"Yes, sir. I want to own my own business one day. I'm hoping to build houses or perhaps have a bicycle shop." Alan's boldness surprised both Mr. Williams and himself.

"Well, do you now?"

"Yes, sir. I'm not quite sure how to get there yet, but that's the direction I would like to go. I would like to be able to hire folks and help them as well, I mean, with a job and all."

"Good for you, Alan," he replied as he stood up. "That's a very admirable goal. Now, let's see if the ladies are ready to go to dinner."

The rest of the evening and through Thanksgiving Day, Alan felt a bit more relaxed. He spent most of his time sitting and talking with Annalisa, except when she was showing him around Walnut Creek. Friday they drove to the top of Mt. Diablo, then down to a town named Pleasanton, on the far side of the mountain. They loved every minute of their time spent together.

Saturday morning the family gathered in the family room after breakfast. The topic of discussion was evident shortly after the conversation started. It seemed that Mr. Williams was determined to get his daughter back to Walnut Creek, one way or another and the sooner the better. Mrs. Williams wasn't disagreeing with her husband but merely thought his way of communicating in absolutes wasn't taking into consideration their daughter's feelings.

The discussion was right on the edge of getting heated when Mrs. Williams, who was sitting next to her husband on the sofa, turned to him and motioning toward Annalisa with one hand persuaded,

"I know our daughter, honey. And when I look into her eyes, they tell me all I need to know. So let's work this out together, okay?"

Her voice was soft and caring, yet had a unique tone that seemed to communicate, enough is enough.

The discussion went on for more than an hour and ended abruptly with the suggestion from Annalisa that Alan consider moving to California. Alan had contemplated this very thought himself, ever since first meeting Annalisa on the church retreat that Memorial Day weekend. However, now that it appeared to be a very real possibility to solving their problem, he wasn't quite sure he was ready for that drastic of a life change.

There was a pause in the conversation followed by Annalisa asking Alan, "If we could find you a job and a place to live, would you move here, Alan?"

Before he could stop the words from leaving his mouth, he blurted out, "Sure!"

He was, in fact, excited at the possibility, at all the wonderful possibilities, but how could all the details fall into place? He determined he and Annalisa should pray about this huge change. Before they left the house that afternoon, that's exactly what they did. Subsequently, he purposed to telephone his parents for their counsel as well.

After lunch on the pool deck with her parents and her sister, Annalisa and Alan headed out for a drive. She was determined to show him the California College of Arts and Crafts where she would be attending again in January. On their way, they passed through the small burg of Lafayette and stopped at a bicycle shop to do some browsing. It was a small shop with a store front right off the main boulevard. The owner, an older gentleman named Rudy, was a short, slender man, who combed his thinning, silver hair straight back and sported a fuzzy goatee of matching color. Rudy told Alan he had owned the shop for nearly forty years but was thinking of closing,

"It's just too much to care for any more."

The two talked for nearly thirty minutes; it was like they had known one another for years. When Alan mentioned he worked in a bike shop in Virginia but would be moving to Walnut Creek in a couple of weeks, Rudy plied Alan with many questions and even challenged him to three tests. The first of the three tasks, was to repack a bottom bracket, the second, to true a wobbly wheel, and the final, to change a flat tire. Alan was happy to accommodate, thinking that maybe this would lead to a job of some sort. Little did Alan know that Rudy was timing him as he performed the three exams. When he finished the final test, Rudy inspected Alan's work.

"That's mighty fine work there young man and rather quick too."

"My boss in Virginia told me repairs are where every shop makes its money. The more repairs accomplished in one day, the better off the shop is financially. I also learned the greater volume of parts purchased for repairs, the smaller the margin the shop has to pay on those parts, thus making each repair more profitable."

"That's true," replied Rudy. "It appears you have a head for business as well. Alan, when will you be back in our area?"

"In about two weeks."

"Okay, I'll tell you what, how does nine dollars an hour sound? And I'll throw in a commission of five percent of the profit for each bike you sell. You can start two weeks from Tuesday. We're closed on Sundays and Mondays."

"I think that sounds perfect," smiled Alan as he thrust his hand forward to shake Rudy's.

The two went on to talk over a few details then shook hands again as Alan opened the door to leave. When Alan finally got in Annalisa's parents' car, where she had elected to wait the last twenty minutes or so, she seemed a bit irritated. However, with the first words out of Alan's mouth, her mood changed dramatically.

"Well, I need a place to live," he stated frankly in somewhat of a monotone.

"What?!"

Alan had learned that her high pitched "what" usually contained more disbelief in what he had just stated, than belief. Regardless, he smiled as she yanked on his shoulder begging, "What, Alan, what is it?"

He turned to her, gave her a kiss, and laughed, "I need a place to live, honey, because I already have the job! Rudy just offered me a job and at a much higher wage than Frank, or even my Cousin Dan is paying me back in Virginia. So I need a place to live because I start work two weeks from Tuesday."

The two of them laughed and talked all the way to Annalisa's college. They were amazed at how it appeared God was working all of the details out. They even drove through the little town of Moraga on the way back. Annalisa had suggested that rent might be less expensive there. Indeed, it was, and Alan secured a one bedroom apartment for a reasonable rate.

The following day was filled with conversations of how to get their belongings, Annalisa's Datsun B-210, and Alan's Toyota pickup truck, back to California most efficiently. The discussion continued on the flight back to Virginia, and right up until they left for California the following Saturday. It was determined Alan would rent a trailer to tow behind his truck, and Annalisa would drive her little car ahead of him. The entire drive took four and a half days. When they finally arrived at Annalisa's home in Walnut Creek, they were exhausted.

The very next afternoon Alan moved into his new apartment. This gave him a long weekend to set everything up and hopefully get some much needed rest for his first day of work on Tuesday. But first, he needed to purchase some used furniture and a few other odds and ends, including a necessity called food. Before he knew what had happened, it was Tuesday morning, and he found himself at the front door of Rudy's Bicycle Shop.

He quickly discovered that his new employer was a very exacting type of person. He wasn't a micromanager, but certainly after so many years in the business he had his strong opinions of how things should be done. It suited Alan just fine though. He too, was very precise in his repairs and adjustments to the bicycles that came through the door in need of attention. In fact, after a few weeks, Rudy left Alan alone to watch the shop and began working fewer and fewer hours. For the most part, Alan enjoyed working for him, but more than that, he really enjoyed living near Annalisa.

Between the work at the shop, and evenings and weekends with her, he hadn't even noticed the passing of the months. Until one day, while at work alone, a student from Saint Mary's College in Moraga, dropped by needing some repairs done on his commuter bicycle.

The student laid his small backpack on the sales counter while he watched Alan adjust the rear derailleur, install the freewheel, and replace the chain. After he finished the repairs, Alan calculated the bill for the student. As he handed him the invoice, he noticed something familiar on the young man's backpack. There, embroidered on the side, were small letters no more than a half inch in height spelling out the word **rojocki**.

Alan stuck out his hand, "Hi, I'm Alan Browne."

"Gary Morimoto," came the reply.

Alan pointed to the word on the backpack, "What does that word mean, Gary?"

"Oh, that's a small group I'm in at college. A counselor at school organized it years ago, and a few students participate every year. There are only eight of us this year."

"Yes, but what does it mean?"

"It was a small group of Christians back in the late 1700s that wanted to . . ."

Alan interrupted, "Yes, I know about the history. But why do you spell it with a 'k' instead of two 'c's'? I've only seen it spelled like this," Alan pulled out Stanley's little leather satchel from his front pocket and showed it to Gary. The student looked closely at the item in Alan's hand.

"Yes, I've seen it spelled that way before. Apparently some of the members of the **rojocki** fellowship decided to change the 'k' to a 'c' shortly after the end of World War II. There was a group, who had been gaining popularity since the 1930s, building structures they called kingdom halls. And as you may be aware, the **rojocki** fellowship doesn't have buildings. Therefore, those in the **rojocki** fellowship didn't want to be identified with something like that, so they changed the 'k' to a 'c'. It was a minor change but was a perfect solution to their concern."

"So what does the 'k' stand for?" Alan asked again.

"**Kingdom**," Gary stated frankly.

"Then what does the 'c' stand for in the **rojocci** spelling?"

"Well, I can't tell you that. I already told you the meaning of one letter, and as you must surely be aware I can only reveal one letter to any seeker like yourself." Gary stated with somewhat of a gleeful pride.

"Oh, for Pete's sake, I didn't want to know the 'k' in **rojocki**, I wanted to know the second 'c' in the word **rojocci**. Now would you please give me that word?"

Alan could feel his impatience rising and was getting ready to burst out with some sarcastic remark when the student replied,

"Look, I can't tell you that, but I'm sure you'll be able to figure it out." Apparently Gary's delight had a bit of impatience as well.

"If I guess it, will you tell me if I'm right?" Alan asked with a bit of a forced smile.

Gary smiled back, "Yes, if you guess it, I'll tell you whether you are right or wrong. Come on now, just think it through."

-eighteen-

Although he tried, Alan couldn't come up with a reasonable alternative before Gary had to leave. Therefore, Gary promised to come back to the bike shop the following week, right after he finished up his final exams. This was somewhat comforting to Alan, but trying to figure out the mystery caused no lack of consternation. He decided to discuss it with Annalisa at her parents' home that evening.

After dinner, the two enjoyed the beautiful May evening out by the pool. Alan told her the whole story regarding Gary and the different spelling, as well as the letter "**k**" discovery for the word "**kingdom**" and the letter "**c**" mystery.

"So, I'm really stuck. I tried all sorts of combinations with the words I already know, and nothing seems to fit. You have any ideas, honey?"

Annalisa looked out across the hills over the fence in her backyard. "The '**k**' meant '**kingdom**', so from what you're telling me, '**c**' must be somewhat synonymous with the word '**kingdom**'. They just substituted a '**c**' word for the '**k**' word."

"Ok, good. So what are some words that start with '**c**' that are synonyms of the word '**kingdom**'?"

"Country?" suggested Annalisa.

"Or, Virginia is a commonwealth," retorted Alan. "How about commonwealth?"

"Alan, really? Do you think it is commonwealth? Where are those other words you have? Didn't you write them down on some scraps of paper?"

"Yes, I have them right here in Stanley's little pouch." Alan pulled the satchel from his front pocket and opened the little draw tie. He removed each piece of paper with the utmost of care. Stanley's handwritten one came out last. Once he had them laid out on the table by the pool, he aligned them to match each word on Stanley's note.

"There," he said with a bit of satisfaction in his voice. "Now, let's see . . ."

"Christian," announced Annalisa. "I think it stands for the word Christian."

"Why on earth would you say that?" asked Alan with a hint of sarcasm bleeding through his most sincere effort at sounding nice.

"Because."

"Oh that's a great reason, my dear." Now his sarcastic tone was clearly evident. "Why? says he. 'Because', says she." Alan laughed, "That makes absolutely no sense at all."

"You didn't let me finish, Alan," she defended with a twinge of disgust in her voice.

"So sorry, honey," he stated sincerely. "Really, what do you mean? Why do you think it's Christian?"

"Well, the whole **rojocci** fellowship is Christian right?" Alan nodded in agreement, "But . . ."

"Now let me finish, Alan." She looked directly at him as if to say, "You interrupt me again and there's going to be trouble."

"So," she continued, "if we know that the 'k' stood for 'kingdom' but was replaced by a 'c' word, then that word must have something to do with the Christian kingdom. Why not just drop the word 'kingdom' and leave the word 'Christian' in its place? Look at your papers," she pointed to the little pieces on the table.

"The letter 'r', we don't know yet."

"The 'o', we learned from A Dub means, 'of'," she giggled. Alan rolled his eyes.

"The 'j' letter is obvious," she continued.

"What?" smirked Alan.

"The 'j' is always 'Jesus' in anything that's Christian, sweetheart," Annalisa smiled. "Now, we know from Stanley's paper that the second 'o' is for 'overlooked' and the first 'c' is for, 'cherished'".

"Granted," replied Alan, "but we don't know what the second 'c' stands for, nor do we know the final letter, which is an 'i'", argued Alan. "And you're guessing that the 'j' stands for 'Jesus'."

"Well, let's put it all together to see what we have at this point, okay, Alan?"

"r"-"of"-"Jesus"-"overlooked"-"cherished"- "christian"-"i"

Annalisa continued, "Assuming the 'j' stands for '**Jesus**', which I'm sure it does, and the second 'c' means '**Christian**', then all we have left to figure out is the 'r' and the 'i'."

"That's a lot to assume, honey. Let's first check with Gary to determine if, in fact, the 'c' means '**Christian**', okay? If you're correct with that one, then we can move on to the next assumption," chided Alan.

"Okay," she smiled. "Fair enough, but I'm right, dear. I'm telling you, I have it figured out."

A few days later, Gary dropped by the shop and confirmed what Annalisa already knew. The second "c" did in fact stand for "**Christian**". Alan then determined to dig into the mystery of the final three letters even if Annalisa claimed to already know one of them. But a week turned into a month, and a month, a season, and that season was extremely busy at the bike shop as Alan's work had become very popular with the local cycling community. Before he knew it, summer was over, and he was quickly approaching the one year anniversary of his move to California.

As the calendar turned over from 1979 to 1980, Alan and Annalisa's relationship had grown substantially. They had even talked of marriage on multiple occasions. This was sparked by the offer Rudy had made to Alan, a few months back, to sell the bike shop to him. They had worked out an agreement, and the closing date for the buyout deal was set for January 1, 1980. That was the first day Alan realized a longtime dream of becoming a business owner. Less than a month later he had a long, private talk with Annalisa's parents. After obtaining their blessing, he purchased an engagement ring.

On Saturday night, January 26, 1980, Alan took Annalisa out to dinner at a charming seafood restaurant on the marina in Jack London Square. Later, they drove up into the hills and across Skyline Boulevard to Grizzly Peak Road above the city of Berkeley. They stopped at an overlook where they could see the entire Bay Area, including San Francisco and the Golden Gate Bridge. It was a beautifully clear night, though a bit chilly. Getting out of her car, to take in the view, they scrambled up on a large boulder that Alan had picked out on his reconnaissance drive a few days before. It was just like the boulder above the lodge where they had first met at the church retreat almost two years ago.

He directed the conversation toward how they had met, recounted the memorable time they spent on the boulder in Western Maryland, and mentioned that this boulder would also have a significant role in their relationship. Next, he told her of all the unique circumstances that had brought them along together to this point in their lives. Finally, he mapped out how he hoped the future would unfold over the next few years. She listened quietly to his every word, recognizing this must be a very special moment for him to be giving such details. After a few minutes, he slid down off the boulder. Then, with Alan holding her hands to help her, she descended until they were both on the ground, face to face. He dropped to one knee.

"Annalisa, my darling, I love you with every ounce of my being. I cannot even imagine a life lived without you. I love the thought of being your husband and very much want you to be my wife, my life partner. There's no pressure on you to say 'yes', but would you, Annalisa Michele Williams, please marry me?"

Alan had not yet revealed the engagement ring, which he had hidden in an inside pocket of his down vest (the same vest he had refused to let her wear not five minutes ago, when she said she was getting cold.) He wanted the answer to be from her heart, free from any other influences. He knew a sparkling diamond could be a very attractive lure, and he didn't want to drag her in with rod and reel. No, he wanted her, of her own free will, to leap in the boat, which would be their life together.

"Of course, I'll say yes, Alan. I love you with all my heart and want to spend the rest of my life with you too. So, yes, my Alan Michael Browne, I'll marry you."

With that, Alan rose to his feet and while still holding her hands, he prayed a quiet prayer of blessing upon their marriage, their lives together, their future children, and their life endeavors. As he said the amen to their prayer, he reached into his vest pocket, pulled out the engagement ring, and slid it onto her finger. Her mouth dropped wide open. She threw her arms around his neck and started laughing and weeping all at the same time. She shed tears of deep joy and after a minute or two, lovingly kissed him several times. Then, through the tears, she whispered in his ear, "Do you know why I am so happy right now sweetheart?"

"Well, I think I could guess."

"No, no, I am so very happy because back on that boulder, at the lookout above the lodge, I knew."

"You knew what?"

"I knew it was you, Alan. Do you remember when you looked at me and asked, 'What are you doing'?"

"Yes, I remember that."

"I was praying, quietly praying . . . and this is what I was praying for—for you and me. I saw in you everything that I knew I wanted and needed if I were ever to give my whole heart to another in marriage."

She kissed him deeply and tenderly as they held each other close in the chilly, night air. "Maybe we could get in the car, honey. It's rather cold out here," she coaxed. "Do you have a date in mind, Alan?"

"Do you mean for the wedding? I was thinking sometime in May, after you finish school."

"That sounds good to me too, but not Memorial Day weekend. How about the Saturday before that weekend? Let's see, I have a little calendar in my purse here somewhere. Yep, here it is, how about Saturday, the seventeenth of May?"

"Sounds perfect to me." The two hugged again. Then Annalisa declared,

"Let's go tell my parents and my sister!"

The next several months were a blur to Alan as he and Annalisa were busy planning their wedding. They had decided to have the ceremony at their church in Pleasant Hill with the reception in the adjacent fellowship hall. Alan went along on all the shopping trips for everything from flowers to table cloths to the wedding cake. In fact, the only trips where she didn't encourage his participation were her frequent visits to the local bridal shops for her wedding gown. "That," she affirmed, "is reserved for my mom and my sister."

It was a magnificent spring California day, a perfect day for a beautiful wedding. The church Annalisa had attended since childhood, was simply, yet stunningly decorated. As her father walked her down the center aisle of the quaint sanctuary, Alan thought Annalisa looked absolutely radiant in her elegant white gown.

They had written their own vows and recited them to one another with smiling faces and tearful eyes. The entire ceremony, as well as the reception that followed, was genuinely perfect in every way. They would cherish the memories for decades to come.

The day had gone off just as they had hoped and planned. Before they knew it, Alan and Annalisa were husband and wife embarking upon their honeymoon. They had decided to stay the first night in a hotel by the San Francisco International Airport, since their flight would leave early the next morning for the city of Victoria, British Colombia, on Vancouver Island, Canada. They had reservations for the week at the majestic Empress Hotel.

Heading north along the coast, Alan wished he had obtained seats on the left side of the plane so they could take in the scenic coastline. However, about halfway through the flight the captain announced on the intercom,

"If those of you seated on the right side of the aircraft will look out your windows, you will see the Mount Saint Helens volcano."

As Alan and Annalisa peered through the tiny window, they could see the smoking summit of the mountain. At that precise moment, Mount St. Helens erupted, spewing ash and smoke thousands of feet into the sky. Although it was more than a couple dozen miles away, the size of the volcanic plume dwarfed their Boeing 727 aircraft. Everyone on board was in a state of astonishment. They were transfixed by this magnificent and dreadful sight. Alan glanced at his watch; it was precisely thirty-two minutes after the hour of eight.

"What an awful and terrible sight," Annalisa whispered to Alan. He nodded his head in agreement.

Their honeymoon, however, was filled with the joy and wonder of starting their new life together. They enjoyed one another as well as the peaceful, beautiful surroundings of the island. Their only complaint was that the time alone was too brief.

Once they arrived home, they quickly settled into life as a married couple. Annalisa thoroughly enjoyed decorating their little apartment. Alan remained very busy at the shop hiring two employees to keep up with the volume of customers, one to help with repairs, and the other to answer phones and deal with customers who visited the shop. His humble bike shop was thriving.

In fact, in the summer of 1984, he heard of a shop in Pleasanton that was looking to close its doors. He approached the owner and negotiated a purchase. Now, Alan owned two bicycle shops. He called them his babies, as they often needed his constant attention.

That same year, Annalisa announced to her adoring husband that he would soon have a third baby to add to his bicycle shops. This one, however, would be more cuddly and lovable. The couple was thrilled with the news and overjoyed when their first baby girl was born the following October. Less than three years later, another little bundle of joy arrived, this one a boy, and another baby girl two years after that. The little Browne family was now five members in all.

Almost as much as he loved being a husband, Alan absolutely loved being a father. Nonetheless, he was really feeling the pressure of all the responsibility and how quickly it had piled up on him. There was the payment for the house, which they had to buy because the space in their meager apartment was barely enough room for the two of them and their one child, much less for all three of their children. Then, there were the payments for the minivan, insurances, utilities, food, food, and more food, not to mention the multitude of diapers.

By 1989, it was all weighing very heavily on Alan. The results caused him to begin visiting a doctor on a regular basis for the first time in his life. Although there was nothing wrong with him physically, other than some moderately high blood pressure, he would commonly complain that he felt he was close to having a heart attack. During the World Series earthquake that same year, he was sure he had had one.

In the spring of 1991, Alan and Annalisa made it their practice to get out every day for a walk of two to three miles. This was quite a juggling act with their three little ones at home requiring childcare. Even though this was no small expense, Annalisa decided it was cheaper than Alan having a lengthy stay at the local hospital due to a heart attack.

On one such walk in March, they were hiking a trail in Mt. Diablo State Park, when they came upon a middle-aged man and woman standing at the base of a cliff watching two rock climbers about eighty feet above them. As Alan and Annalisa continued by, Alan noticed, on the back of the man's ball cap, the word **rojocci** embroidered in a half circle around, what Annalisa called, the ponytail hole. Alan immediately stopped. Upon introducing himself and Annalisa, he asked the man about the word.

"Oh, that," the man answered nonchalantly, "I've wanted to put some more time into researching the meaning of the letters, but with all the busyness, I just haven't been able to. It's really hard to find a quiet place, you know?"

The man's reply came as somewhat of a shock to Alan as he heard his own voice in the words that fell from the man's lips. The two acquaintances shook hands. Then Alan and Annalisa continued down the trail. But, those words festered within Alan's mind for years to come.

Instead of setting aside a quiet time each day, however, he was becoming busier than ever. By the end of the summer of 1992, he owned three bicycle shops: the original one in Lafayette, the one he purchased in Pleasanton, and the new one he had just opened in Danville that he had employed a contractor to build for him. It was on a vacant lot he had purchased the year before. He called it his flagship shop; it would turn out to be his waterloo.

The construction costs had gotten way out of hand as it neared completion. This was partly due to Alan's insistence on everything resembling what he had loved about Dan the Man's office back in Virginia. But it was also because material costs had skyrocketed due to a horrific hurricane, named Andrew, which had come ashore on the opposite side of the country. This, combined with the remodeling of the other two shops within the same eighteen months, had depleted all his capital and had caused him to take out a business loan on the Lafayette and Pleasanton shops.

At one point in late 1994, everything was getting so far out of hand, Alan was considering filing for bankruptcy protection. Instead, at the urging of his attorney, he applied for an equity line of credit on their home, having convinced himself that with the upcoming summer season he would be able to pay this bridge loan back by next September. He closed on this line of credit in February 1995.

However, before he knew it, his initial draw on the line, to catch up on his bills, became another draw he had to use for payroll, then another, and another. A few months later it was evident he would not be able to pay the balance back by the end of the year. By late September, his line of credit had a mere few hundred dollars available. This burden was becoming more than Alan could bear and it was absolutely relentless.

Then came the news that sent him over the top. His sweet, precious wife of more than fifteen years announced to him she was pregnant again, this time with their fourth child. He just couldn't handle any more pressure and barked out at her,

"Oh, great, that's just what we need right now, another mouth to feed!"

Little did Alan know at the time, but this drove a huge wedge between the love of his life and himself. It was something, under normal circumstances, he would never in a million lifetimes want to happen. He loved her with a deep, abiding love that, at times, seemed to him, more than life itself. He would never want to hurt her and would certainly never want something to come between them.

However, the news came as more of a burden than a joy to both of them, although for entirely different reasons. Feeling especially vulnerable, Annalisa was in dire need of his acceptance. She needed to know he would be there for her no matter the difficult times. For Alan, the news reminded him of how close they were to losing everything: to living on the street or in a campground somewhere with three children and a pregnant wife, while he tried to scrounge up some menial work. "Surely, she would leave me," he convinced himself.

As he dwelt on these thoughts, his mind began to race again, like it always did when he was confronted with a difficult situation. He couldn't stop the anxious ramblings of his imagination. Irrational thoughts flooded his mind like his precious wife leaving, taking their beloved children to live with her parents, an old boyfriend coming along, the two of them falling in love, then demanding of Alan a divorce. Losing everything, he envisioned himself living alone in a broken down shanty with an old crotchety, cantankerous cat named Cattila the Hun. Alan wasn't particularly fond of cats and this last thought was just overwhelming. It sent him immediately to the phone to make an appointment with his physician because his chest was feeling incredibly heavy, almost like an ache, a deep, heavy ache.

Dr. Rajandra, Alan's physician, was a first generation immigrant from India. He was tiny in stature, at least to Alan, who was more than a foot taller than his doctor. Alan had decided years ago that this man must have the smallest bones of any adult male he had ever seen. But he was also one of the kindest men he had ever known. He had been very patient with Alan's many stress related ailments, except the one time when Alan had a kidney stone. On that occasion, Alan asked if the sharp pain he was feeling was going to let up any time soon. He was experiencing extreme discomfort. The gentle doctor, in his very thick accent, while tapping the tips of his fingers together several times, just smiled, "It's only going to get worse."

But now with this visit, the latest in a long line of appointments, his physician made a comment that perhaps Alan needed a different type of doctor, one who dealt with illnesses of the mind. This was a slap in Alan's face and a much needed wake-up call. After many questions from Alan regarding his condition, which consequently led to more questions than answers from Dr. Rajandra, Alan was at the end of his rope.

The two sat quietly in the cramped exam room for several seconds. Then Alan, who was seated on the exam table, shifted in his seat as if he was ready to say something. Before he could get the words out, Dr. Rajandra held up one of his tiny fingers and said, "I'm going to write you a prescription for a vacation. However, you are to go on this vacation alone and to someplace where you know no one at all."

"That's impossible, Dr. Rajandra, I have way too many responsibilities to take some time off right now."

"Alan, I'm telling you, if you don't take time away from those responsibilities, they will end up killing you. Now, do you want that?"

"Well . . . no, of course not."

"Then here is your prescription and my serious, heartfelt advice with it. Take the prescription and go fulfill it sooner rather than later. The medicine will do you much good. It may even save your life!"

~nineteen~

Sitting upright in the porch hammock, Alan allowed his feet to fall on either side until they touched the floor. It was dark, and so very quiet at the Morgan's cottage. He determined he must have dozed off for a few minutes. All his fretting and daydreaming of the past week while at the cottage hadn't really solved any of the problems that he believed caused him to need this time away. However, though the storm had raged on the outside, he had a new found calm, a peaceful rest on the inside. In his heart he had never known such stillness his entire life. He decided he loved this new tranquility, and needed more. The only place he was able to find any clues to this new discovery was in the Scriptures. So back to the kitchen table he went. Once there, he calmed and quieted his heart and mind, waiting on that still small voice to speak within his thoughts.

He found a candle and some matches in the box of supplies given to him by the folks in the Red Cross van earlier that afternoon. After lighting the candle, he glanced at his watch and discovered it was after two o'clock in the morning.

"Wow, I must have been really tired from doing all the work in the yard and removing the storm panels from the windows. I think I've been asleep since six or seven o'clock last night. I'll get a bite to eat and then sit down with the Scriptures."

Noticing a little check in his thoughts, Alan determined it was somewhere inside of him, deeper than his thoughts. It wasn't on the emotional level either, it was of a spiritual nature. "I wonder if what I'm sensing is in my spirit?"

Quickly opening his Bible, he turned toward Hebrews. "Where was that verse?" he questioned aloud. This is the book where he was encouraged to look for an answer by that small voice in his heart yesterday, so he thought to try there again.

"Ha, here it is . . . yes, I figured it was close by." His finger ran along the words of the twelfth verse in the fourth chapter.

". . . as the division of soul and spirit . . ."

Alan's eyes glanced across at a reference in the margin, First Thessalonians, fifth chapter and the twenty-third verse. Upon finding it a few pages away in his Bible he read it aloud,

"Now may the God of peace Himself sanctify you entirely; and may your spirit and soul and body be preserved complete, without blame at the coming of our Lord Jesus Christ."

Alan's eyes opened wide as it was difficult to see in the candlelight. "There's no question," he declared, "The Scriptures are clear. There is a definite distinction between my spirit and my soul. But, what does it matter? If it does matter, then why does it matter?"

Reclining back in his chair, he closed his eyes. He reasoned that if there was a difference in the Bible, then it must matter because it was actually written in the Bible. Therefore, he concluded, this must be something that was important because God had it recorded in the Scriptures long ago, saving it through the generations for him today.

"Thoughts," he declared aloud. "Thoughts seem to be such a major part of all of this." He checked the tiny concordance in the back of his Bible. "Whoa, look at this!" he shouted. "Proverbs, the seventh verse of the twenty-third chapter says,

'For as a man thinks within himself, so he is.'"

Then he noticed another few verses, this time in First Corinthians, chapter two, verses thirteen and fourteen:

". . . combining spiritual thoughts with spiritual words. But a natural man does not accept the things of the Spirit of God; for they are foolishness to him, for he cannot understand them, for they are spiritually appraised."

"Well, there appears to be something the Scriptures call 'spiritual thoughts'. I wonder where they come from?" Alan thumbed back through his memory banks to determine if he had ever heard anything remotely similar to these words he was now reading. He recalled a conversation with Betsy where she had expressed to him that there are more than one source of thoughts. The very voice he believed he sensed, just the day before yesterday, she had called a still small voice. This source for thoughts was unambiguously different than the one, or perhaps several, he had been accustomed to heeding.

In fact, he was fairly certain he may have perceived something positive before. For example, he recalled the time he had offended Annalisa with a sarcastic comment in front of their friends. The still small voice suggested he should apologize to her and to their friends also. After a time of wrestling back and forth between thoughts that seemed to justify his comment, and thoughts of the hurt he had caused her, he chose to follow the gentle nudging within, to make things right. Not only had he asked for their forgiveness, and was so grateful to receive it, but they too apologized for their participation in the incident. They all grew much closer because of Alan's initiative in acting upon what he had heard. Annalisa later confided to Alan, her respect for him had grown tremendously because he had humbled himself for her benefit. Needless to say, Alan was very glad he had listened to that quiet voice in his heart that particular day.

Sitting in silence at the kitchen table with his Bible open, he felt compelled to turn to the Book of Romans. As he flipped back and forth in the Scriptures and made notes of his findings, he had a thought flash across his mental screen,

"... here a little, there a little."[1]

"It really does take time, doesn't it Lord?" he prayed while he turned to the eighth chapter. His eyes scrolled down the page much faster than before, as if he really knew what he was looking for, even though he wasn't quite sure what it was. Then something caught his eye in the fifth and sixth verses:

"For those who are according to the flesh set their minds on the things of the flesh, but those who are according to the Spirit, the things of the Spirit. For the mind set on the flesh is death, but the mind set on the Spirit is life and peace."

Alan glanced in the margin to find a reference to another verse. This one was in the Gospel of John, chapter three, verse six:

"That which is born of the flesh is flesh; and that which is born of the Spirit is spirit."

Continuing through the rest of the Gospel of John, Alan jotted down whatever verse or passage he sensed God was highlighting for him, like the one in chapter six for example:

"It is the Spirit who gives life; the flesh profits nothing; the words that I have spoken to you are spirit and are life."

Alan recognized these words in verse sixty-three as the words spoken by Jesus Himself. But more than that, they were words directly penetrating into Alan's own spirit. And there he ruminated upon them all, pondering what the Lord was communicating to him personally. He also purposed to fast, pray, and study the Scriptures until Friday. That's when he was to meet with his new cycling friend, Joseph Hinote, at Bayview Park, across the bay in Pensacola.

Before Alan blew out the candle, he discovered one more passage and was convinced it needed a place in his notebook. It was found in the Book of Galatians, the fifth chapter and the sixteenth and seventeenth verses:

> "But I say, walk by the Spirit, and you will not carry out the desire of the flesh. For the flesh sets its desire against the Spirit, and the Spirit against the flesh; for they are in opposition to one another . . ."

Alan sensed that God was trying to express something very important to him. He glanced out the front window from where he sat at the kitchen table. It was getting light outside and a new day was dawning, just like the one in his heart. He determined, as he gazed out the window, that every action whether a sarcastic comment, a loving remark, a selfish reach at the dinner table, or a helping hand repairing a broken toy—every action begins with a thought. And from what he could determine from the Scriptures today, those thoughts have at least two wellsprings. More importantly, those two sources are absolutely opposed to one another.

When the thoughts are followed through to actions, the fruit or results of those actions are entirely different.

In fact, he discovered later in the Book of Galatians, that one line of thinking, if taken to fruition, leads to some pretty severe consequences and results. In contrast, the other train of thoughts, if allowed to develop, births some very beneficial fruit, spiritual fruit. Fruit, he determined, that wasn't just to his advantage, but to others as well, and even to the One who is the Creator of the fruit Himself. "Thoughts," he reasoned, "are very powerful things."

Leaning back in his chair, he gazed up at the ceiling as if there was an answer written on it. He recalled the time, even the exact moment, one Sunday afternoon after dinner, when Annalisa was in the kitchen washing dishes. He was seated on the sofa waiting for the 49er's game to come on the television. When suddenly, he had the thought to get up and go help her in the kitchen. He remembered it was immediately followed by another thought . . . the thought that the game was coming on at any second, and he didn't want to miss it. He had chosen to remain on his comfortable sofa. A decision he later regretted.

It seemed to Alan that just about any time he had had a thought to do something for another person; it was almost instantaneously followed by a different thought of an opposing viewpoint, a more self-centered perspective, cancelling out the first notion to help someone. This dawned on his mind as a revelation of light, like a sunrise filmed in fast motion.

"Yes, Lord, I think I'm beginning to understand," he whispered as if there was someone there in the room with him.

"I've been trying to control my actions and have almost always failed miserably because that's not what needs changing . . . it's my thinking. By focusing on changing my actions, I've lost the battle because it has already been won by the opponent in my thoughts. I remember making some cutting remarks once because I thought someone was being snarky or sarcastic. When in reality, they were just being friendly. However, in the fight waged in the trenches of my mind, I had already been defeated before the words ever proceeded out of my mouth. My thoughts were controlling what my mouth was spewing. All these years . . ." Alan paused for just a moment to let the next words register deep down, to saturate his soul at such a depth he would never forget them.

"All these years I've been listening to the wrong thoughts." Alan sat there at the kitchen table slowly shaking his head from side to side.

"All these years, Lord. All these years. All the foolish words I heaved out of my mouth at so many people. Why did you let me continue? Why, Lord? Couldn't you have told me to stop years ago?"

Sitting very still, he kind of half-prayed and half-talked to God. He closed his Bible then his eyes and quietly placed his head on the kitchen table. Just then, he sensed a very soft voice in his thoughts.

> "I had many more things I wanted to say to you, but you could not bear them then."[2]

"But, Lord," Alan pleaded, "I was a Christian back then. I mean, I prayed to receive you in my heart way back on that ninth grade retreat at Skyland Lodge in Shenandoah National Park. I read my Bible and went to church. I even gave tithes when I made some money working summer jobs. Why didn't you tell me these things way back then?"

Waiting for a reply for several minutes, he tried his best to sit quietly before the Lord and listen. Finally, a thought came. "That sounded a bit like I was defending myself rather than actually wanting to know what You have to say to me, Lord. I'm sorry, my dear Father, please forgive me. Please speak what You want to say, when You want to say it, okay?" Alan knelt at the table seeking forgiveness for his latest offense.

Within seconds, a Scripture so loving and gracious, came into his thoughts. Immediately his eyes welled up with tears.

> "My thoughts are not your thoughts, neither are my ways your ways . . . I love you with an everlasting love and spoke to you in parables because you did not have eyes to see or ears to hear what I was saying."[3]

With this last statement, Alan dropped to the floor with his face down in his hands weeping. "I'm so sorry, Lord. Please forgive me for being so arrogant and proud that I couldn't hear You. My most sincere, heartfelt apologies, Father."

"Alan, 'I am the Light of the world, walk in this Light as I Myself am in the Light and we will have fellowship one with another and I will talk with you as a man speaks with his friend.'"[4]

With this last affirmation, Alan began to sob uncontrollably. He felt as though he were covered and surrounded by a comforting cocoon of warm, supernatural love that had a most calming and peaceful sensation deep within him. It was absolutely heavenly.

Little by little, a thought of gratefulness came into Alan's mind. He immediately expressed it out loud as if to let the Lord know that he did, in fact, hear it. This was followed by a song of praise, then a chorus of thanksgiving, along with a hymn of worship, as he knelt there on the floor. It was a wondrously precious time that he never wanted to end.

However, the songs began to quiet down, and the Scripture verses, which had flowed from deep within, like a wellspring down inside a cave, quieted to a hush. Remaining was a unique peace of the kind he had never experienced before. Alan remained there, basking in it for what must have been hours. When he finally got up off the floor, he glanced at his watch; it was half past one o'clock in the afternoon.

Upon rising to his feet, Alan stretched by reaching his finger tips to the ceiling. He then lengthened his legs like he used to do before track practice. Placing his hands on the kitchen countertop, he completed several pushups before noticing his mobile phone a few feet away.

"I really need to call Annalisa and let her know how I'm doing," he stated as he turned on his phone. "Man, still no service. I wonder if there's a working pay phone at Bruno's market."

With this, he donned his cycling clothes, inflated the tires with air, and walked his bike to the asphalt road at the end of the Morgan's gravel drive. Within minutes of turning the pedals, he realized how wonderful it felt to be on the bike again. The air was warm and balmy with several, big, fluffy clouds floating overhead. The ride to Bruno's took a mere ten minutes, but it did Alan a world of good.

"Just to get the blood flowing again feels good," he proclaimed out loud. He passed by a line of cars waiting for gasoline at one of the local stations. There was a line, at the hardware store also. And, as he pulled into Bruno's Market parking lot, he noticed a line there too . . . for the payphone.

It took nearly two hours, but Alan eventually had the phone in his hand. He was very disappointed to reach the answering machine at their home, instead of his sweet Annalisa. Regardless, he left as long a message as the answering machine would allow. Just before being cut off, he made sure she knew he was okay, and that he loved and missed her with all of his heart.

Wanting to see how others had fared after such a terrible storm, Alan decided to ride his bike the long way back to the Morgan's cottage. As he continued along the back roads of Gulf Breeze, he noticed he was becoming quite weary. This caused him to remember he had been fasting, so he decided it best to cut his little tour short before becoming too drained to make it back to the cottage. Arriving shortly before dusk, he got settled in at the kitchen table just as the sun was setting.

That evening and the next few days were filled with wonder for Alan. He wrote down dozens of verses from the Scriptures and also had quiet times of prayer, along with worship and singing. Sometimes he sat at the little kitchen table, and other times he walked around inside the tiny cottage, turned sanctuary. He loved every blessed moment of his stay and was beginning to actually wish he wasn't leaving in a day or so. However, the very next day he would be riding over to meet with Joseph Hinote in Pensacola. Knowing how much energy he would need to accomplish the bike ride of several miles, he decided it was time to end his fast.

The following morning, dawn broke with cooler temperatures and sunshine aplenty. It was an absolutely perfect day for a bike ride. Previously, Alan had purchased a local map, so he knew which roads to take to get to his destination. He left the cottage early, just in case there were any unexpected delays in getting to Bayview Park. He arrived there about ten minutes ahead of their scheduled meeting and sat down at a picnic table, under the shade of a large oak tree. He swung around so he faced outward, resting his elbows back on the table top. Looking around, he noticed that the park sloped downhill to a beautiful body of water, named Bayou Texar. A well-kept lawn covered the hill with a mixture of pine and oak trees scattered throughout. To his left stood a large white cross, standing some thirty feet tall. At the top of the hill, fenced tennis courts could be seen, one of which was being used by a man and woman attired in tennis outfits.

"What a nice park," he exclaimed out loud. "I would guess this is a great place to live. Hmmm, I wonder . . ." Just then a cyclist rode by, and Alan sat up to determine if it was Joseph Hinote. The rider continued on around a corner and out of sight. "Must not have been him," he mumbled.

Once again resting back on his haunches, and tilting his head, he gazed straight up through the branches of the oak tree to the brilliant blue sky above. The dark barren branches, against the cobalt color made the backdrop seem an even deeper hue. It reminded him of the days before the storm, when he sat by the Sound with his old friend, the giant oak. His mind began to drift off and to muse upon the events of the last several days. He thought of his experience during the storm and how he had been so certain of his peril, "But, lo, I'm here," he smiled aloud. "Thank you, my Father. I am so appreciative of your kindness."

He recognized with the verbalization of these last words, that he had never really acknowledged the whole episode in the cottage. "I will call it, 'My Awakening', and boy, that was some waking up."

At this point, a thought came to him in the form of a question. "Do you think establishing some disciplines would be a good idea? You are a disciple of the Lord's and disciple means disciplined one." He no sooner admitted it a good idea, than his mind was off and running with all the things he should be doing. Before long, he had a list of several items he should be practicing every day and an equal amount for Annalisa and the children. Then, he recognized another thought, "Perhaps, before mentioning them to someone else, you should work on your own convictions and implement these disciplines in your life. Remember, the Lord asks for volunteers. He never coerces anybody. If He did, it wouldn't be love. Besides, He didn't force you, so how can you justify forcing them?"

Alan sat up and gazed out across the bayou. "Wow, that's an amazing revelation. When I get home, I'll tell Annalisa all that has happened, but I won't push her into any of it. Let's see if You can work some miracles in our lives, Lord. Oh, I can't wait to get home and share with her all You have done." A huge smile broke across his face as he allowed his mind to think of his beloved Annalisa. "I love her so much, dear Lord, I really do."

The delight of thinking of his cheerful wife, however, soon faded into thoughts of their home, his three bicycle shops, and his struggle with the lack of funds to pay his bills on time. Those awful, anxious anticipations of all that going back to California held, began to overwhelm him. He found himself slipping into the black hole he very much dreaded, the same chamber of despair he had visited so often in the past but which had been absent since the storm. It was a terrible, claustrophobic feeling. One he had always hated but had never seemed able to avoid. He needed a change of topic quickly, before this got out of control, way out of control.

"Where is Joseph Hinote anyway?" he barked. "Where is that guy when I need a distraction?"

-twenty-

Within a few minutes, but what seemed to Alan like an hour, a rider swooped down the hill, into the park, and right up next to Alan.

"Alan?" asked the rider who was hardly recognizable under his helmet, sunglasses, and cycling clothes.

"Yep, that's me," quipped Alan. "Joseph Hinote?"

"Yes, sir," stated the man as he took off his helmet and sunglasses stretching his hand out to shake Alan's.

"Call me Joey, though. Have any trouble finding the place?"

"Nah, it was pretty easy to locate. How'd you and your family fare in that storm?"

"We did fine," replied Joey. "It's a lot different here in Pensacola compared to out on the island, or even in Gulf Breeze. Those guys take a bit more of a beating than we do over here. I'm glad the power and phones are back on though. How about you?"

"Uh, I made it through okay, I guess. Where are the phones back in service?"

"All over the city. Why, you need to call home?" inquired Joey.

"Definitely! I can't wait to talk with my wife and kids. So you have phone service at your house?"

"Well, not yet, but they do just up the road a ways."

"Where do you live?"

"I live in a little town. It's more of a village really, out west of Pensacola called Hurst Hammock."

"Are you serious?" quipped Alan. "There's actually a place named Hurst Hammock?"

"Yeah, if you go west out of town on Highway 90 until you come to a crossroads called Beulah, turn south on Beulah Road, and in about five to six miles you'll see the Hurst Hammock town limit sign. It's a quaint place right on Perdido River, where it flows into the Perdido Bay."

"Sounds nice, is it quiet there?"

"Oh yeah, it's extremely quiet there. In fact, after I nearly went broke in a business venture, my wife and I decided it was the perfect spot to kind of hunker down for a few months. That was almost seven years ago. We love it there."

As he was speaking, Joey's face showed evidence that whatever had happened in the past was still painful to talk about. So Alan determined to avoid any discussion of business affairs, even though his mind kept wandering back to his own. He purposed that he must find a way to get the discouraging thoughts under control. They had way too much sway in his mind.

"Uh . . . where're you from Joey?"

"I grew up here in Pensacola. My family is originally from Virginia, but my grandparents moved here when they were first married. The family has been here ever since. My parents are getting up there in age, so they're in an assisted living home on the north side of town, by the University of West Florida. My brother and sister both live on the west side of town in Myrtle Grove, with their families. I have another brother out in Vegas. He's kind of the maverick of the family." Alan noticed how Joey smiled almost the entire time he talked.

"Where in Virginia?" quizzed Alan.

"Around Lynchburg, I think. I'm not quite sure. By the way, here's my address and phone number for future reference." Joey handed him a business card. "Sorry I didn't have one the other day."

"Here's mine," Alan slid a scrap of paper across the table that he had prepared with all his contact information. "I'm from Oakton, Virginia although, as you can see, I live with my wife and children in San Ramon, California. The rest of my relatives live in Virginia. That's why I asked."

"Yeah? I'm pretty sure my family is from Lynchburg. Is that close to Oakton?"

"No, I think it's about a hundred and fifty miles or so away. Do you have any kids?" Alan asked.

"Yeah, two daughters, the oldest, Sandra, is a straight-A senior at Pine Forest High School, and the younger one, oh she's a stinker, but the apple of my eye, is in junior high. Her name is Tanya, but we all call her Sissy. It's because my wife's name is Pam and sometimes when I would call across the house or yard for Tanya, my wife, Pam would answer and vice versa, so we decided it was just easier to call Tanya, Sissy. How about you Alan, you married? Any kids?"

"My wife, Annalisa, and I have three kiddos and one more on the way."

"Oh, congratulations," interrupted Joey.

"Uh, yeah, thanks. We just found out about it a few weeks ago. It's kind of a surprise and comes at somewhat of a difficult season, so I guess I have some mixed emotions." Alan's tone sounded very apologetic, if not outright guilty. "I mean, don't get me wrong, Joey, I love my kids dearly. I love being a father, but I'm going through some tough times in my business. Oh man, I didn't mean to bring that up, but somehow when you're always thinking on something, it tends to come out of your mouth. Kind of like a pot on the stove. If you don't ease up on the heat, at some point, it's going to boil over. You know what I mean, Joey?"

"I understand," Joey replied frankly. "More than you know, I understand Alan."

"I'm sorry, Joey," apologized Alan. Joey nodded in acknowledgment. "Anyway, we have three kids: Julie, who is our oldest, Richard, and little Emily, who we call Emma. I miss them and look forward to seeing them tomorrow night, God willing.

"What do you do for a living, Alan?" Joey appeared ready to discuss business matters now.

"I own and operate three bicycle shops. The first two were small ventures that were turning a profit almost immediately. But the last one I built on a lot I had purchased, and it pretty much ate my lunch. It's my fault. I mean, I made the choices, the mistakes, but it doesn't make the failures any more palatable. I'm sure when I get back I'm going to have to make some pretty drastic decisions. I'm hoping to hang on until I can sell. That's if I can find someone to buy me out. I'm in a real mess." At this point

Alan could visualize the rim of the black hole he so dreaded and decided to stop talking.

"Don't worry about it, Alan. I went through something similar, and all that worrying gets you nowhere. In fact, it almost landed me in the hospital."

Alan snapped to attention as this last statement hit home with him.

"Yeah, I was worried about everything," continued Joey. One day I thought I was having a heart attack. But, you know what, it was just my emotions. They had been ruling my thoughts, and all I could think of were solutions that were so emotionally charged, that none of them made any sense. Those were awful months for my family and me. Now, with the perspective of time, I can see it was more about controlling my emotions and learning how they influenced my thinking, than it was about the actual difficulty of losing my business."

This was precisely what Alan needed to hear. He was absolutely astounded Joey had put into words the very issues he struggled with deep within himself. It was like the time in Betsy's backyard when she had accurately described the hidden battle that raged in his mind. While Joey continued to give some of the graphic details concerning his business failure, Alan's mind fought to cling onto the positive side of the war. Listening to Joey with one ear, he desperately wrestled to stay on the offensive. He was determined to prevent the inevitable from creeping into his thinking. He labored mentally to keep some vestige of hope. He appreciated the story that unfolded from Joey, but as the soundwaves of his voice crossed the picnic table and entered

Alan's ears, they were somehow, enigmatically transformed into words which became personal scenes of Alan's own saga. It was as if Joey was speaking a language of hope, but Alan's mind was interpreting it into another language, one of despair. Finally, in what felt like his last dying effort, Alan remembered the stormy night in the cottage. It brought a flicker of hope. Nonetheless, when he just couldn't listen to Joey's story any longer, he interrupted,

"Since that night, the most astounding things have happened. I mean extraordinarily remarkable things. A change in my thinking, or at least an initial shift, but I'm still struggling with this great dilemma I'm in. At this point, I'm really having difficulty expressing all that happened. I'm not quite sure what to do or where to go or how to . . . uh, or anything else. So if it's okay with you, could we talk about the **rojocci** fellowship and all?" Alan glanced over and pointed toward Joey's bike with the custom **rojocci** insignia.

"Sure, I'm sorry, man. I know you're probably a bit raw right now. I'm sorry, Alan."

"No, no, it's not your fault Joey. I'm just way out of my element here and missing my wife and kids, so things are a bit exaggerated right now, okay?" Alan was trying to make it clear that he was the one who should be apologizing, not Joey.

"That's okay, Alan. Look, I don't know that I understand any more than you, but I do love to discuss all things **rojocci**," smiled Joey.

Alan had noticed the quarter inch tall letters on Joey's polo shirt above his left chest pocket. Although they were the same bright red color as the shirt, Alan could definitely spell out the word **rojocci**.

"By the way, I really like your shirt. Where'd you get it?"

"Oh I had a few made a number of years ago. I mostly wear them now when I'm riding. I like them though, bright colors make you easily seen by motorists, you know?"

"Yeah, that's a good thing," declared Alan. "So Joey, how many years have you been in the **rojocci** fellowship anyway?"

"Hmmm, I don't think anybody is ever actually in it. But I've been searching for a little over nine years now, shortly after I started having business problems. It's just a lifestyle of searching the Scriptures and discovering what the Lord says to me, then purposing to do my best to do it. You know what I mean?"

"Yes, I do. I'm finding that it's most assuredly a lifestyle. I kind of like it. But do you know what all the letters mean? What each one represents?" Alan was leaning forward across the wooden picnic table.

"Well, most of them, but not all. I don't know the second 'o' or the two 'c' words. How about you Alan?"

"I can help you with one of those, Joey. But I don't have a clue as to the very first letter. However, I have a guess for the last letter. Although, it sounds like you may know them both."

"Yes, I do, my brother. Which one would you like to know?"

"Actually, I think the 'i' would be easier to narrow down than the 'r'. In fact, if I guessed correctly, would you tell me?"

"Uh, yeah, I guess so . . . I mean, if you said the word, I wouldn't deny it or anything."

"Then let's do this," negotiated Alan. "Since I'm almost positive I know the 'i' word, please tell me what the 'r' represents. Then, I'll simply confide in you what I think the 'i' means, okay?"

"The word is '**receiving**'; that's what the 'r' stands for," resigned Joey.

Alan quibbled, "Then the 'i' means '**insights**', doesn't it?"

Without saying a word, Joey nodded in agreement.

Alan paused as he looked up into the clear blue sky and pulled Stanley's leather satchel out of the back pocket of his cycling jersey. As he sheltered it with one hand, he used his other to write down the new words on the small piece of paper he pulled from the pouch. Then he silently recounted what each word meant;

"receiving-of-Jesus-overlooked-cherished-christian-insights"

"What's that?" inquired Joey pointing at the old, leather satchel Alan found all those years ago in Stanley's toolbox.

"What? Oh, that's where I keep my **rojocci** papers," replied Alan as he held up the leather pouch. He then stuffed the paper that noted his recent acquisitions into the satchel and turned his gaze upwards again.

"Hey, Alan?" Joey broke the silence. "What does the second 'o' stand for? I've been really curious about that one for a couple of years now."

"It stands for the word '**overlooked**'," replied Alan, gazing into the sky, deep in thought.

"**Overlooked**?" Joey sounded like he didn't believe Alan, but quieted down as he pondered this latest revelation. "Hmmm . . . that's a bit odd, Alan. It doesn't seem to make much sense. I thought I could guess the meanings of the last two letters I'd been searching for, but now I'm not so sure. How long have you been searching for the answers to these letters?"

Still staring off into the sky, Alan blinked his eyes a couple of times and then looked down at Joey.

"Sorry Joey, I uh . . . was just reflecting. It's been since the autumn of 1977, when I first heard of this way from a dear friend. He passed away shortly thereafter. Now I'm wondering if it all has been worth it. I mean all the searching, all the inquiring of others, and all the pondering, was it all worth it? You know what I mean, Joey?"

"Oh, it's definitely worth it. There's no question about that," retorted Joey. "But now that you're at the end of your quest, don't think it was all for naught. On the contrary, think of all you've learned, the multitude of invaluable insights you've gained because you continued to search out more of the hidden answers. Think of the character, the precious character, you have developed because you didn't quit, you kept going even when, I dare say, you thought it was pointless."

Joey continued, slapping his hand down on the picnic table. "Alan, listen to me. Think of all those believers you never would have met otherwise, who you now consider brothers and sisters. Some, I'm sure you grew to love because of this adventure, this journey that you never gave up on. Oh, no, my brother, don't you think this was all for nothing!"

Alan eyes were transfixed on Joey's face.

Then Joey pointed out, "This silly, little word, **rojocci**, has added so much more to your life's journey than you may have realized just a few minutes ago when you found out those last letters. It has promoted so much more meaning, so much more substance, so much more value to this odyssey we call life."

"Alan, you just agreed it was more than a word. It is a lifestyle—a lifestyle of hope, of discovery, of adventure in an unseen realm. This isn't just an acronym made into a pronounceable word. No, this is an allegory, a parable of our walk with the Lord Himself. It's a metaphor of the tenacity developed over the decades of a life lived in searching, discovering, and implementing all that He reveals to you."

Joey paused long enough to notice Alan was looking directly at him. Then he said something Alan would never forget.

"You thought you were looking for letters to a word. But God had something entirely different in mind that He was developing within you, deep down inside, hidden within you. Something that is much more important, something eternal, something everlasting. Alan, He changed you!"

A smile slowly broke across Alan's face as he nodded his head in agreement. He jumped up and hopped on his bike. "Thank you so much, Joey. I really mean it, thank you. You are a good friend, and I can't tell you how much I appreciate what you've said, but I've got to go. Can you get together for lunch later? I'll call you, okay? But right now, I have to get going."

"Where are you going?" called Joey.

"I have to call Annalisa. I have so much to tell her!"

-epilogue-

Shortly after finishing his story, I contacted Alan. We had kept in touch over the years. However, the distance between our locations made it no small task to get together for a visit. We set a time, a few days later, to meet at a Cajun seafood restaurant in a coastal town that's about the same driving distance for each of us. He arrived with the ever cheerful Annalisa, as I arrived with my bride, the lovely Mrs. Graves, who I call Susie.

After hugs and pleasantries, I got down to business sharing the manuscript with the two of them. I showed them where I had highlighted certain sections I wasn't quite sure were as accurate as he had communicated to me a number of years ago. Although I had taken copious notes, some of my scribbles, from those many wondrous visits together, appeared more like the handwritten words on a physician's prescription, than the orderly notes of one writing a book. He assured me, therefore, that he and Annalisa would go over it with "a fine-toothed comb", correcting any discrepancies from the actual events and circumstances.

I had determined to pry him a bit about a topic I thought was very important to the continuity of his incredible

R. J. Graves, Jr.

adventure. However, before I could broach the subject, the waiter arrived with our seafood gumbo and crawfish etouffee'. If you have ever eaten a good Cajun gumbo and etouffee', then you understand why the conversation ceased temporarily.

After we finished our meals, Annalisa and Susie perused the manuscript. They paused at various sections, sometimes giggling, and other times eyes brimming with tears. This gave Alan and I the opportunity to catch up a bit, the very thing I had been hoping for since tidying up the first draft of his astonishing chronicle.

He told me several things the Lord had been teaching him lately and how, if it hadn't been for good old Joey Hinote, Alan may have quit altogether. He related how he will be forever grateful to that dear brother for his encouragement that day at Bayview Park.

"He was sent by our loving Father to help me in a very up and down time in my life," he confided. "We remained close friends and fellow explorers until he passed away just short of two years ago. He was a good man and a trusted 'friend who is closer than a brother'."

"Uh, Alan? I really want to ask you about . . ."

Just then, the waiter showed up with our Key Lime pie and hot tea. For those of you who have ever tasted a good key lime pie, well, you can guess why the conversation was temporarily put on hold again. However, once I had finished my delightfully delicious dessert, I was prepared to continue my courteous inquisition.

"Alan?" I pried, "What about that dream? You never told me the rest of your dream."

"Hmmm . . ." Alan rubbed his chin and took a sip of his tea. "I don't know about that, I'd really have to pray about it. That's a very private matter."

"Alan, it's been over twenty years since that night. I know you didn't feel comfortable telling me back in 2005. I understand that. It was a very personal experience between you and the Lord. But Alan, I think many folks who read your story are going to want to know exactly what happened that stormy night in the Morgan's cottage. What do you say? Are you ready to tell me the story?"

I knew I was really pressing upon a sensitive nerve because I had recognized many years previous that Alan was a very private man. He felt, above all else, most uncomfortable talking about himself. He had also learned over the years, the danger of his quick wit in group settings. He had declared to me many times before and now reiterated, "My tongue has caused me more burdens than I could ever carry, and I would just as soon not accumulate any additional baggage."

"I understand Alan. I really do. However, please consider perhaps explaining to me the parts that you feel aren't as private. Maybe we could start there. Then, when you feel more comfortable, we could move into that which you hold more private. That might be a good approach for you. What do you say?"

"Well, let me pray about it, and we can talk when we get together again to go over this manuscript, okay? It's not that I don't want to share the dream with others. It's more that I don't want to violate what He may have entrusted to me. Do you understand?"

"Yes actually, I really do understand how you feel, Alan. It's a sacred trust, right?"

He nodded his agreement.

Annalisa, who had obviously been listening to Alan and me, interrupted.

"Honey, it's been a long time since that night, and I'm sure there are many hurting folks that need to hear what you experienced in your amazingly, vivid dream. You were desperate to hear from Him, and He met you. Why not help others by sharing the dream with them. I know it's a very private matter to you, dear, but if it could deliver just one person, who may be in bondage as you were, why not allow the message to do its work?"

Smiling lovingly at Alan, she wore the same expression that caused her eyes to arch upward as her smile lit up the room.

"It helped me sweetheart, remember?"

Footnotes

Chapter Seven

1.   1 Kings 19: 11-13; John 10:27

Chapter Eight

1.   Ephesians 5: 22-32

Chapter Twelve

1.   Matthew 19: 4-6

Chapter Thirteen

1.   James 1: 17; Ecclesiastes 8: 17

2.   Psalms 46: 10

3.   2 Timothy 3: 16-17

4.   Jeremiah 29: 13

5.   Isaiah 28: 10

Chapter Fourteen

1.   Luke 17: 21

2.   Isaiah 28: 10

Chapter Nineteen

1.   Isaiah 28: 10

2.   John 16: 12

3.   Isaiah 55: 8; Jeremiah 31: 3; Matthew 13: 13

4.   John 8: 12; 1 John 1: 7

About The Author

R.J. Graves, Jr. and his wife, the lovely Mrs. Graves, who many call, Susie, met on the mission field in 1978. They have six wonderful children, three of whom are married and have blessed them, to date, with three precious grandchildren. Over the years, R.J. has been on youth staff, taught Bible studies and Sunday school classes, and has been in church leadership. He enjoys walks with Susie and their dog, Pumpkin, and when he finds the time cycling, and some woodworking.

During his career, R. J. has held positions as, Journeyman Carpenter, Law Enforcement Park Ranger, and Construction Inspector as well as several management and executive positions in commercial construction and the homebuilding industries. However, his heart always leaned toward ministry within the work environment. Today, he feels called to encourage believers in discovering greater capacities of faith, hope, and love in their daily walk with the Lord. Oftentimes, he employs natural stories to express spiritual truths.

You can contact us on Facebook at www.facebook.com/rojocci or at: www.therojoccipapers.com if you have any questions or just need someone to pray.

Look for the next book in the

the rojocci papers

series...